MEMORIES
OF THE
KHASSOS

MEMORIES
OF THE
KHASSOS

LEAH FLAHERTY

Badalia
PUBLISHING

Printed in the United States of America.
ISBN-13: 978-1-7369513-4-7
LCCN: 2021907244

Badalia Publishing
Clemmons, North Carolina

For Bonita Aurelia

You are the purest joy I have ever known

PROLOGUE

Ash rained down from the crimson sky. Sounds of falling rock and explosions boomed in the distance. Father and son stood in silence as they watched from the safest vantage point—a mountain range overlooking the valley called Madera. The torrid heat hung heavily in the air, threatening suffocation to what little life remained here. At their height, father and son saw most of the expanse of land.

The place crumbled in dramatic fashion; fires blazed, torching the remains of what had once been homes of its inhabitants. Tahrell, standing next to his son, could barely take his eyes off the destruction. There was a deathly stench about the air around them; it made Tahrell's stomach lurch with every shallow breath.

Brief wind gusts helped clear his nostrils and blew his hair into his face—momentarily obscuring his view. They would not be able to observe from this spot for much longer, and Tahrell knew he should not have brought Rahm here in the first place. His child looked down, awestruck by their surroundings. Tahrell watched his son's posture straighten and his look of awe transform to one of concentration upon noticing his father's gaze on him.

"Have you deciphered what the flaw in the design was here?" Tahrell questioned his son, not wanting the dangerous lesson to be wasted.

"Yes, Father, I believe so," he replied.

"Let me hear, then."

"I believe the most detrimental flaw was the size. Celadon was far too small to accommodate such a rapid expansion."

"And after witnessing what lies before you now, what would you have done differently?"

The child pursed his lips, thinking for a moment before answering his father.

"I suppose the obvious answer would be to make it larger."

He could see that his son was confident in his answer, and this pleased him.

"In time, we will see if you are correct. Perhaps the simplest answer is the right one," Tahrell said.

The wind howled as the gusts grew unbearable to withstand. Rahm took Tahrell's arm to anchor himself.

"We must leave now," Tahrell told him.

The sky flickered above them. Tahrell turned away from the ruin, making his way toward their exit, his son clinging to his arm.

His son stopped to look back. "Will they all perish?" his child asked, more out of curiosity than concern.

"They must," Tahrell replied without hesitation.

Tahrell led Rahm away, positioning himself behind his son so that his own body shielded his child's from the wind. Tahrell looked back once more to watch the scene; his eyes were the last to see this place.

The narrow path filled with battered soldiers seemed to go on forever. The sunset left an orange glow in the distance as if to highlight that my destination was just out of reach. As the sky darkened, it seemed to siphon both the light guiding us and what little energy remained to this nearly broken troop.

This body was aging. Muscles that I didn't know existed ached now with my every move. I knew I had put these old bones through a lot. I couldn't expect to fight as long as I had without showing signs of fatigue.

The rhythmic movement of my horse made me drowsy despite the sharp pain in my side. I was bleeding through my dressing, which I was reminded of with every step my horse took as we traveled in a large caravan. At that point, every part of me felt too heavy to hold up, including my eyelids. Surely we would stop for the night soon. I was thirsty and exhausted.

I noticed a young man making his way down the line toward me. Finally, the water carriers made their way to me. I never knew how far I could push these bodies I inhabit. I forgot the limits. I counted the others in front of me as I tried to pass the time until I could drink. The other soldiers were at a much earlier point in their lifespan than I was. They pushed themselves harder and hopefully took less time to drink. When the water carrier reached me, his eyes traveled to my seeping wound. He grimaced.

"You should have a healer see you," the water carrier said.

I said nothing, then grabbed the water sack from him. I greedily drank before handing the sack back. I knew he was thinking he shouldn't have to waste water on a warrior who didn`t look like he would make it through the night—let alone long enough to make a difference in the next battle. I've seen that look before, and it doesn't affect me. Not much does anymore.

"We resting for the night?" I asked, looking up briefly at the darkened sky.

He shook his head slightly, clearly disappointed with my casual demeanor toward my obvious injury.

"Just beyond that bend in the path, there is a healer," he said. "Go and see her before you take a rest."

I rolled my eyes for him to see, and winced at the pain. I knew he was right; my body was failing me. I felt weaker by the minute. I attempted to swing my leg around my horse to dismount and nearly fell to the ground. The water carrier steadied me, but I felt the impact of the ground reverberate through my body. I held my side, blood leaking onto my hand. The pain was sharp, yet it throbbed in time with my breathing as I shuffled my way toward the direction the water carrier pointed.

As I got to a structure, I smelled a strange aroma wafting around me. The shelter was made from cloth and marked with the treelike symbol of the healers. Still holding my side, I maneuvered my way through the opening and saw several men lying on the ground moaning. One man toward the back of the tent was motionless. A man, very early in his lifespan—compared to me, anyways—ran back and forth fetching supplies for a woman. I presumed she was the healer.

The young male had blood splattered on his clothes, but he didn't seem to notice. The female, however, looked as though she bathed in a pool of blood. Only her pale face was clean, except for a few speckles of red. Small jars, as well as cloth and binding materials, were splayed around the ground. A mixture boiled over a small fire, producing the same aroma I noticed upon entering. The female healer was stirring it.

Trying to catch someone's attention before I lost consciousness, I called out to her. "Healer, I would ask for your assistance."

She glanced at me just long enough to see who had spoken to her, then moved further away from me. She knelt next to a male lying on the ground, his head covered in blood. She placed her hands on each side of his head, examining his eyes, then looked for the source of the bleeding.

"Penn, go assess the elder there," she said to her male helper as she motioned toward me. Then she continued her examination of the male on the ground.

"Just a skull crack," she reassured her patient. "I will come back to ye. Just need to clean the wound and dress it. Probably a good idea to lay here a while, but try not to sleep. You might be concussed."

The man gave her a brief brow raise as if to think to himself: *Whatever that means.*

I felt helpless as I watched the healer move to her next patient. He looked bad off and moaned uncontrollably, but the healer had a determined look on her face.

"Not much longer now," she said. "Be strong."

The healer hopped back up to her feet and made her way toward whatever was boiling. She stirred it once, then scooped up a ladle of liquid, blowing on it in an attempt to cool it. She returned back to the man's side with it.

I stood, struggling to hold my side and remain upright, as I waited for the young one to come and assess me. I began to feel faint. I didn't know if it was from the pain or the blood loss.

I watched the slender boy dart back and forth, picking up his supplies before rushing toward me.

"Sorry elder, busy time for us as you see. Why don't you have yourself a sit down."

"I will if I can manage one," I responded.

"I can help you, elder. Nice and easy now," Penn reassured me as if he was talking to a frightened horse.

He moved to my good side so I could transfer my weight onto him. Then he helped me down to the ground. I was positioned to face the male who the healer was with. Penn was on my opposite side.

"It will be a lot easier for both of us if you are lying down like so," he explained. "Now, let's have a look-see."

I moved both of my arms down to my sides to give him better access to the wound and watched as he pulled a small knife out from the healer's belt around his waist. Penn used the blade to cut my blood-soaked clothing away from my wound. I looked down at my torso and saw the cut was much longer and deeper than I thought. I felt sick, so I looked away and trained my thoughts elsewhere. I watched the male fight to drink down the liquid the healer served him.

The healer stroked the man's hair. "You will sleep now," she said.

The man continued to moan a few more moments. Then, his eyes closed and he drifted into unconsciousness. His previously clenched hand now lay still and limp. The healer took his hand into her own, holding it with both thumbs, and counted to herself. She stretched his arm out toward me, then got up and moved just behind us. The healer was out of my line of sight. I wondered if she had gone over to the man I thought was lifeless. Perhaps he still lived, after all.

I could feel Penn still trying to stop my own bleeding, but each time I watched what he was doing, I felt worse. So, I concentrated again on what the other healer was doing.

"Forgive me if I don't understand your ways," I said, "but why isn't she helping those who still live before examining the lifeless?"

"Oh, she is helping them, elder," Penn replied.

I was confused, but I realized that my mind was not as sharp as it was in my earlier years. Plus, my thoughts had become considerably more foggy since my injury.

"Did she put that other one back there into a sleep as well?" I asked, gesturing with my head back toward the healer. I winced at the pain my slight movement caused.

"Try not to move, elder. This is going to be tricky enough business without you squirming," Penn said. "Yes, that man back there Nan is seeing to now has been out since just before you came to us."

Nan returned to the other male's side with a basin and began chanting over him. I didn't understand the words she was saying, but her chanting grew louder as she moved the basin closer to her. She produced a knife from somewhere on her person. I watched in horror as Nan lifted the knife and cut into the male's chest. I found it hard to breathe.

"What is she doing to him!" I shouted.

"Lie still, elder." Penn firmly held my arm as he continued to work on me. "She is a very experienced healer."

If I thought seeing my own wounds made me sick before, I was wrong. It was nothing compared to the shock I felt as I watched that so-called healer pull an organ from the other male's chest.

I wanted to close my eyes, but I couldn't look away. I *needed* to know what she was doing.

Still chanting, the healer reached into the large basin and lifted a mass out with both hands. She raised her hands high above her head and howled the same chant. That's when I saw it. It was only slight, but the organ in her hand moved on its own. The realization flooded in. I looked on in shock as she placed the object in the male's chest, and I knew I would be sick. I turned my head just in time, but when I looked down, it was not bile that I had coughed up—it was blood, and quite a bit of it. Penn's facial expression told me the situation was grim. I now knew this healer is who I was sent here to see.

"Best come quick, Nan!" Penn called out.

My body has failed me and I will soon be lifeless, but it doesn't matter. I am not afraid. I have died many times before.

CHAPTER 1

CARRICK

What was a memory worth if you were the only one to hold it? Did that memory touch other lives and change the tide of what was to come if it remained locked away? When you became a Watcher—as I am—you became just that, a memory lost. You no longer had the life you once led. You were no longer your own. All that remained was the memory of who you once were. Being a Watcher transformed you into different people and took you to distant realms.

My life as a Watcher had revealed unfathomable things to me—things I otherwise would never know existed. I had seen multitudes of life forms, technologies, and ecosystems that seemed unreal because they were so different from what I knew. I had seen the good in people and had certainly seen the corruption as well.

I experienced a rebirth and a new purpose in each new life I have led. It was never a life, however, that I made for myself. Each new life was designed for me, written into my very being. I remember every life and place I have traveled. Some journeys were more important than others. Other journeys changed everything.

My current journey had brought me to a place of remembrance and—I hoped—redemption.

I was in a wide-open expanse of land, far from any other inhabitants except for the young Erretas woman in front of me. There were no

1

landmarks of note around me, just rolling, green and brown hills as far as I could see. The air around us seemed still, as though holding its breath in anticipation for what would happen next. It seemed almost impossible that just a short time ago, my captive and I had nearly been overcome by a mass of people in the city streets.

I allowed my head to hang for a moment, unrestrained tendrils of hair fell over my eyes. My heart and mind raced as I thought back over the chaotic events of the day. The weight of my head on my shoulders seemed heavier than ever. I took in a deep breath and hoped that when I lifted my head again, the weight I had carried for such a long time would, at last, be lifted.

I was finally alone with the one I had sought after, and yet I felt no relief as I faced my unlikely captive. Silence stretched between us as my mind searched for a solution to our predicament. The Erretas woman's eyes met mine. Her eyebrows were raised as if she's asking, "What now?"

I turned away. *What now, indeed?*

I remembered a talent that might prove useful, one that had previously been lost to me. After all that had recently happened to me, many of my abilities had changed. It could be possible, I thought. It might just work—if I could remember.

Wasn't that ironic? If only we could remember, then anything would be possible. Many talents I thought were lost forever were now returned, but so much time had passed since I used them. I wasn't sure I knew how to use them again.

I once possessed a form of communication that might help me now. I could try it and hope that the ability had returned to me. Tightness spread across my chest as I mentally prepared myself for my next move. I forced myself to look at my captive, but I found it difficult to control my feelings when I locked eyes with her.

The Erretas was still. Her golden hair, frayed into wild strands around her face, was the only evidence of the chaos we experienced. My chest further constricted. I had to be cold-hearted, as I had been many times before. I reached for her hand, desperate to find out if my plan would work. Then, I hesitated. *I should explain myself before commencing,* I thought. I tried to clear my voice of emotion before speaking.

"When time passes as it does for me, it is difficult to remember the beginning, but I will try." I hesitated, looking into the woman's eyes. "For your sake, I will try. After all of the pain I'm sure I have caused you, I owe you that much."

Her brow furrowed in confusion.

"Perhaps it will give you comfort," I said. "To hear the pain it will cause *me* to retell it now."

There was still no hint of recognition in her eyes. I felt as if I were speaking to myself.

"I believe there is a way for you to view my memor—" I stopped again. That didn't seem like an appropriate way to describe what I wanted to attempt. "What I mean to say is ... there may be a way for me to let your mind see what I have seen—just as I have seen it—or experienced it rather." Embarrassed by my stammering, I kept going. "But you must allow yourself to relax, if you are able. I need to form somewhat of a link between us in order for this to work."

I looked into the Erretas' fearful eyes, wide with terror. I needed to put her mind at ease. I needed to try a more soothing and confident voice. I needed to stop stammering and sound more assured of what I was doing—for her sake and for mine. It had been a long time since I attempted this talent and I had never attempted it with an Erretas.

"I know you have no reason to trust me," I implored, "but if I can make you understand, then everything that has been happening to you will make sense. You see, I need your help."

Before I could lose my nerve, I took the captive's hand in my own. Immediately, she pulled her hand from my grip.

"It won't hurt," I tried to assure her. I could see she wasn't convinced. She took several steps back from me, creating a gulf of space; her eyes were wild, darting back and forth as if looking for an escape.

My plan wouldn't work if the Erretas couldn't relax and quiet her mind. How could I calm her down if I couldn't even calm myself? If I expected her to trust me, then I had to be vulnerable myself. So much was bottled up inside me. I would have to explain myself to the woman if this was going to work.

"I am different from you," I said. "I know you've realized that much."

The Erretas woman was apprehensive, but slightly dipped her head to show acknowledgment.

"How did I come to be this way? I cannot remember, which is ironic since I'm the one who can't forget," I allowed myself a brief laugh. "I wasn't born as you were. I think that I have always been—or at least the Khassos within me has. Time is not linear for everyone. Some things are eternal, as inconceivable as that may be to you. There were others like myself. Once, I even had a partner. No," I corrected myself, "I really was only part of a pair. Now I am alone, yet never truly by myself. My whereabouts are monitored. I supposed I experience many beginnings, but I will never have an end. It is my curse, but I resolved to make my penance a distraction after enduring it for so long. That is—until now. One day, it will be the means to an end that I have long been denied. That is what I must tell myself to go on. And I must go on. They've made sure of that."

I'm rambling, I thought, which was making it harder for the Erretas to follow.

"One ending just brings about another beginning for me," I said. "It has been this way for countless lifetimes. A long time ago, I tried keeping count, but somewhere along the way, I lost track. I've lost hope and regained it again. I can no longer tell if the hope is my own or another's. Such is my curse."

I let my gaze fall back to the young stranger's face. She remained silent and looked at me with earnest. She waited for me to go on.

"I think perhaps I should start with the last time I saw her," The word "her" stuck in my throat as it always did when I referred to her. My heart ached only slightly less when I used the pronoun to refer to her. I couldn't bear to say her name. I looked down, attempting to hide my pain. I couldn't say her name to anyone, but now I must. I closed my eyes and spoke.

"Let me tell you of the last time I saw Eirene."

By saying her name out loud, I felt a little relief. It was as if I'd been holding my pain as a prisoner and now released it. Once I said "Eirene," I saw her in my mind. I remembered our last encounter and prepared myself to recite what happened. When I opened my eyes, I saw a different expression on the Erretas' face. She no longer looked terrified. It had been replaced with a look of concern—not for her own well being, but for mine. I decided to be as frank as possible.

"I know you're afraid. I am too. But time is running out, and if you know what I know, then I think we can fix our situation. I think you know we don't have time for me to explain. If you allow me to do this, I can relay information in a matter of minutes."

I extended my hand out to elicit her response. I could see the woman mulling over her options. She gave a brief head bow to grant her permission. The Erretas woman still looked uncertain, but she moved toward me, each step was a calculated decision on her part. When she got close enough, she reached out her hand. My large hand engulfed her petite one, and I attempted to reach into her mind.

"I will not start from the beginning," I communicated. "That would be too difficult to grasp now. Instead, I will start by explaining my penance, and maybe after learning what I have been through, you can learn to forgive me for what I did to earn it."

CHAPTER 2

CARRICK

Weaving a link with someone was tricky business, even when conditions were perfect. What happened with the Erretas woman was far from that. Her brain was a maze filled to the brink compared to what I usually found when trying to attempt a connection like this. My mission would prove difficult. I felt a surge of energy course through my body as the linking current extended from my body to the Erretas woman. At the first jolt of energy, I felt her grip relax, and then there was resistance. The woman tried to pull away from me, both mentally and physically, her eyes were wild again. I tightened my grip on her hand, overpowering her, forcing her to stay with me.

"Do not be afraid," I said.

I couldn't soothe her. She tried to jerk her hand away again. I refused to let go of her, so she shifted from fear to outright fury. Before completely losing the connection to her, I grasped the sides of her head, my hands flat against each of her temples. This time, the energy jolted us both.

"Stop," I instructed. This time, I tried to speak directly to her mind.

With eyes still wide and expressive, she looked up at me. I could sense all of the emotions—anger, fear, and confusion—running through her. The fatigue she emitted from her mind was overwhelming.

The Erretas' brain was more intricate than I knew. Did I dare make further connection between us?

Her head felt so small in my hands; it didn't seem possible that a mind could hold so much. I communicated feelings of calm and my reassurance to her before exploring the complexities of the Erretas' brain.

A strange sensation came over me—like a chill running through my body—as I searched her mind. I closed my eyes to focus, but I only saw blackness. I was locked out, blocked by a darkness that made my stomach churn. I had to find a way around the barricade. I knew the woman held so much information. I could feel it, but it was hidden away by a force I had never experienced. My mind searched hers for the ending to the darkness. I tried to push through the barrier, but that proved useless.

I couldn't gain access to the Erretas' mind as I'd hoped. If I could find a memory within my own mind that we both shared—maybe that would work.

I concentrated. What caught my attention the first time I saw the Erretas woman? What made me notice her? I was in conversation with another Erretas, a man wearing a uniform, and then ... *ding*. A bell rung. Wait, it wasn't a bell. The elevator reached the bottom floor. And the *ding* I heard was the notification that the elevator had arrived. The noise made me turn around, which is when I saw the Erretas woman. I needed to find that exact moment in her memory. I quieted my mind, thinking only of the ringing noise, searching for it among all the darkness that enveloped her.

I pushed harder. Then ... I saw it. A faint light emitted from her mind. It stuck out against the darkness. The light pulsed with the ringing I heard in my own memory. I had almost missed it. Once I saw the light, I made the connection. This time, I didn't feel resistance, and no jolt or shock as I'd expected.

After finding that overlapping memory, I merged her version and mine—as if they were the same. I would be able to communicate this way, after all.

The connection was easy now, like riding a calm wave or floating weightless through the air. I was at ease and momentarily forgot the task at hand. My mind lulled into a safe slumber like nothing existed except the two of us. I felt drowsy—like I'd been drugged—but some part of my mind urged me to act. I heard a gentle voice say:

Find her. Reach for her within yourself. Time is running out.

A shiver ran through me.

"Quiet your mind and listen only to me," I instructed the Erretas woman. I vaguely recognized my thoughts in the hypnotic tone I used. "Let my words wash over you. Let me direct you so you may see as I have seen." I felt the woman's mind relax.

I thought back to one of my more chilling stories and knew it was the one I had to share. I braced myself for what would come. The story was about the last time I saw Eirene. I felt a surge of energy, as if the memory physically left my mind as I shared within our link. I immersed myself in the memory, taking the Erretas' mind with me.

It's funny how one penance had developed into many. My mind shifted and it became more difficult to catch a steady thought. For someone so young, I had very old thoughts.

My mind always jumped from thought to thought right before I was given a new life. For a brief time, I was given the mercy of forgetting who I really was and what I've done. I *was* someone new in that moment, and the real me slipped my mind as I transformed— gradually, at first, and then all at once within the memory.

My consciousness slips into my new role, and I do not know how much time has passed or what world I am in. All of a sudden, I am a young boy named Aquilo, and I am freezing cold. It is so cold that I can think of nothing but the cold.

The rain no longer falls.

"The gods have turned everything to ice," the woman called Taiga tells me.

I like her, I think. She has a warm smile and tells me stories to lull me to sleep. We have walked for a very long time. My feet are tired and my stomach calls to be fed. I must make sure to keep my eyes forward and follow so as not to get lost in the frozen lands. It is too cold for plants to grow or animals to live, so we search for better land. Most importantly, we seek food. I do not remember how many sleeps I've had since last I ate, but I look forward to the new land so I can eat a great lot.

There are many of us traveling together. I tend to spend time alone as that is how I came about them. I don't remember my existence before I met the people I travel with now. The other children have families, but I do not. I am not allowed to cause trouble here, and no one will miss me when I'm gone, so I'm on my own. Somehow, I know this like it's part of me.

I joined the others on their journey—in the middle of the frozen land—from their home place to their new land. I appeared with food for them one night as they made camp. Some of the group says I was sent from the gods to help them. I think Taiga started spreading that information upon my arrival so the others would take more of a liking to me. Others in the group say I am a nuisance because I'm one more boy to look after and an additional mouth to feed. They tell me I am good at surviving despite my young age. I have found things to eat when they thought there was none. It has been too long since I have found anything useful though, which makes me nervous. I can travel with them, but I am my only source of protection. I don't have allies out here.

What are allies, I wonder. I stumble on strange words and thoughts sometimes. As soon as I think them, they are gone.

Once I am no longer useful, I will be left behind—or worse. Taiga has warned me of this.

Taiga has a sister, Neva. She is not as friendly as Taiga, but I once stopped Neva's son from falling off the big edge. This is what we call the steep drop-off along the path we walk. Since then, she at least no longer hates me being in her presence.

Neva has two sons; she calls them Fox and Bear. They are bigger than me, but it is fun to play with them. Taiga does not have sons, and I think that makes her sad. She smiles when she tells us stories though, so we sit with her and listen before we sleep. Sometimes, I lay closer to Fox and Bear. It makes me feel safe and warm, but they always ask me questions I do not have the answers to.

"Where is your mother?" they ask, but I do not have a mother. Taiga makes a sad face whenever I say that I don't remember. But it's the truth; I don't. They say I had to have a mother, but I know somewhere deep inside that I never have. Some things you can't explain to people who don't understand. So, instead, I just shrug my narrow shoulders and always reply the same way when asked about my family. "I don't have one."

After the first day I came across the others, an older man—whose name I don't know—asked me where the rest of my people were. I told him that it was only me. Taiga tells me the group fears me. She says they think I will lead my people to hers and hurt them. Taiga, however, knows I am good and would never betray her.

"One day, you will tell me about your people," she says every so often. Some nights, I hear the men talking about their plans. Sometimes they even talk about me when they think I'm sleeping. They all ask, "What will we do with the boy, Aquilo?" and I am scared.

We walk all day, but our surroundings never change. Fox, Bear, and I play a game with our steps, and we get excited when we come across something new. We are happy to see anything that isn't white or ice, but that hardly ever happens. We count everything. We count our sleeps, our meals, how many times we make water. We count the moons—everything.

"How long have I been with your people now?" I ask.

"Hmm," Bear ponders. "I think at least a hundred sleeps."

"No, more than that I think," Neva corrects. "You have been with us for eight moons. I have been counting too."

Something about those numbers makes me nervous. We have not seen anything new in six sleeps now. I think it is time for me to explore by myself. The others will only slow me down. They are not good at climbing, and they cannot run as fast as me. Something inside me says tomorrow is the day I must go.

Once we stop for the day, I make myself sleep.

It is still dark above when I wake. The others are sleeping. Bear makes a rattling noise when he sleeps, so it is easy to slip away. I walk until it is light out, counting my steps along the way. I am relieved that the sun is coming out. I can see better, except there isn't much to see besides bright white. I walk and walk, which seems like such work now that I walk alone. I feel like I have been walking for many sleeps, but I know I have not since it is still bright. Just when I think I can walk no more, I hear it.

I stop in my tracks—waiting to hear the noise again.

Silence.

I fear my mind is playing tricks on me, but I wait longer.

More silence.

I make myself as still as possible.

There it is!

The faint noise of a bird cawing. Where there are birds, there will be other animals. There will be food.

I have to figure out where the bird is and follow it back to where it made its home. I close my eyes so I can concentrate only on the noise. My instincts tell me I would hear it before I see it.

There it is again! Louder this time. The bird is closer. I move toward the noise. I count one hundred more steps. Then I look up. I found it! The great bird soars above me. "Show me where to go," I whisper. The bird hovers in the air—almost in the same place—my eyes meeting its own. "Show me," I plead. The bird makes a move.

I run as fast as I can while still looking up, hoping I don't trip, fall, and lose sight of the bird. I run so fast that I forget to count my steps. I look too high into the light, then all I see are spots. *Where is it?* I panic. I see spots of light; I can't tell the spots apart from the bird. Even worse, I have lost count of my steps. *How will I ever find my way back to the group?* I stop running and close my eyes. I strain to listen, but all I can hear is the loud beating in my chest and my rapid breathing.

I am lost and know I will die out here alone with no food and no warmth. Hot tears well up in my eyes. I blink them away, worrying that they, too, will freeze. Alone I began, and alone I will die.

Such an old thought for one so young.

I think strange thoughts sometimes.

My vision grows blurry and my thoughts became hazy. I feel strange. The wind picks up. I am freezing. I hear Taiga and the others' voices in my head. They ask, "How could you not have any people?" "You are too young to have survived on your own. A boy so young and so small would have frozen to death long ago surely." "Where is his family?"

"Aquilo," whispers a voice in my head. With my eyes still closed, I decide it is only the wind howling. Nonetheless, it gives me comfort. I open my eyes, refusing to cry any longer. The wind *had* whispered to me. It whispered through a tree.

A tree! It is barren, thin, and blowing in the wind, but the tree is beautiful. The bird has guided me, after all. I smile. I smile so big that it hurts my face as the frost cracks away and falls to the ground. A tree! I rejoice to myself.

I eat the pieces of the tree that I can break off and carry more with me before setting out again. I walk and count my steps, and have three more sleeps before the ice thins enough for me to see a color other than white. I see the brown of more trees and the dirt on the ground. I eat whatever I can find and continue to walk.

After five sleeps, I wake with a start to another noise, but it is not an animal or the wind I hear. It is the scream of another person. I immediately recognize who it is.

It hurts my heart to hear Taiga cry out. I run as fast as I can toward the screams. I don't know what I will do once I get to her, but I have to help her. I can not stand for her to be hurt, not Taiga. She has such a nice smile and is so kind to me when no one else is. I run to her as fast as my small legs carry me—faster than I had run after the bird. I think that she might have been attacked by an animal or that she had fallen, but when I find her, a man is standing over her. I have never seen him before.

I could help her if she fell and I could scare an animal away, but I don't know how to shoo people away. I thought I could help Taiga, but how can I face a man? I am just a boy. I wasn't just a boy though, was I? *What does that mean?*

Think, Aquilo! Don't let your mind jump about again. Taiga stops screaming; her body lays limp in the snow. I see a color that I have not seen in a very long time—red. It is everywhere. My eyes can only focus on the red. That is it, I thought. Color.

Look for something that isn't white. She always loved color. Stop your strange thoughts, Aquilo. Help her!

My eyes search as my panic escalates. It is hard to breathe. The man notices me.

"What are you doing here, boy?" The man's deep voice sounds angry, and I become scared.

My heart pounds in my chest until I feel like it will explode. *Look for anything that sticks out from the snow.*

The man moves toward me, leaving Taiga bleeding in the snow behind him. I have nothing. I can see her body lying on the ground. I am too late. She will die now. I will never see Taiga's smile when I bring her people to the land they can live in. I will never hear her stories again. Nothing matters without her, so I stop being afraid and anger takes hold of my body.

I know I could do nothing— I am just a boy—but I don't care. I run at the man as hard as I can, hate coursing through my blood. I want to hurt him. The man freezes. But I run with my head down until I hit him with an impact that hurts my entire body.

I knock him to the ground. The man is big compared to me, but he was weak from lack of food or from fighting with Taiga, and I have taken him by surprise. I get on top of him, hitting him as hard as my frail arms let me. He shakes me off like I am a crazed animal, then slams me into the ground. My head hits the hard earth.

He stands over me. "That was stupid of you, boy," he spits. The man kicks my stomach and the air leaves my body. I struggle to breathe. He kicks me once more, then takes my head into his hands and pounds my skull into the ground. My mind blurs, but I try to focus. I see more colors and don't know if I am seeing them because they are actually there or because I have a head injury.

I see the light, violet sky that is almost white. I see the brown of the man's clothes, and I see blood in the snow. Is it my blood? I see the outline of where Taiga's body had fallen in the snow, but I no longer see her laying there. *Where is she? Have the gods taken her away like she told me they did when someone died?* I will die soon too, I think. Maybe I will join her again in the afterlife.

"You may never be with her again," a voice whispers. The man hits the side of my head and my vision blurs.

I brace for another blow to my head, but the man stops.

A rock falls next to my body and hits the white snow. I see a blur of red. The man's full weight drops on top of me, knocking out what little air I still have in my lungs. I am trapped—too weak to move, even if he was not on top of me. I see hands reach down and then feel the man's body roll off me.

I close my eyes, waiting for the gods to take me, too. Nothing happens.

Opening my eyes, to my delight, Taiga appears in front of me. She did what I could not, she found the color. She found the rock and saved me from the man.

I try to get up, but can't. Taiga collapses on the other side of me, and I turn my head to look at her. I try to get up another time, but my body fails me. It has failed me before, I thought. I was going to die and Taiga would as well. For some reason, I believed the voice that had said Taiga and I would not be together again in the afterlife.

"Sweet boy," Taiga stops, unable to speak.

"I failed you, Taiga! You will die!" I cry out. I sound every bit the young boy I am.

I am not him though, not truly. It makes no difference if I was Aquilo or anyone else. I cannot bear to watch her die. My mind fully returns to me as I look into her kind eyes.

"You are a hero, Aquilo," she whispers. "You gave your own life to save me and to save my people. The gods will surely bless you in the afterlife."

"I only wanted to save you," I reply. "Why did you follow me here? Why do you always find me?" I plead.

She tries to laugh, then wheezes as she sucks air into her lungs.

"You were sent to us. I knew you should be with us in the new land, so I followed you to bring you back."

"There is no new land. I only led you to your end!" Tears stream down my face as pain burns in my chest from memories lost to her. I cannot stand watching Taiga live a nightmare next to me.

"You don't understand," I say.

Taiga reaches her hand out to stroke my hair, comforting the child she never had in this life.

"You are the one who does not understand. Don't you see, boy? I have seen it. We have found a new land for us to inhabit. Our people will go on now."

What did she say? Like a key into a lock, her words click into place. I am not here to witness the end of these people. I am here to ensure their survival. They have found a way to live on.

I know I don't have much longer. I have to find the strength to move. I fight with all my might to inch my body closer to her. I prop myself up and take her head in my child-sized hands.

"Eirene?" I whisper.

Sometimes it works, and she returns to me—even if just for a short time. At times, I do everything I can so she will not remember because it is too painful. Right now, though, I want her to remember. I want her to agonize with me in this cruel joke they have played on us. It is selfish, but I don't care. She looks back at me—a bemused look on her face—but no recognition.

"I don't know that word, Aquilo. What does *Ah-ren-ee* mean?"

"Please remember me," I plead.

"I will remember you in the next life. You don't have to be afraid, Aquilo. The gods will favor us, and we will look down on our people as they live in the new land."

"Damn it, Eirene!" I shout into her face.

My anger gives me strength, but my body will give out soon—as will hers. I blink a tear away and watch as it falls onto her. Inspiration strikes.

"You asked me about my people, Taiga. Remember? You said one day I would tell you about my people. You were right. I want to tell you now."

She gives me a kind smile, as she always does.

"You wait until now to tell me, boy? Well, go on and tell me your story. I have told you enough of mine."

"My people are not from this land, and neither are yours. You know that. Deep down, you know that, and you know me."

"You know me, Eirene," I repeat with as much conviction as I can.

I see her eyes widen just a fraction, but it is there. Her eyes look into mine and she sees, but she sees too late. I take the boy's last breath and then I am gone.

I found myself gasping for breath as I crouched down at the entrance of the Great Corridor. This happened every time I used up my form's lifespan. I returned to this very spot, but the times I encountered Eirene left me angry and broken. This time was no different. How long would she lie there with the horrible knowledge of our past before she lost it again? I did not know. I saw her as Taiga, lying in her own blood on the snow, who adored me as the boy she thought I was.

I let my mind go back to the memory of her looking at me with much different eyes. I saw the look she gave me when I betrayed her. I could not think about it now. The pain never went away. It changes to different types of pain. Now, it was raw pain. I allowed myself to get too wrapped up in the form I took. That was the only way I could forget. I had let myself go too often as of late. How many times had I relived this pain?

I had to force myself to walk to the end of the corridor and report what I observed as Aquilo. I would not give the Council the satisfaction of seeing me on my knees and lost in despair. They cared not for what I suffered. They already knew it was the same over and over again when it came to her, but my punishment was the Council's source of information and, therefore, extremely important.

As such, the process worked efficiently. Once I had the information I was sent to retrieve, I found myself back in the Great Corridor to report my findings to the Council of Five. My job was to relay pertinent details, then move on to another life. It was time now to begin again. Had I known then how many more times I would have to begin anew before seeing her, I might have tried less to forget Eirene.

CHAPTER 3

LYRIS

A cool breeze shot down from above, breathing new life into the oppressive heat of the market streets. Finally, they managed to turn on the air cooling system to break up some of the artificial heat pumping into the common area. A slight chill ran through my body as my sweat-soaked shirt began to cool. I readjusted my hair on top of my head, but dark tendrils still stuck to my neck.

The market was sparse these days, too hot out for the gentle temperaments of those who had the money to purchase anything. Wiping sweat from my brow just before it could drop into my eyes, I spotted my signal from a short distance ahead. I continued meandering down the brightly lit walkway, remaining as casual as I could. My knee still ached from the last time I was forced to flee from a similar trade. Best not think about that now though; it added to my nerves and all.

From the corner of my eye, I tried to notice anything out of the ordinary. I kept a slow stride toward the entrance of Severin's new meeting place. A woman I've never seen before restocked her kiosk, slowly unboxing children's trinkets, but that particular kiosk had high turnover. It was hard to sell cheap toys when the majority of children were wealthy and unlikely to make it over to our area of the market. Another woman I knew to be called Hilli wandered around the corner searching for her next prey. She was blessed with the sleight of hand talent and was very good at it. Plus, she was adept at never getting caught.

The oculi were stationary, directed toward their standard positions to observe the walkway. The only thing out of the ordinary here was me.

I took the last few steps to the door, then hesitated. I peeked to my right one last time. No one around, not a single oculus had moved—nothing should seem strange here. As I entered the small eatery, I was hit by a waft of cooking smells and spices. The artificial air was much cooler inside, and the dim lighting lent to the atmosphere.

Severin's light-haired man who gave me my signal sat toward the back. He looked up only to make eye contact with me. His movement was so slight that no one who watched him would even notice. Severin's man stretched his arms above his head, letting out what I assumed was a fake yawn, then his head bent in the direction I was supposed to go. I tilted my head in acknowledgment, then moved in the opposite direction. I took a seat at the counter to order.

After taking my time to eat, I asked for the location of the facilities. The man behind the counter pointed me in the right direction, and I made my way. I couldn't help but notice Severin's man trailing me. Toward the end of the hallway, just past the facility room, Severin's man caught up with me and opened a door using an old key code entry and his thumb print without saying a word. As quickly and quietly as the man appeared, he was gone.

The door he opened led me to an empty room. It was dark, but not so dark that I could not see Severin's private oculus above me. The machine pivoted down toward my face. Seconds later, a second door opened for me.

Severin was seated behind a large table. His short hair, slick with sweat, looked darker than his natural color. Two other men I didn't recognize were with him. One was positioned next to Severin, the other stood behind them. There was nothing notable about their dress or appearance. These men looked just like Severin's typical guards for hire, except Severin didn't dismiss them upon my arrival as he usually did.

It's strange that he'd let them listen to us. We didn't usually have an audience. Tension coursed through my body as I thought of all the implications. Once my eyes adjusted to the brighter light in the room, I noticed the coloring of Severin's face was a tinge gray, and he was sweating more than he naturally would as if he was ill.

"Hot one out there today, eh?" Severin asked me. "You'd think with what we pay to keep our power on around here that they could give us a break from the heat season they've deemed so necessary."

"*Mm*," I responded, not trusting our spectators. "Who are they?" I motioned my head toward the two men.

The man behind Severin smirked, but it only gave me pause. The whole situation felt staged. Swallowing, I felt my pulse thrum in my throat.

"Just one of my employees, and the other is a mutual friend. Nothing to worry about. They seek the same information I do. So, please, have a seat. Let's talk."

Well, that certainly wasn't the deal we worked out. Not to mention, I charge more money for extra ears—as Severin well knows. Something is amiss.

"I have nothing to say to strangers," I said at the same time I slipped my right hand into my pocket. "Perhaps you and I can have our discussion at a later date."

I pressed my right thumb to the lambent in order to lock the records, then checked the time.

"It's almost market closing. We wouldn't want to miss our curfews, would we?" I took a step back. "Another time, Severin." Then I turned on my heel and told myself to remain calm.

As I reached for the door, an olive-skinned hand, similar to my own coloring, closed around my wrist. That was where the similarities ended.

I looked up into a man's large grey eyes and could tell he meant business. He was nearly as wide with muscle as he was tall, and his head was shaved bald. I saw every bulging vein along his skull. I hadn't noticed him in the room, let alone heard him get up. *Where did he come from? This wasn't one of Severin's men.*

"Sit down," the large man commanded. He guided me back over to the table. Severin was still seated. He was profusely sweating and looked as nervous and ill as I now felt. The other two men appeared unfazed. The two men peered at me with interest.

I aimed to remain standing, attempting to show what little defiance I could. The big man, however, slammed me down into a chair and clamped his hand like a vice around my wrist. The force of it caused more of my fine black hair to loosen from the knot on top of my head and fall down around my face and neck as I struggled.

"Severin, what is going on here?" I asked, no longer able to hide my panic as I continued to struggle out of the big man's grip.

"We need you to do what you were hired to do, Lyris. Talk," said the man seated next to Severin. His voice was calm and soothing, like he was trying to tame a wild animal, which was what I felt like as I thrashed and fought to no avail in the grip of this boulder of a man. I stole a glance at Severin; he still looked nervous.

I stopped thrashing, but I didn't respond.

"You can talk of your own free will or we can find ways to make you talk," said the same man with the soothing voice. "The choice is yours."

I spit on the table. "You can't force me to do anything. It is an extreme violation of my rights to detain me, especially by force," I said. "The Council has a zero-tolerance policy for violence! You can't strong-arm me into acting against my will!"

Beads of sweat dropped from Severin's face and pooled on the table in front of him. His eyes bulged, communicating that I needed to cooperate.

"Lyris, Severin here uses a large network to gain information, which he mentioned to us in a recent audit," the smooth-talking man said. I watched him move from his seat and place a hand on Severin's shoulder. I noticed the lambent strapped to his waist. It glowed with the enforcement's symbol emblazoned on it.

They were enforcements all along? How can they break the law like this, and with violence too? These are corporal offenses.

"Now," gesturing to my lambent, he said, "we need to see what you brought to share with Severin."

"You'll never be able to hack my lambent, and you can't detain me here," I said. "What kind of enforcers don't know their own laws?"

"Oh, Lyris, we're the kind you don't hear about. The kind that aren't bound by the same rules as the average citizens." He paused long enough to flash a devious grin. "You see, citizens like yourself, and Severin here, who bend the laws a smidge to make a not-so-honest living have made it necessary for us to patrol areas the oculi can't see. What the oculi can't catch doesn't get back to the Council unless we want it to. So, that strict no-violence policy you mentioned ... Well, let's say—when no one is watching —Otto here doesn't *always* follow that rule." With that, the man pointed to the boulder with the death grip on my wrist.

As if rehearsed, Otto released his grip from my wrist and grabbed me by the throat. My body left the chair and slammed into the nearest wall. I slunk down to the ground in pain. I'd experienced my fair share of injuries due to running escape routes all these years. But I had never felt the pain that came from another person hurting me like this. Bodily harm toward another citizen was strictly against the law; now I knew why.

The air barely returned to my lungs when Otto grabbed a chunk of my hair and lifted me back to my feet. I grimaced and managed to contain a shriek as the sharp pain seared my scalp. This time, however, I was smart enough to avoid struggling. Otto held me face-to-face with the enforcer.

"Do we understand each other now?" The enforcer asked me.

"Yes," I replied, trying to move as little as possible since Otto still had me by the hair.

"Good. Place your thumb on your lambent and open the recording."

CHAPTER 4

CARRICK

It took time to regain my composure after I had linked with the Erretas woman. I relived what happened, but I wasn't really there now. That story was the past, and my present was in a much different time and place. Sharing my past through linking made it more than a memory; it felt as though it happened to me all over again.

I took a deep breath, allowing the shared memory between the Erretas girl and me to fall back into my mind —like a file returning to its proper chronological order—where it belonged. Without breaking our connection, I focused my attention on the next occurrence I needed to share. I hoped this memory would be easier for the Erretas to grasp as it happened in her own time. I spoke into the Erretas' mind, hoping to explain myself before moving on.

"I lived lifetimes in other forms, in other worlds, before I finally made it back to the world the Council had banished Eirene to. Even then, there was no guarantee that I would see her. There were too many people in her world for me to have an encounter with her every time, which was my only true mercy. In truth, it was easier not to see her. I could concentrate on my new role and go places where other people didn't know who I was. I needed to let myself forget her. After all that time, surely I deserved at least that.

"Maybe that is why I hadn't seen her in many cycles. Maybe the Council wasn't so merciless, after all. At the beginning of my penance, each time I returned to them screaming and crying like a maniac, they assured me they had no control over whether or not I saw Eirene. They would tell me that I went where I was needed, but I didn't believe them. I could never trust them—not after everything that happened."

I reached into my mind for another memory to share. I felt that slight shiver again as I did so; then I accessed the memory I needed.

"My next life form of note is what ultimately led me to you," I shared.

I looked to the Erretas woman, trying to gauge her reaction. Her eyes were locked with mine; there was an unreadable expression on her face. I feared the connection between us could falter due to the barrier, but for now, it seemed to work. Contrary to the woman's physical state, she appeared to be absorbing the information.

I needed to move on, but there was more relevant information to divulge here before we got further.

"These brief reports to the Council of Five were the only communication I was allowed with my own people, and they all hated me. Most wanted me dead, but I was too important for them to be truly rid of me—or so I was told. All Watchers, including myself, serve a penance designated by the justice system for criminals. I haven't always held this position; I once had quite a different occupation, if you can even call it that."

I had to stop myself before my emotions got the better of me.

"But I can't dwell on that now. In the present, my job is to communicate between this world and my own. I'm dispatched as a Watcher in order to study life on each realm and report findings back to my people. Whenever an important event is about to occur or, I should say, whenever an event that is important to *us* is about to occur, I know in my Watcher form that I have found the information needed, and then my time in that particular life form ends. I travel through a mechanism called a Panoptis, which transports my consciousness into other existing bodies to observe. I'm very similar anatomically to those I become. We are all interconnected to some extent, but we share a common energy within us that allows me to ... *uh* ... bounce between different people and places without altering my own atomic makeup."

I'm sure my stories were confusing to the Erretas woman because she was unfamiliar with the travel of a Watcher. I needed to put this in Erretas' terms, but I couldn't find the words. Hell, the best way for her to understand would be if I just showed her. I needed to show her, but I felt I was losing control of our connection.

Concentrate! This is important, I told myself.

"I suppose the best way to describe what happens is that I am always me, I just play the role of someone else. Most of the time, as a Watcher, I don't know I am playing a role as it happens. It has taken me lifetimes of practice to know that I am a Watcher and not whoever I am operating as. In the beginning of my penance, I completely forgot myself until I got back to the Corridor.

"Watchers are immediately integrated into the architecture of other people's everyday lives. I became a person who fit into the situation that needed to be observed. This way, my arrival did not cause alarm and I could slip away when it was time to go. As I said, I am told we are automatically sent where we are needed to observe. Given the magnitude of my crimes, though, I suspect I am used as a Watcher more than others."

I stopped myself again, wanting to move on from these dark thoughts. *Explain the process and then get out of here,* I thought. My grip on the present was shaky. Truth be told, the connection between the Erretas woman and me still had that drugged effect on me. That made it difficult to not slip into this next memory. I had to resist slipping in order to keep from being sucked into the vortex. I struggled against my mind, and realized that the Erretas woman seemed to be directing us both into the memory.

The same blank expression remained on her face. If she was controlling anything within our connection, there was no outward sign. Something within her wanted to go into my next memory, whether she knew it or not. I tried to look at her, tried to regain control of our connection, but I couldn't overpower her.

Impossible. But it was possible with her. I knew this to be true.

We were both pulled—as if by some unseeable force—into my memory. I wanted to resist, and then I didn't. I felt that same floating sensation and relaxed, the tension vanishing. I found myself letting go, slipping into the memory until that was all that there was.

I study my new reflection in a small bathroom mirror to see what I look like now, although I am still very much aware that I am a Watcher. I am slender in build with pale skin. I have dark brown hair and blurry vision. I squint until I find a pair of glasses lying on my nightstand. *There, that's much better.*

I walk back to the mirror and see more clearly that I am actually *very* slender with a slight slouch. My eyes are large and brown. I am intelligent too; I realize this as if my brain has just been awakened. I am a professor at the university near my house. My house is small, but I don't spend much time here. I also notice that I have a very happy and upbeat attitude.

I stagger, dizzy, as though hit with a wave of strange awareness. Flashes of colors momentarily blind me, then disappear. As I reach for the sink to hold myself up, I realize that I'm not alone in my mind. This hasn't happened before—or at least I don't think it has. My mind is more than a little hazy.

The Erretas woman ... I vaguely had an awareness of her observing in the back of my mind. It's not like when we were connected before, but more like she was here with me along for the ride in my memory. *Well, this is certainly different.* I had just enough time to note that she was there with me before my mind relaxed again, allowing the memory to take over.

My form glances at the large digital clock on my dresser and realizes he is running late for work. At least they sent me to a body that is already dressed. My form wears dark slacks and a short-sleeve white shirt with very worn black shoes that lace up. The belt holds up my form's pants, which are much too large for his slight frame. My form grabs the keys from the hook near the front door and walks outside.

Another wave of dizziness hit, this one was a little less jarring than the first. I was in my own memory, and yet I could sense the Erretas woman was there too. I could barely tell if I was thinking to myself or speaking to her in my mind, but she was there, and now she could truly experience what I had encountered. I tried to concentrate, but my body kept going through the motions, and I was in my memory, feeling just as I did when it actually happened.

I walk outside and get hit with a wall of heat as the humid air fills my lungs. I live in a small town, so my neighbor waves at me as I get into my vehicle, which is clearly more than a decade old. That's what happens in small towns, friendly people wave at you even though they barely know you. What any of this has to do with my real job I haven't quite figured out at this point.

An astonishing number of important people hail from sparsely populated areas just like the one I find myself in now. Of course, the definition of what constitutes a small town has drastically changed over time as well. But for this place and time, the town is considered small. *Good thing I'm smart this time*, I smirk. You always have to find the humor in your situation, no matter how bleak it seems.

I hurry since I'm running a bit late. I wonder why they would have me running late. I look at my name tag, which appears to double as an access card. I am James Umbridge. Oh wait, Dr. James Umbridge, but people call me Jim—I think—as it pops into my head like it has always been there.

I have gotten better at controlling my thoughts when in character. I no longer lose as much of my true self as I did in the past, but it's hard to block out the overwhelming positivity that I feel in this new life. The person I've become today is happy, and I have to say, it is an unfamiliar sensation. It will fade once I move on, but I embrace it while I can.

I pull into my faculty parking space and make my way to the side of the building. I have always been Dr. Umbridge to everyone else involved in this life, but I am someone different each life form, so it takes a little while to register all of my character's information. Once it does, the character's mind blurs with my own. At times, it's difficult to decipher if I'm actually thinking something or if I'm lost in whoever I am supposed to be. More and more comes together for me as I walk into my office.

Today, I am supposed to meet with a student before class. He is an exceptional student. Perhaps he will lead me to the reason I was sent here. My job is to figure out that reason.

"Understand that I cannot really alter what happens," I communicated to the Erretas woman. "I can merely assist or guide, but never change an important event. I am only there to observe and communicate whatever is pertinent back to the others like me. As I said before, we are all interconnected, and so we must know what the other realms are doing and how it will affect us. What I witness in a realm can change my peoples' future."

I walk into the office at 7:33 a.m. I am only three minutes late. Very unlike me, and by me, I mean Dr. Umbridge. He is painstakingly punctual. I see my student, Andrew Whitfield, already waiting for me. I realize now that I work closely with him on my research project.

Andrew is a similar build as me, but he has lighter hair and a string of freckles on his nose. That makes him look younger than his age, which I believe is around twenty. Right now, however, his excitement makes him appear like an eight-year-old child. Andrew jumps out of his seat when he notices me.

"Sorry I'm late, Andrew," I say. "I know you have a class at eight."

"Don't worry about it, Dr. Umbridge. I have wonderful news!" Andrew exclaims. His face shines. "I've found her!"

The adrenaline pumps throughout my body. For a moment, my true identity blurs with my character's. *Her?* The pronoun always grabs my attention. For a fraction of time, I forget that this student doesn't have the same interests I do. The "her" he's referring to is not mine.

It takes me another moment to recall Dr. Umbridge's memories and his work with Andrew. Dr. Umbridge spends most of his nights using the university's equipment to study the stars, and the "her" that Andrew mentioned is the star they were tracking.

Andrew stands up with what appears to be a rolled-up blueprint in his hand. He uses his other hand to clear a space on my desk. As Andrew unrolls his map, he asks me to hold the other end.

"See, Dr. Umbridge! There." He points toward the center of the map. "It's much larger than we initially thought, but more importantly—look at its movements. Here you can see its position in relation to this cluster, and here is where it showed up in past documentation on the Schaleski report. But look where it is now!"

It's not the first time, but I am still astounded to realize how much information I hold from a character's mind. It is a strange sensation to have memories of a life I never lived and knowledge from past experiences that didn't happen to me. This is especially true in Dr. Umbridge's very capable brain.

"Is this accurate? Did it reverse its direction?" I question.

Gauging my incredulous reaction to this news, Andrew clears his throat. "I've checked and rechecked my work multiple times, but it's always the same result."

I let out a breath I didn't realize I was holding. I feel a bit giddy. This is not a feeling old Jim Umbridge is used to.

"I would like you to look over my notes, but there's more I need to show you," Andrew pauses. "*Um*, give me just a second." Andrew lets go of the map, and the paper naturally rolls back into a coil again.

Andrew moves toward his bag, which is on the other side of my office. He rummages through it and takes out a notebook and folder.

"Let me show you a closer look, sir."

He opens the folder to reveal a stack of glossy photographs. He places the first photo in front of me.

"This is the one that was developed years ago." Andrew skims through the photos until he finds the one he wants and places it next to the first one. Both are directly in front of me.

"This is the image I captured two nights ago. You see, there. Look at the color." Andrew points.

I gasp, but say nothing as I study the picture. Jim Umbridge's vision is truly terrible. It dawns on me that this star is why I was sent to observe in this specific time and place. Usually, it takes months, sometimes years of a character's life to get to the point where something important happens. This must be a record of some sort. And to think I was almost too late for it! *Something is strange. Why was I almost late?* Before I can think too hard on that, Dr. Umbridge's mind takes over and studies Andrew's work.

"It's not a star at all," I hear myself say. "It's a planet." A big grin spreads across my face. "Tell me everything."

Andrew proceeds to tell me how he came upon a planet everyone else in our field had assumed was a star.

CHAPTER 5

LYRIS

I awoke with a jolt and moved into an upright position, taking in my surroundings as I sat up. I was lying on the floor of a dark room. My body was cold and sore. It took a few moments to register where I was. When I did, a shiver ran down my spine. *Oh, Lyris, this is not good. Not good at all.*

My head ached. Actually, my entire body ached as I scooted toward a wall. Every movement caused more pain; it was as if each particular body part that was bludgeoned had awakened now as well.

"You look like hell."

The unknown voice rattled me, and I nearly knocked my head against the wall.

"*Mmmph,*" I gritted my teeth in pain.

What I wanted to say was: *Who the hell are you?* But my mouth didn't want to work. As I tried to manuever my jaw, it dawned on me that it might be broken. *Am I the first person in Anatan to have my jaw broken by force?* I turned my head to look at the man who spoke to me, and was rewarded with more shooting pains for my effort. I realized I was in a cell adjacent to his. I was relieved that we were not in the same cell, but I could see straight into his cell from mine.

There was a thin, clear barrier between us. It was as though I looked at him through a layer of water, flowing slightly in ripples of translucent waves until the eyes were able to focus on what was within. The inside of his cell looked much the same as mine—dark floors and a small cot of the same grayish color in the corner. I could barely make him out. His cell was enveloped in shadow. I tried to look past his cell to the next one, but I didn't see anyone.

The outline of the man moved toward the barrier between us. It became easier to make him out. He was an average-sized man, who walked with a lot of confidence for someone locked in a cell. As the man came closer, I noticed his brown hair; it was cut short and stuck out every which way at the top and shaved close on the sides—not like any Anatani hairstyle I had seen before. His skin was paler than the highborns, more like the Sators of legends, and his posture was that of a man in charge—not one trapped in a cell.

"Wasn't sure you'd wake up, kid. Must've been one nasty fall you had," he said.

Though it pained me to do so, I made my mouth move. "*Whrrr* we?"

He grinned and his green eyes became more vibrant as he inched closer.

"Where are we? Why ... you're the envy of every Anatani, kid! You're just mere rooms from the Great Corridor itself."

The Great Corridor? That meant I was going to trial. It also meant my situation was serious. No one *goes* before the Council of Five.

"You must've done something pretty awful to be in here with the likes of me, huh? Or maybe you did nothing at all. Sometimes the Council operates that way as well. Which is it? Are you a hardened criminal or just in the wrong place at the wrong time?" He asked. He tapped his finger to his chin as he looked me up and down.

"I think you look pretty innocent, so my guess is you probably deserve to be in here just as much as I do. Looks are usually deceiving. Don't tell me though; let me guess."

He stared at me as if just looking at me would give him the clues to my innermost thoughts.

"Alright, you've definitely got the highborn hair, even if it is a mess, but your skin is darker and your eyes ... or eye rather ... that right one looks a little swollen. Anyway, your eye is much larger and lighter in color than those of our illustrious leaders who are born into greatness with their dark beady eyes. Still you have a bit of their look. *Ah!* Is that it? Are you some highborn's dirty little secret? A love child they want forgotten?"

I turned my head away, attempting to ignore him.

"No. That's not it, you wouldn't be here if that was the case. They would've just gotten rid of you. *Hmm* ... fairly good build by the looks of you—not too thin and frail—not overweight. *Ah!* Were you selling yourself? That's illegal, you know?"

The anger shot through me during the man's ranting monologue, which made me forget the pain I was in. That was the only pleasant thing about this moron interrogating me.

"Enoughhh!" I managed to shout. I felt my eyes blazing with fury.

"Oh, that one struck a nerve. Don't worry, I realize you'd need a working mouth for that."

At that, I forgot my situation and lashed out. I tried to jump from my sitting position toward him; instead, I toppled over on the floor when I reached the clear barrier between us. I didn't know which I would regret more: the rushing motion I made to strike at him or the painful landing I made on the hard floor. I heard the man laughing but refused to look at him.

"What? Did you think you could move through walls now?" he continued laughing at my expense.

My left arm, I realized, was nearly useless as I tried to brace my weight on it, and slumped closer to the floor. *I'll be damned if I let this bastard criminal see me cry.* So, I bit my lip to hold back my tears as I pushed myself back up with my good arm. As I righted myself, the man's demeanor changed.

"Sorry, kid. I don't get much entertainment here or much company at all, for that matter." He used a gentler tone. "I forget you're new. You'll get used to it."

I glared at the ground rather than him as I scooted my aching body back toward the wall. I needed to prop myself up in a slightly less miserable sitting position.

"You know they'll heal you, right?" He asked. There was a tinge of regret in his voice.

I looked up at him with my good eye.

"Yeah, yeah! Seriously, kid, they do. It's the law. They have to heal you before you appear before the Council, or before they release you. So, just hang in there. It can't be too long now," the man said. "They don't like to leave people in these cells, especially not around people such as myself." He smiled down at me and gave another wink.

"You look young. First-time offender?"

I nodded, holding my clenched jaw as I did. *Well, first time I've been caught.*

"See! You'll be fine. Didn't kill anybody?"

I shook my head no, still staring at the ground. My hair fell around my face, but I was too weary to push it back.

"Yeah, you'll be just fine. Crime is so rare these days; they'll practically lock you up for anything," he said. "They're low on Watchers too. They'll take what they can get and frame it as criminal just to get those numbers up. The last time I was in these cells, a woman next to me had her child on her hip! Can you believe that? They arrested her with her child, and she claimed all she did was spit on the collector when he came asking for her tax payments. She said she couldn't pay them *and* feed her child. They told her that was ludicrous and that everyone in Anatan had sufficient funding for all living expenses. They really are out of touch with what the rest of us deal with. Anyway, they let her go. She didn't have the blood to be a Watcher. They say most don't nowadays, but they test us just the same."

I heard of the Watchers before, but imagined it was the highest punishment for true criminals—not mothers. My nerves frayed again. My new, talkative neighbor sat down next to the barrier. He got as close to me as he could. As the barrier rippled then made itself clear again, it was almost as if he were sitting beside me.

"I'm Balor," he said. Maybe the brief silence between us was too much for him. "If I could shake your hand, I would, but *uh,* obviously that's not possible. Sorry about before. I shouldn't have messed with you. It's just ... I'll never get out of here, so any company is good company. You know?"

Exhausted, frustrated, and more than a little scared, I realized this might be my only acquaintance or source of information in here, so I had to take what I could get. I opened my clenched jaw as much as I could.

"I'm Lyrith."

He smiled that same mischievous smile as before, but the moment was short-lived. A deafening scream sounded in the distance. We both stood up, then moved toward the edges of our cells to get a better view of what was going on. I tried to ignore the shooting pains that ran through me.

The source of the screams moved toward us. It was a dark-skinned man, round in build and of a similar height to me. A lean, taller woman with jet black hair tied tight at the top of her head, and another muscular man with olive skin and his dark hair slicked back—both wearing the dark green guardian uniforms—dragged the screaming man down the hall. As the group came closer to our cells, I could see the screaming man's eyes rolling around as though he was possessed. Spittle hung from his dark lips, spraying out as another agonizing scream escaped from him. I nearly jumped out of my skin.

The guards marched silently, never looking at us or him, as they escorted him past us. The sporadic screaming turned into a drawn-out moaning and ranting. I couldn't make out any of the words the poor man tried to get out. After they were out of sight, I turned toward Balor; my eyes wide with shock.

"What the hell *wath* that? I mean—what'd *thhey dooth* to *im*?" I asked as best as I could.

"That is what happens when you don't have enough of the blood," he responded.

"*You'vth theen* others like *thhat* before?" I asked.

"Yeah. It's been happening more lately. Like I said, they're low on Watchers, so they test everybody now."

"What *doth* that mean?"

"Well, kid, you can't be a Watcher if you don't have the blood in you. They'll take a sample from you when they heal you, I'm sure. For some reason, you can't use the Panoptis system if you don't have a certain gene. You can't travel right, but lately, I think they've been trying to push it. I think they're experimenting on people, trying to see if they can travel even if they have a little bit of the blood in them. If it works, then they've got another Watcher they can use in the system. If it doesn't work ... well ... you become whatever he is."

My heart pounded.

"Now, it's rare to have any of the genetics in your bloodline that allow you to become a Watcher, especially at your age. So, I wouldn't worry too much about it, kid."

I heard footsteps in the distance. The same guards who dragged the man by us made their way toward us. Each heavy step grew closer in time with the thudding of my heart.

The lean woman stood directly in front of my cell; she pulled out her lambent to scan. She scrolled through, apparently reading, while my heart felt like it would burst out of my chest at any moment.

"Balor, back so soon," she said.

"What? Did you miss me, Rhetta?" he quipped.

"Oh, you know I never miss. Ask your ribs if you don't remember."

"They remember. Can't blame a man for trying though, sweetheart," he teased. Then he blew an air kiss toward her.

With a slight cock of her head, the male guard moved behind her and opened Balor's cell. The guard walked straight in, and without hesitation, dealt a powerful blow to Balor's side. Balor bent over in pain. The guard marched back out and locked the cell behind him as though nothing had happened.

"Alright. Lyris Suttor, is it?" Rhetta asked.

I nodded, clutching my useless arm while trying to make eye contact with the eye that wasn't swollen shut.

"You look like a girl who has learned her lesson. Are we going to have any trouble here? Did your new neighbor, Balor, teach you his tricks already?"

"No *troubble,*" I mumbled.

"*Ah,* well at least this one won't be a talker. Let's get her up for testing, Len."

She opened my cell door using her lambent. The larger guard restrained me before leading the way. I had just enough range of motion left to look back at Balor. He was still crumpled over on his cell floor. He forced himself back to his feet, leaned up against the clear barriers that were his cell, and mouthed what I think was, "You'll be alright." Then Len turned my head back around for me, leading me away from the comfort of my cell.

CHAPTER 6

SENIA

I tapped my foot as anxiety overtook my body. I waited in the doctor's office for my name to be called. There were two other people seated in the waiting room with me, both much older. I fidgeted with my hair like I usually did when I was nervous. My light brown tresses had grown long. I had waited several days for my test results, and I didn't think I could wait much longer.

I picked up a parenting magazine, glanced at it, then put it back down. What did I need to look at a parenting magazine for? I didn't have children.

I had noticed the symptoms more frequently now, which was why I came to see a doctor in the first place. The headaches were getting worse, and I was starting to forget things. I couldn't ignore it any longer.

The door into the waiting room opened. A female nurse wearing colorful scrubs with little cats all over them came out.

"Mr. Wallace? She'll see you now, sir," she said. They both disappeared behind the door.

I tried to watch a morning talk show on the television, but I couldn't concentrate on that either. I glanced at the clock. *I have been here more than twenty minutes now.* My frustration continued to grow. I briefly thought about what the doctor might tell me, but those thoughts were too scary. *What if there was something seriously wrong? What if there's nothing wrong with me at all? That is the more likely scenario*, I reassured myself.

"Senia Sha-le-sky?" I heard the woman mispronounce my name.

"It's Ska-le-skee," I corrected.

"Sorry 'bout that, dear. Dr. Reynolds is ready for you."

"Okay," I responded. I tried in vain to squelch my nerves.

"Let's get your weight here first, hun. Step up on the scale, please."

I stepped onto the scale and the woman slid the metal weight across the scale. To my surprise, I lost nearly ten pounds since the last time I weighed myself. That was only just last week at my previous appointment. Something was wrong.

The nurse in the cat-covered scrubs escorted me to an examination room and told me to sit so she could take my blood pressure.

"Looks good, hun. Dr. Reynolds will be in with you in a few minutes. Just sit tight."

"All right, thank you." I felt like I had cottonmouth.

I didn't have a good feeling. I could hear the large clock ticking on the wall as I waited. My mind wandered as I stared at a poster diagraming artery blockages. My heart raced, yet I sat still in the chair as Dr. Reynolds walked in.

Dr. Reynolds was a middle-aged man with a receding hairline. He was a straight shooter, which I liked. I didn't want to beat around the bush.

"Good morning, Senia. How are you feeling today?"

"My headache is just a dull throb today, not as bad as last week."

"Good, I'm glad to hear that. Sounds like the medication is working for you. Now, let's talk about your test results. As you know, we've done a lot of bloodwork and scans over the past week." He displayed my results for me to see.

"As you can see right here," he pointed, "the scan does show a growth."

My heart dropped. I forced myself to keep listening though.

"The mass is likely creating your headaches. Now, we have several options for a course of treatment; however, your tumor is in a very difficult place to reach. Surgery is out of the question due to that."

I could barely hear what Dr. Reynolds said. His voice became white noise, and the fluorescent lighting blinded me. *How does one sit and listen to someone telling them that they have an inoperable brain tumor?* The last thing I heard him say was something about six months. *Six months to live*, I thought.

My vision went black.

I didn't know how long I was unconscious. The next piece I remembered was the white light above me. White light, then I heard a voice. It was a man's voice. He was asking if I was alright. *Where am I?*

As I scanned the room, it all started to come together. I fainted in the doctor's office. I was listening to Dr. Reynolds a moment ago. *Am I dying?* That last thought stung enough to snap me back to reality.

"Senia, try and sit up, but go slow. I have some water for you. Take some sips. It will make you feel better."

Before I could help it, a giggle escaped my mouth.

"Water? That's your cure for me? I think I need something stronger than that to feel better."

"I know this is a lot to take in, especially for someone so young, but we will provide you with every available treatment to make you as comfortable as possible."

Young, I thought to myself. *Yes, I am very young, only twenty-six years old. I don't have any children, a significant other, or any real family to speak of. I've just barely started a career after college. I've never traveled or done anything great in my life, and now it was ending. How could this be?*

"Is there someone we can call to pick you up?" Dr. Reynolds interrupted my thoughts. "I don't think you should drive yourself home."

"No, there's no one close by I can call."

The reality of that hit me harder than I thought it would. My mother was dead, and my father lived across the country—not that he was the most reliable anyway. I only had a few acquaintances here since I moved for my new job. I didn't have a friend I could call and definitely not anyone I could call for something as serious as this. I had no one, and that was the hardest part to think about.

"I'll be fine. I can drive. I'll sit here for a little while longer. You're right, the water is helping." I tried my best to smile and believe what I said.

Dr. Reynolds looked at me with true pity in his eyes after that, something I didn't think he was capable of with his closed-off demeanor.

"I will prescribe several medications for you. I urge you to fill *all* of them."

I couldn't help but notice Dr. Reynolds stressed the word "all."

"This will be a difficult time for you, and though you may not realize it now, you will need all of the medications for different symptoms going forward. Each one will help you with your condition in different ways, and I can explain them all to you. First—"

My mind faded again, but I drank more water and forced myself to listen to his instructions.

This was my reality now—a lifetime of pills and mere months left in my lifetime. I had to be brave and face the truth. Wherever I went, I couldn't run away from my diagnosis.

CHAPTER 7

LYRIS

Each delicate step I took shot pain through my body. It started in my feet and ended in my jaw. I took in my surroundings with my good eye. I hoped Balor was right and they would have to heal me soon.

Rhetta and Len guided me through halls that had bright—almost white—light illuminating from the walls. It took my good eye a little time to adjust to the shock of it after leaving the darkness of my cell.

When we made it to the end of what—in my humble opinion—was a much too bright hall, Len and Rhetta opened a solid wall using their lambents and some type of facial recognition scan. Just when I thought the lights couldn't get brighter, we stepped into the brightest room I had ever seen. I had to squint. Len all but dragged me. My good eye tried to adjust. *Are those machines? Is that a white bed in the middle of the room?* My stomach dropped. This was it. This was the testing room.

A new person entered the room from another unseen door. This person wore a light-blue, robe-like gown. "*Ah,* there you are," Rhetta said. "Garron, this is Lyris Suttor. The Council has ordered testing for her. She needs a full scan, and, well ... here. Just read the file, will you? Haven't got all day."

Rhetta used her lambent to send the file to Garron, but before I could read it, Garron snatched it from the air above and entered it into his own lambent.

"You want to get her properly clothed, Guardian Lynnea?" Garron directed his question to Rhetta. He scrolled through his lambent, his eyes never leaving what I presume was, my file.

With a bit of mumbling, Rhetta grabbed my arm none too gently and released my restraints. She directed me behind a small privacy curtain.

"Hands up," she ordered. Then Rhetta lifted the hem of my blood-and-sweat-stained shirt and pulled it over my head. Pain shot down my left arm. I winced through it and finally changed into a stark white top. It was slightly large for me. I continued to help Rhetta redress me in matching boxy, white pants with my good arm. My hair was still in disarray, bare feet now cold as they touched the bright white ground. Once I was dressed in my new, not-so-fashionable attire, Rhetta put the restraints back on me. I cradled my bad arm as I walked all the way back toward the tester.

The tester's hair was slicked back in a similar fashion to Len's, though not quite as dark in color as his. I sized him up, wondering if I could take him if left alone without the guards. With my current condition, I doubted I could fight my way across a room. But, if they healed me …

"As Guardian Lynnea said, my name is Garron. I will be conducting your assessments. First, you will receive a full body scan. Then, we need a blood sample. After that, we will take you to the healing chamber— if you cooperate with questioning. Understood?"

"*Yeth*," I replied, grateful that I would be healed, after all.

Garron addressed Rhetta and Len next. "Doesn't do much good to question her if she can't speak properly now, does it?"

"She had a terrible fall, landed right on her mouth when she came down," Rhetta responded.

"I'm sure," Garron answered; he seemed unimpressed. "Alright, step outside, you two. I'll let you know when I need you."

The two guards stepped out of the room before Garron addressed me. "You'll need to be seated for the first portion. We need to monitor your heart rate and other organ functions. Please be seated now, Lyris." He motioned me toward the bed-shaped object in the center of the room.

I watched Garron fiddle with one of the machines next to me. He entered information from his lambent to the much larger machine. He scanned through the data and paid very little attention to me.

If I could just get these restraints around his neck ... but then what? I don't even know how to get out of this room with its disappearing doors, and I'm sure that Rhetta and Len would be really happy to see me escape and fall on my face again. No, I should just sit here and get my scans done so they can heal me, and then I can figure out what to do next.

It didn't feel like anything happened, but Garron swiped away over on the machine. His brow furrowed as he read the information produced from my scan. That made me even more nervous.

"Alright, Lyris, your first scan is complete. For the next one, please lay back and we'll begin."

"*Itth* done already?" I asked. "I *thidn't* even *notith* anything happening."

"Yes, the scanner is very efficient. Now, just lay back," he instructed.

As I did what I was told, the bed came up to meet me. It molded around my body to hold me up.

"There, great," Garron said. "Now, both arms down at your sides."

I moved my left arm down, cringing as I did. Again, the bed molded around each arm in a cradling position.

"Now, let's be very still for this part. Try to relax your body, and we'll begin the scan."

Try to relax? I laughed to myself. *Sure, this is completely normal and not at all a terrifying situation to be in.* I tried my best to remain still, and looked up to the ceiling with my good eye. I squinted at the bright light until the scan was complete. I heard Garron mutter under his breath. Then I saw him towering over me.

"All done," he said. "Sit up slowly, please." Garron helped me up, and I think the bed thing did too.

"I just need your blood sample, then we're done here."

My heart pounded; flashes of the crazed man screaming down in the cell area ran through my head. I hesitated. Then held out my hand to Garron. My fate was sealed with a quick prick of my finger.

Would I have the blood and become a Watcher?

I barely knew what that meant, but if Balor was right, there was a very small chance. *I'll be fine.*

"Feeling alright, Lyris?"

"Yeah, I'm *juth* great."

Criminals weren't privy to their own medical records until deemed necessary, so I had to wait until my hearing was scheduled with the Council of Five. That's what I was told before Garron scurried off with whatever information he gained from my scans.

Still barefoot, and in my new stark clothing, Len and Rhetta escorted me through those brightly lit halls again. I thought maybe I'd be lucky enough to go back to my cell, but we seemed to be going another direction. Garron mentioned questioning after the scans, and I felt a rush of adrenaline.

"*Whrr* we going?" I asked Rhetta. She seemed to be the talker of the two.

"Questioning."

I dragged my feet a little when she said that.

"Taking longer to get there will only delay the inevitable. If you're brave enough to do something to get you in here, then you're brave enough to answer questions about what you did."

Great, if the questioning had gone anything like it had with the enforcements, I wasn't going to make it much further.

Rhetta and Len used their lambents to open the door at the end of the hall. Thankfully, this room was not quite as bright. It had an eerie, calming effect I couldn't quite explain. Once I was seated, I started to feel at ease. I let that calming sensation fall over me, entranced for what seemed like no reason at all.

"It's kicking in," I heard Rhetta say. Her voice sounded a little fuzzy.

"Hello, Lyris," someone greeted me.

The room seemed to fade around me, and all I could focus on was that new voice. I felt like the two guards were still there with me, but that didn't matter. All that mattered was this new voice that came from a form in front of me. I can't quite make out what that voice looked like.

Heh, a voice doesn't look like anything. I mean, I can't make out what the source of that voice looks like. It's just a shadowy form sitting across from me. I glanced up to see the guards, but they were just shadows now too.

"*Ello, voith,*" I heard myself say.

The shadowy thing looked over me to the guards, then tilted its head back to me.

"Are you in pain, Lyris?"

Pain? Yes, pain. I was in pain all over, but I can't quite feel it now. It's just I can't quite make my mouth move right to make my own voice work like the shadow's voice. I thought about it some more before lifting up my hand to my jaw, rubbing it to figure out why it wasn't working properly.

The shadow reached toward me, and I sensed a shadowy arm outstretched to my jaw. There was something in the shadow's hand, but it was all a blur. The shadow used whatever was in his hand, waved it over my head, from the top of my skull down to my neck—back and forth—as my head lulled. I tried to keep it up.

"Lyris, can you try to speak to me now?"

"Sure." My voice sounded a little more clear to my ears, but it was hard to tell if I was slurring my words. My head was still fuzzy, but my face didn't feel clenched anymore. "*Mmm hmm.* I think I can talk now."

"Very good," the shadow told me. "Lyris, you stole some valuable information. The information you took belongs to the Council of Five. Do you remember taking it?"

"Yep." I didn't even have to think about my answer.

The shadow seemed to nod to the other guards standing next to me again. They looked like shadows now too.

Why did they turn into shadows? Am I a shadow? I looked down at my hands, flexing them, and noticed they looked a little blurry, but I was not a shadow. *Whew, that would've been really strange if I was shadow.* I thought my hands still felt stiff like my face did before that other shadow fixed it.

"Lyris?" The shadow voice brought me back. "Lyris, who sold you this information?"

"Rock. Her name is Pearla Rockwell, but she goes by Rock because she thinks—Ha! She thinks it sounds like a man's name and that she's less likely to get caught. Misdirection!"

I felt a snort and a giggle escape from me at the thought of Pearla thinking she couldn't get caught when I had just told them.

"Lyris."

Oh, that's me! "Yes, shadow?" I straightened up and tried to stop laughing.

"Where can we find Pearla Rockwell?"

"She lives ... haha! She lives in the upper quadrant with all the highborns! Because she is a highborn! Her son is married into the E'Trell family. Her own son!"

Tears leaked from my eyes with all the laughter, and I remembered somewhere in the back of my mind that one of those eyes was shut. I tried to touch it, but it felt swollen and puffy, which made me sad.

"We need to get her into the healing chamber. This isn't going to work if her body is this weak. Look at the effect its having on her. We should heal her first, then bring her back in to continue questioning." I heard the shadow tell the guards.

Heal me first? Yeah, heal me! That's sounds really great. My head lulled again. My chin rested on my chest now. I didn't think I wanted to pick my head back up yet. It felt nice to rest it.

"Lyris?"

"Yes, shadow." I jerked my head back up.

"Lyris, I just need you to answer a few more questions and then we can heal you."

Yes! Healing sounds good.

"Were you hired by a man named Severin Eilish to take this information?"

"Yes! Severin is who I sell most of my information to! I work with Severin a lot, but then he got me stuck in here. He shouldn't have done that. I'm good at what I do."

"I'm sure you are. And I take it that means you've done this before? Sold information to Severin?"

"Yeah, a bunch of times."

"I see. Well we can talk more in depth about that later."

"*Uh huh,* good. Later."

My head hung down, weary from all the questions and truths.

"She's starting to go again. Let's bring her to the healing chamber."

All three shadows moved toward me as I tried to hold my own head up. I thought they picked me up because I kept trying to sit back down. It didn't seem right that I should be standing when I weighed so much. I felt really heavy and like I needed to sleep.

One of them carried me away when I heard the shadow voice again.

"One last thing, Lyris. Do you know what's on that recording?"

The word "Sators" popped into my head, but something held me back. My foggy brain resisted and kept the answer to myself.

"*Hahaha!* I guess you'll never know, shadow!"

He'll never know, I thought. My vision cleared up a bit. I saw that the shadow was actually a woman. Then, the shadow looked blurry again, and I was carried away.

CHAPTER 8

SENIA

I turned the key in the lock of my apartment door. I was gasping for breath after climbing three flights of stairs. It became more difficult for me each day to make that climb. I balanced the bags of groceries and my purse on one arm as I nearly fell through the door. I flung my purse on the couch and dropped the groceries and keys on the floor, then ran to the kitchen sink and threw up for the second time today.

I turned the water on, splashed some on my face, and cupped a handful into my mouth. I collapsed on the couch, winded and frustrated, before sobbing with my head in my hands.

A few days had passed since Dr. Reynolds delivered my diagnosis, but I still couldn't find the strength to call my father. *Get up*, I told myself. *Stop feeling sorry for yourself and get up.* Groceries sprawled across the floor and the ice cream had surely started to melt.

If you're going to die soon, you might as well eat whatever junk food you want, I thought. I really had no appetite, though; so what did it matter if ice cream melted on my floor? Soon, it would be someone else's floor. Someone else could walk from their front door to their bedroom in a few steps, and accidentally knock things over, trying to cook in this tiny kitchen. Maybe the next person who lived in this studio apartment would have a more fulfilling life. Maybe they wouldn't just live to work like I had. Maybe they would go out with friends or fall in love. I hoped they would enjoy life more than I had.

Lightning flashed outside the window, and then a huge crack of thunder made me jump. I peaked through the blinds and saw that it was pouring rain outside. There hadn't been a cloud in the sky a few minutes ago. *That came out of nowhere. Yes, Senia, that's what came out of nowhere—a storm. Not to mention the unbearable headaches and memory loss that hit you. Not this brain tumor in your mid-twenties.* My mind seemed to wander all the time now.

The next thing I knew, I was lying in bed, watching television in my pajamas and glasses.

I didn't recall changing or moving there at all. I got up and moved back to the living room, and noticed that there were no longer groceries spewed across the floor. *I must have cleaned it all up, after all,* I thought. If I had to forget things, at least I could forget having to clean. You always had to find the humor in your situation, no matter how bleak it seemed, right? *Oh, please, there's nothing humorous about this.*

I filled up a large glass of water and took my many medications before going back to bed. *I have to stop this,* I thought. *No more moping around. Tomorrow, I will call my father. Tomorrow, I will do things differently. Tomorrow, I will live.*

I was restless the entire night, waking from dreams that made no sense. In one dream, I was lying in a field of red grass. My hair was longer than it had ever been and spread out around me. I laughed at a tall, blonde-haired man as he juggled some strange fruit before tossing one to me. Such kind eyes the man had, I thought. They were vibrant and almost violet in color. It felt like he was my family, but—except for my father—I had no family left.

I looked up at a pale pink sky and saw three moons, which I pointed out to the man. A shadow blocked out the moons as it crept over the sky. Another man stood above us and looked down where we sat. I could not make out his appearance, but I was terrified.

I awoke with a jolt.

The dream was so vivid and felt real, but it made no sense. I supposed it had to mean something. Maybe the three moons or the pink sky were symbolic. I didn't really know, but when I slipped back to sleep, I saw the same blonde man smiling back at me again—this time, he was in a large hall, which seemed to glow all around us.

I spun around and around, looking up at the breathtaking scene surrounding me, but when I turned back toward the blonde man, he frowned, and the shadow returned along with the other man. This time, the other man stepped out from the shadows and looked right into my eyes. Everything around us seemed to explode, and I felt a falling sensation.

I woke up again, this time panting with a sheen of sweat on my forehead. Then I ran to the bathroom and vomited again. I was almost glad of it this time. I didn't want to fall back asleep after those dreams. I couldn't put my finger on why they bothered me so much. I couldn't get the image of the blonde man out of my head. Every time I thought of him, it made me happy and then overwhelmingly sad.

The other man in the shadows, however, I could not recall. I remembered everything else about my dream—as if it had actually happened to me. Yet, I couldn't recall anything about his appearance—except that his eyes bored into me—and that he had frightened me so much.

I will stay awake, I thought. It was just a dream, but I was still afraid. I turned my small bedroom television on and clicked through the channels. I looked for anything that wasn't an infomercial. The next thing I knew, it was late morning. I was dressed and preparing myself to make phone calls to any of my few friends who would care about my condition.

I had skipped ahead again. I was losing time. Had I blacked out? That didn't seem fair since I had little time left in the first place. Even if I was just watching crappy television at four in the morning, I still wanted *that* time. I deserved that much, at least. Try as I might, I couldn't recall what I had done. Even if I had merely fallen asleep, I didn't think I had started dressing myself and making plans for the day while sleepwalking. The last thing I remembered was watching television after a bad dream. I felt childish as I tried to reassure myself that I was safe. But I wasn't safe, was I?

I couldn't remember the dream that had frightened me—only that I had been scared. What did I need to be afraid of? I am going to die soon anyway. What could be more frightening than that? At that moment, the thought of calling my father was the most frightening, but I took a deep breath, and just as I was about to touch "Dad" on the screen of my phone, I noticed a small note on my kitchen counter. RE was all it said, and it was in my handwriting. What did RE mean?

It was a long and draining day. I finally called my father to tell him the news of my illness, but when I heard his voice, I couldn't make myself tell him. I was his only child, and I was dying. Maybe it was selfish. Maybe it would hurt him more to be shocked when I was gone than to know what was coming. Either way, I didn't want any more pity. I'd received enough of that from my other calls.

My new friends— more like acquaintances—all had a similar reaction. I knew I could expect at least one of them to show up with a casserole any minute. *Screw this*, I thought. *I'm done telling people my sob story, and I'm done working. What's the point?*

I opened up my laptop and pulled up my bank statement. If ever there was a time to splurge, it was now. I wanted to escape. I wanted to use whatever time I had left and be someone new. I looked at location after location on my laptop before I finally decided where I wanted to go. I purchased my airline ticket. I wasn't going to sit around wasting time any longer. I choked back feeling nauseous and ran again to the kitchen sink. When I stopped gagging, I filled a glass of water.

"Screw this too."

I got another glass from the cabinet, then stretched up on my tiptoes to reach a bottle of scotch that was still unopened from my past birthday. I rarely drank. I never cared for it much, to be honest. But no time like the present. I twisted the cap off and poured the amber-colored liquid into the glass. I threw the scotch back in one gulp, nearly gagging again. I kept it down, though, and felt it burn down my throat, warming my entire body. I shivered a little, then smiled. I started to pour another glass.

"Screw it," I said again. I took a gulp straight from the bottle before setting it back on the counter.

I glanced over at the rows of pill bottles lining my dingy worn-in counter next to the kitchen sink. I thought about what Dr. Reynolds said during my visit. "You'll need these in the weeks to come." He said it so matter of factly—as if he *actually* knew me.

I picked up one of the medication bottles and threw it across the length of my tiny apartment. The plastic bottle hit the sliding glass door to the balcony. I watched the cap fly off during impact—the pills broke free and littered my cheap shag carpeting like shattered glass. I grabbed the rest of the medication bottles and hurled them, one by one, across the room.

"Screw these pills! I'm done being sick! I'm done!"

It felt cathartic to see those pills scattered across the floor. I was not going to take medication.

I marched toward my closet door and discarded everything that was in the way of my suitcase. I flung the suitcase on my bed and grabbed random clothes to shove in before I zipped it up again. I reached behind my nightstand for my phone charger. I glanced at the framed picture of myself on the nightstand. In it, I was a little girl with my hands folded sweetly in my lap. My mother sat beside me. She was still so young and beautiful before she got sick.

No, I wouldn't dwell on that either. *Only good things for me from here on out.* I turned and marched right back out of my room—suitcase rolling behind me. I grabbed my purse and tossed the phone charger in. Then I flung the shoulder bag over my shoulder. I walked out of my front door, not bothering to lock it. My suitcase bumped down every step of the three flights of stairs.

At the bottom landing, I pulled out my phone. I only had one call left to make.

"Yes, I need a ride, please." I used my perkiest phone voice. "Going to the airport. *Uh huh.* As soon as possible. I live in an apartment complex. Yes, I have the address."

CHAPTER 9

CARRICK

The Erretas and I continued reliving my most recent memory. I returned to the entrance of the Great Corridor as I always did after my time as a Watcher, and made my way toward the Council. I was still reeling from the information I gained during my time as Dr. Umbridge. My footsteps echoed through the large halls as I walked the great length to where the members were seated. Their eyes were fixed on me. The weight of my stride and the Council's reaction to my presence alerted me that I was back in my own body. I was strong again and had my wits about me.

When I was in another world, my mind and my surroundings always seemed a bit hazier than when I was back where I ought to be. Though, who can say where I ought to be? According to my people, I should be serving my time elsewhere. Others thought I should no longer *exist* at all. No matter them, though. I was fit and strong, so I strode with the confidence that came with being myself.

The Council members' uneasiness created tension in the room. I could feel it grow the closer I got to them.

I was told I didn't speak with them the way other Watchers did. Rahm's black, contempt-filled eyes bore into me as I came to a stop in front of the semicircular barricade separating us. While it was made to appear that we were in the same room, I was not even in the same realm as the Council. The barrier between us looked like a waterfall from a distance, but as you got closer, the barricade became more transparent and still. At the closest point, you felt like you were face to face with Council members, but you couldn't reach out and touch them. My guess was the barrier served as protection for them. Watchers could try to harm one of them; I knew I had been tempted a time or two.

The Council consisted of five members—three male and two female. These were not the same Council members who held these seats at its origin. Long ago, the Council consisted of a male and female pair called the Khassos, another pair called the Sators, and a fifth member, who was a citizen of Anatan, serving as the swing vote. The pairs were tasked with creating for our kind.

Legends said we all descended from the Sators. They created all we knew, but there was a need for balance, and a means to conserve energy. So, the Khassos were put on the original Council to maintain that balance. The Khassos later betrayed the Sators. As a result, we lost the power to create.

Since our kind could no longer make things new—as we once did—we had to search what was already made to ensure our kind lived on. The Council had to decide where—and more importantly, when—to inhabit, based on the Watchers' findings. In truth, it was rare for Council members to go against the will of the Lead member, Rahm.

With the loss of the Khassos and Sators, the Council now served as a decision-making committee, comprised of five members. Each member gained his or her seat through election, birthright, or conquest. While the Council had five members, it was also called the Council of Five because it represented the five empires and the decisions to be made for all of them.

Rahm held the Lead position in the Council, and always casted the first official vote. The others tended to follow suit. Rahm's father, Tahrell, held the Lead position before him. Tahrell abdicated at some point, I can only assume. One day, I came to report my findings, and

Rahm was in his father's place. I must admit I was happy to see Tahrell gone. He and I did not share a pleasant history.

Ashala was Second position. She had been a Council member longer than the others. Then there were the twins: Lyde and Latham. When they were younger, they won their spots on the Council by warring their way through many kingdoms for our people. They settled disputes as they went. In truth, they could've ruled over any of the realms they wanted, but they eventually opted for the more peaceful approach and rejoined their own kind. Lyde and Latham retired their armor to rule on the Council.

Lyde and Latham both had blue eyes that sparkled, and golden hair that gave them an ethereal glow. Though Lyde is female and Latham is male, they seemed to think with the same mind; it was as if they were *always* one. From what I had seen, they communicated without words, so they were able to make decisions just by making eye contact with one another.

Last was Cade. He took his position as Council member more serious than the rest. He weighed each option and calculated what the best outcome would be. He never blindly followed his peers. That is why Cade had the final vote. He was not tied to the other members, and always served as the impartial vote. He was also not one of *us*, which added to his impartiality.

Cade came from one of the realms created by the Sators. He won the Council over with his discoveries about his own world, and was intelligent enough to take the offer of joining the Council when his world ended. He was highly regarded as one of the most intelligent life forms we had come across. He rarely displayed emotion. They said that even as his own realm died, he watched on without a single tear or word of lament. It meant a great deal to our people to watch something created by the Sators fall apart—even if we never lived there ourselves. Cade's lack of emotion was not something that would soon be forgotten.

His amber-colored eyes always seemed to appraise his surroundings. Cade almost always had a serene look on his face too. I, however, knew that on the inside, Cade's mind worked to solve a great puzzle only he could see. His ebony skin contrasted greatly with the golden twins he sat beside in Council meetings. Cade was very large, with a formidable presence and a mind to match.

I reported my findings to Rahm, Ashala, Lyde, Latham, and Cade. They weighed the information they received from Watchers, and decided what our kind must do. Sometimes I was allowed to hear their input. Most of the time, however, they dismissed me. They would enjoy my findings while being Umbridge. A big discovery from the realm of Erreta always pleased me, and this news would please the Council as well.

"Greetings, Watcher," Ashala declared. "I trust your journey was enlightening."

She was not really welcoming me. This was just the formal greeting to all the returning Watchers like myself.

"It was expedient," I addressed the entire Council. "I almost enjoyed it."

"Their world is not for you to enjoy, Watcher," Ashala responded.

She'd never been a fan of mine. I suppose that none of them really had been, not after what I did. Who was I kidding? None of them had ever *truly* been my brethren. What would they know? They were from another generation, a much different time than the one I came from. All the Council knew was what had been passed down to them from previous generations.

Ashala looked down with her dark eyes; it was as though I was an insect. Her hair was so black it shined almost blue in the bright light. If she ever wore her hair down, it would surely hit her knees. Ashala was very proud of her position as Second in the Council of Five. Her arrogant posture as she sat behind the dais showed it. As Second position, she spoke to me—more like interrogated me—about the circumstances I witnessed. It was her job to ask most of the questions so Rahm could concentrate on his decision as Lead position.

"Get on with it," Ashala prompted. "What news do you have for us, Watcher?"

The sooner I could get the information to them, the sooner I could get out of their sight. They did not enjoy dealing with me.

"Andrew Whitfield is a scholar of astrophysics in the realm of Erreta." I contained my smile as I emphasized *Erreta*. "He found a planet that can sustain life."

The Council members shifted in their seats and looked back and forth to Rahm. He only stared me down.

"I remained on with him as long as I could before I was sent back to you. From what I have witnessed, though, he will be the one to lead them to the planet. Not likely in his lifetime. By my approximations, it will take them several lifespans to get there. He will not live long enough to see it happen himself, but he will get the credit for the discovery, and it will work. The Erretas will go on."

I stood, waiting for a response—a barrage of questions from Ashala—anything. But the silence lingered, so I went on.

"They have made the discovery themselves; they will endure. You understand, Council members, do you not?"

More silence. The tension in the meeting place grew. The Council did not seem astounded or pleased. They merely looked back and forth at each other, but deferred to Rahm to be the first to speak.

I suddenly realized this was not new information to the Council. So, why was I sent there? Something went wrong. Rahm stood as if to vote. I was confused. They didn't ask a single question. The Council didn't discuss anything. A system typically filled with pomp and circumstance got reduced to a mere head nod before being taken to a vote.

Rahm looked down at me. "They will not endure if we inhabit it first."

He could not be serious.

"There are rules," I said.

"Rules which we vote upon, *Watcher*." Rahm made sure I remembered my position. "The Council conferred previously to your report. We have decided we will inhabit this new realm."

"How is it you came by this knowledge of a new realm in the first place?" I asked. "Why was I dispatched if you were already privy to this information?"

"That is not your concern," Rahm said.

"Not my concern? Of course it's my concern, it's my—"

"Watcher, it is your duty to report back to us and you have done so," Ashala interrupted me. "Therefore, you are dismissed now."

I took a deep breath and tried to gather my thoughts. I wanted to speak more carefully this time so as not to upset them. "I am a servant to our realm, Council. I understand my duty to you and to our people, but is it not also your duty to explain your decisions to *all* members of the realm? Whatever I may be, I am still a member of the realm. What are your intentions for the Erretas, if you mean to make that planet ours?"

"If I'm not mistaken, I believe you lost that privilege long ago," Rahm said.

"Perhaps I have, but my lost privileges do not grant you the right to wipe out the entire Erretas species. We cannot make another realm like it. It is unique, and the Sators are lost to us, if you recall."

I could tell Rahm was trying to contain his anger. "How could we forget the demise of our people, *Carrick*?"

My real name was a curse upon the lips of those who used it. Rahm made it sound every inch the ugly word that it was.

"The Council is not required to divulge the details of its decisions to Watchers," Rahm reminded me. "Now leave and report back to us when you have more information."

"I will not be dismissed." I didn't budge from my spot on the floor. "We are not to touch the lives of the Erretas, and you know this."

"My sister and I have fought many wars for our people, and we could battle again if needed, but you need not worry, Watcher," Latham interjected. "We do not break any laws in what we plan. We will not battle the Erretas for the planet. We will not eradicate them in the new world, for they will never make it there."

"You've said enough, Latham," Lyde said.

I'd been through enough of these to know Lyde mustered as much calmness as she could.

"What my brother is trying to convey to you is that their world is already dying," Lyde informed me. "We don't need to fight them or take anything from them because they will never make it that far. Their time will soon end. They will cease to exist. They have done it to themselves. They have damaged their world beyond repair. It has nothing to do with us; thus we have found a loophole to our rule. It is only a happy coincidence that the Erretas have made this discovery, and we will reap the benefits."

"So, you see, Watcher, this is happy news!" Latham said. "We will inhabit it before they do, but their world will end due to their own demise. We do not directly intervene. We simply claim it for our own. What we do is legal."

I could not tell if he was trying to reassure me or himself.

"So you have decided already, then? All of you?" I asked.

Silence.

"But she is bound to their world," I muttered. The gravity of their decision hit me all at once. "How long?"

Tension filled the meeting place again. I realized they were frightened of me.

"How long?" I screamed. I heard my own voice reverberate through the Great Corridor.

"It matters not." Ashala's response was cold. "She is lost to you, Watcher. You cannot save her."

My heart sank. I knew Ashala was right. I could do nothing except what I was cursed to do—watch.

"How did you come about this knowledge?" I pressed. "Which Watcher told you? Was it Arden?"

The Council was silent once again.

"Answer me, Council! I at least have that right!"

"You forget yourself, Watcher!" Ashala shouted. I saw her dark eyes bulge with anger.

"Cade, please. Surely you can see this is a violation of our laws. Say something, please," I begged. "Tell them your thoughts on the matter."

With a mere tilt of his head, Cade addressed the Council, not me. "I have spoken my piece, as the Council of Five has heard during our deliberations. But now, I believe it is time for the official vote. I would ask, however, that this Watcher would remain to hear the vote. It is his right as a member of the realm and as a reporter to the Council."

Cade had done me a small favor. While the others would have me gone, he allowed me to hear the Council's decision. Cade looked at me almost apologetically, as if to say, "This is the best I can do for you."

"Let us take it to the vote," Cade directed the others.

My heart began to race, as it might if I were waiting for an executioner to swing the ax toward my neck.

Rahm rose.

"The Council of Five will now make an official vote on the decision to inhabit the new territory, which will be called *Kallan*, in memory of what was lost to our people," Rahm stated. He knew he was twisting the knife that had already been plunged into my heart. He smirked, knowing full well what he was doing. "May the Sators before us grant us the wisdom to make our decision, and may the Khassos caution us to do what is just. I, Rahm, Lead position of the Council of Five, vote yes in favor of inhabiting the new territory."

Ashala sprang from her seat. "I, Ashala, Second position of the Council of Five, vote yes in favor of inhabiting the new territory of Kallan."

The twins rose as one.

"I, Lyde, protector of the Council of Five, vote yes in favor of inhabiting the new territory of Kallan." Lyde nodded to her brother.

"I, Latham, protector of the Council of Five, vote yes in favor of inhabiting the new territory of Kallan."

I watched in horror as Cade, the final Council member, rose from his seat.

"I, Cade, protector of the Council of Five, vote no to inhabiting the new territory of Kallan."

Cade looked directly at me. "In memory of what was lost," he added.

For the first time, I saw a slight sign of emotion out of Cade.

The other Council members look shocked, but regained their composure when Rahm stood again.

"The decision has been made by the Council of Five. We will communicate it to our people. Until this knowledge is communicated, no one present may utter a word of what has been spoken here today. This I do swear."

"This I do swear," the other Council members repeated.

I was silent.

"Watcher, you must repeat the phrase before you are dismissed," Rahm said.

Fear, anger, and raw emotion pulsed through me as I gathered my thoughts.

"Through this world or any other, I will hunt you down, Rahm— and your father—for what you have done to her ... to our people! You will pay, and you will suffer as I have suffered. This I do swear!"

Before anyone on the Council could respond, I moved to the farthest right pillar and threw my weight into it. The first pillar crumbled, creating a domino effect on the other pillars until one of them slammed into the barrier between the Council and me. My surroundings jostled sideways, and loud cracks of marble slabs busted and fell to the ground, filling my ears. Upon surveying the damage, I saw there was nothing left but the translucent barrier.

As if moving in slow motion, I saw the room right itself from its sideways position. Chunks of marble fell all around me during the shift. I barely had time to watch the barrier ripple before I was knocked to the ground. I laid trapped, watching the meeting place crumble. As the barrier shattered, I saw a warped image of Rahm's face. He was consumed with anger. Our connection severed.

This *could* mean no communication between the Council and the Watchers in my current realm, which also meant no more communication with whoever gave the Council this information in the first place. I would bet my life on which Watcher delivered *that* information. I had to act fast. I had to find her before the Council did. She was the only Watcher who would want the Erretas' world—and me—destroyed. It had to be Arden.

I have to find my sister. That was my last coherent thought before darkness claimed me. This darkness, however, was different. I wasn't in another body. I was in my own.

CHAPTER 10

LYRIS

I was healed! While my memories were a bit fuzzy as to how it all happened, I now walked around pain free. I didn't have that weird twitch in my leg any longer. There was no more pain in my arm. My body didn't ache all over. And my vision was clear again. I could finally think straight without the ringing in my ears or the dazed, sick feeling every time I moved. I felt whole again. I was, however, still wearing restraints and flanked by my favorite guards, Rhetta and Len.

The bright hallways turned into a dark corridor, which meant I was almost back to my cell. I noticed other prisoners this time. The cells weren't so empty.

We stopped in front of the same cell I was in before. I couldn't recall all that happened since I left this cell, but at least I was healed. I felt energized, like waking up from a deep, rejuvenating sleep.

I felt relieved at seeing Balor on his cot in the cell next to mine. Rhetta opened my cell and removed my restraints before leaving my cell to lock the door.

"Rhetta, wait." I said. "What happens to me now?"

"Hell if I know, Suttor. You either pulled some kind of stunt in there or you've got something that helps you avoid questioning." Rhetta seemed unhappy about this. "And let me tell you, no one avoids questioning. I've seen guys twice the size of Len try to resist questioning, and they all end up crying and asking for their mommies by the second question."

My energized feeling wilted. "What do you mean, Rhetta? What did I do in there? I can't remember anything that happened."

Rhetta engaged the lock, but remained silent.

"Come on, Rhetta! What happened?"

Again, no answer.

"Len! Len, what did I do when they questioned me? What are they going to do to me?"

Rhetta wheeled around to face me through the cell barrier. She kept her voice low and spoke close to the barrier.

"You laughed at them. I don't know what they'll do to you now." Then she and Len walked away, leaving me alone with that last terrifying thought.

I walked back to my cot and sat down. I brushed my unruly hair out of my face, trying to smooth it back and out of the way. *What had gone on in there and why couldn't I remember it? I had laughed at the questioner? I wonder if they had gotten any information out of me.*

I barely remembered the healing, and nothing came back to me about the questioning. I didn't know if I would go to trial or rot forever in this cell. Even worse, I didn't know if they would rough me up again to get more information from me. They wouldn't heal me just to break me again. *Would they?*

"Hey, you don't look like hell anymore," Balor said.

"Don't feel like hell anymore either. Though my nerves are pretty fried."

"And she talks too! Glad you've got your voice and your wits back, kid. You sounded like you had a bag of marbles stuck in your mouth before. Looks like you can see out of both of those eyes again as well."

I twisted my hair up on top of my head, trying to tie it in a knot to make it stay there.

Now that I was healed, there had to be a way out of here. I wonder if Severin was locked up in here or if he had sold me out for his own freedom. I needed to work with what I had, and I had a chatty neighbor.

"Balor, you've been to trial before. How long did they make you wait in here before that happened? Did you get your sentencing right away or did they have to force a confession out of you? I'm trying to figure out what I'm up against here."

"Ha! I went to trial quite some time ago, kid. I've been questioned a time or two, though. First time was pretty easy. You crack because you have to. You tell them whatever they want to know without even meaning to. They've got tricks of all kinds in this place. Works pretty well."

"You mean they have some kind of truth serum or something? That's ridiculous. They must have beat it out of you and you gave up the information they needed to put you away," I said. "How are they allowed to do that, though? I thought all bodily harm was against the law. How do they get away with it?"

"Oh, you sweet, sweet, kid." Balor tried not to laugh. "As you found out the hard way, they can do whatever they want; they *are* the law."

"Does the Council know about this though? Do they know the measures enforcements are taking? Do they know about all the testing?"

"Of course they do, kid. Who do you think orders them to do it?"

I got that sinking feeling in my stomach again. *Oh, this is bad.*

"So, you're in here for life then?" I asked.

"Well I'm not in *here* for life." Balor pointed to the floor. "They keep us moving a lot more now that there are so few Watchers."

"Wait, so you're a Watcher?"

"In the flesh. Though sometimes not my own."

They still hadn't told me if I had the blood or if they would make me a Watcher. What if I only had enough of the blood for them to try, but not enough for me to travel? I'd end up like that madman I saw pass my cell.

"Does it fail often? I mean, that man we saw the other day? Do people end up like him a lot?" I asked.

"You're worried you're going to have the blood?"

"Yeah, I guess so. I guess I'm worried about all of it. I mean, I either don't have the blood and rot in a cell, or worse, I do have it and then I'm a Watcher for life."

"Aww, I'm sure you wouldn't get a life sentence. No way."

"You did."

"Well, I'm a different story. You're just a kid. What did you do anyway? Steal some food to feed your family?"

"I did steal, I guess. But it's more complicated than that."

"Kid, you've got nothing to worry about. After your trial, you'll never see me again." Balor ran his hand through his spiked hair.

"I'm not so sure." I tried to hide the emotion from my voice.

"Let me ask you this," Balor's voice was gentler, less teasing now. "Why did you do it? Why did you steal in the first place? Even if you make yourself all the fame and fortune you can find in this world, they're never going to let you be one of them. You'll never be highborn. There's no reason to commit a crime here, not for someone as young as you. So what were you looking for? The thrill? The adventure? I'll tell you this, kid, you'll never have an adventure like what you'll see as a Watcher. I've been male, female, old, young, and my appearance has changed in more ways than I knew possible. I've seen things, felt things, lived and died again through situations you couldn't possibly dream up. There are worlds we would have never even known existed. Life on this bio-dome, its all the same for you and me, but if I could go back ... Oh, kid, let me tell you, I'd leave this place and go."

"You'd go where?" I asked.

The excited look was gone from his eyes. He stopped himself, not wanting me to know whatever it was he almost said.

"Let's just say things have a way of working out. One way or another, you get what you need. It might not always seem like it's going your way, but whatever happens—Watcher or not—you'll figure it out. You've got things left to do, kid. I can tell."

I got up from my cot and paced my cell. Balor was right. Everything would work out.

"Are you ever going to tell me what you did to get in here?" Balor pushed. "I mean, what you really did?"

"Does it matter?"

"No, I guess not."

I realized Balor hadn't told me what he did to get a life sentence. "Balor, what did you do?"

He smiled a big, mischievous grin. His green eyes sparkled.

"Me? I helped hack the Panoptis—the Watcher transport system."

CHAPTER 11

CARRICK

I was in darkness. My eyes tried to flutter open, and all I saw, as they did, was the flashes of light through the dark. There was a faint humming noise somewhere in the back of my mind, and I felt a sharp pain at the back of my head. Color shot through my vision, then darkness again.

Her eyes are beautiful. They are the most beautiful eyes that I have ever seen, and I have looked into and through thousands of them. It's always her eyes that I notice. Her long lashes flutter as the light shines down on her. She is on her side next to me, her head propped up on her hand.

"Well?" She asks. "Do you like it?"

I look up and see two great lights in the emerald sky. For some reason, I can't lift my head off of the ground. "Yes," I think, but she somehow hears me. I am rewarded with her smile, one that makes those perfect eyes sparkle. *Her eyes*, I think, *it's always her eyes.*

Again, I am lost to darkness.

"I have made my decision," I hear my own voice say. Then, I repeat, "This I do swear," until I think my ears will bleed.

The repetition finally stops, and then a deafening silence. I see nothing but black. Suddenly, I hear her voice.

"I still love you," she whispers.

Her hand is in mine, and I am content. My heart is full as we walk through a valley filled with fragrant plants.

"It's beautiful," I tell her.

She smiles at me, and she is both different and the same. *What does that mean?*

Then, there is darkness again.

A tear trickles down her face as I approach her. She looks down on the wreckage. I wait for her violet eyes to meet my own, but she will not look at me. I look at the destruction instead, and am filled with sorrow. All the land is engulfed in flames and rubble as I have seen many times before, but this one was so new, and that makes it harder to bear.

"We have to stop this," she says.

"You know we cannot. They will punish us."

"What punishment could be worse than this?"

Something about that question tugs at me. I know it seems wrong, and then I cannot think at all.

She cries in my arms as I stroke her hair. I'm trying to calm her for what must surely be the millionth time. She is so upset, but all I can selfishly concentrate on is how wonderful it feels to hold her again.

"I thought I had lost you forever, Carrick. I wasn't me. I couldn't remember!" She sobs.

"I know, my love. I know," I reassure her.

She stops and freezes in my arms. Then looks up at me—terrified. "Who are you?" She asks. Why are you touching me? Who are you? She is frantic.

Pain hits my chest as I accept that I will lose her again. She is ripped from my grasp by a force I cannot see, and the pain is unbearable.

"Eirene!" I sob. Then all I know is darkness again.

My vision was blurry as my eyes tried to focus on the ruin around me. There were chunks of marble and rubble all around me. I was still in the Great Corridor. I hadn't left, nor had I transformed into another body. I was pinned underneath a large pillar—one that would crush any of my other more fragile forms. I had a brief moment of fear for my life—my *real* life—which was strange after living so long as a Watcher. Normally, I would not remain in my true form for this long, nor would I remain in the Great Corridor after I'd reported. Something was different. My gamble may have paid off. *Did I really manage to damage the Great Corridor enough to sever communication?*

I lifted the pillar off my body. Making my way to my feet again, I noticed how strong and free I felt. My strength felt like it was back, but that was impossible. I stumbled a little as another huge pillar fell down behind me. I did not have power to the extent that I once had. Still, I had much more strength than I did in any form as a Watcher. I looked to where the barrier was before I shattered it, and though it was clearly broken, there was a flicker of light where the Council once appeared. I inspected the Great Corridor further, half expecting to see other Watchers. Would they be called back? I never quite understood the mechanics of how it all worked. There was no movement save the flickering of light and my own.

I waited for the guards or anyone to emerge and restrain me. Surely, I angered the Council enough for serious retribution, but I remained alone. One thing was certain, whatever I did prevented them from communicating with me now.

What now? I had to get to her. I had to find my sister, though I had no clue how I would do that. A pang rose in my heart, but I had no time to think about that now. I had to find a way out of the Great Corridor, but I was used to breaking things, not fixing them. *How could I figure out how something so ancient worked?* I had to try, though. I cautiously made my way up to the enormous podium in front of the barrier. I climbed my way up and over the top, trying to find anything that looked like a control hidden behind the podium. It was difficult to see with such a blinding white light flickering. My attention was drawn to six translucent orbs crackling as if lightning was inside of them. Two of them were clearly broken beyond repair, and another was cracked, but the other three remained intact.

As I studied each orb closer, my eyes adjusted to the constant flickering of light behind me. Inside each orb, I saw the entire planet at once. Millions of movements from the life forms that I knew to be called Ire reflected in my mind as I absorbed the topography from the orb. It was so much information all at once. I couldn't think about anything but the Ire. Some movements seemed to be highlighted and different from the others. They stood out, but they were few.

The other Watchers ... it was the other Watchers observing the Ire. *Concentrate.* It was difficult to think of anything but the Ire. *Stop thinking about them. Think of anything else.*

I couldn't even think of myself. I was in a trance, unable to function except to process their information. My eyes glazed over as thousands of images flashed in my vision. Just when I thought there was no escape from it, the images changed to a blinding white light. *I know that light. I have seen it before.* Another pillar crashed down behind the podium; it dissolved whatever linked my mind to the orb with the Ire's planet. A pillar hit the orb I was so entranced by, and then it all happened fast.

I was sucked through a vortex of sorts, unable to grasp my surroundings. *What is happening to me?* I saw nothing but black, then instantly, every color imaginable in a flicker of a moment. I tried to focus on a singular thing, but I could not. It was a strange sensation to not be able to think. I never thought it was possible. It was as if I was frozen in time, yet moving. As soon as the vortex started, it was over. I could only recall what happened once it ended.

I was sitting in Dr. Umbridge's office chair, where I was before I reported back to the Council of Five. *Am I going back in time? Impossible.* I looked around for a clue as to what the hell happened. The old, black clock on the wall said 10:21. It was dark outside. I glanced down at Umbridge's wrist where I expected to see a large digital watch. I knew Umbridge could barely see, even though the numbers were huge, but there was no watch on my wrist. It was not even his slender wrist I stared down at. *It's my hand!*

It was one thing to stay in my true form in the Great Corridor, but this ... it wasn't possible to be *here* like this.

I placed my hand on my chest, patting it to make sure this was actually happening. I reached for the pens I knew were always in Umbridge's breast pocket and found nothing. I raised my hand to my eyes and found no glasses. I was wearing my own clothes—the clothes I was wearing in the Great Corridor. They were tattered from the destruction I caused. I panicked.

I was much too large for Umbridge's desk and chair. As I stood, the chair flew backward—as if I had launched it as hard as I could. I walked over to Dr. Umbridge's computer.

I moved the mouse to wake up his computer and typed in Dr. Umbridge's username and password. I hovered over the date and time. It was the same day here as when I had left. So much had happened in such a short amount of time. "A mirror," I thought. I hadn't looked at my true reflection in millennia. I needed to see myself to believe it.

I strode down the hall to the men's room; I completely forgot about the alarm system. The alarm didn't go off; it was as if the sensors didn't pick me up. Strange but convenient, I thought. I pushed the door to the men's bathroom open and stared in the mirror that covered the length of the wall above the sinks. My mouth fell open. I saw my true self looking nearly the same as I had the first time I lost my form. I always went back to it when I reported to the Council, but I never remained in it for long. It was one thing to look down at your body and quite another to see your face.

I studied my reflection, taking in the features I almost forgot. My eyes were the first thing I studied, remembering how they displayed every color that an Erretas eye usually took on and more. They started brown around my pupil then swirled to gold and green, then indigo and blue. My vision was impeccable, which I realized now should have been my first clue that I was no longer Jim Umbridge. My face appeared as most Erretas' faces do, but my skin had a healthy, golden glow that other Erretas couldn't naturally achieve. My hair was longer—falling to my shoulders—than most Erretas men wore it now. It was a chestnut brown color, and laid straight, for the most part, but made me look like I belonged in another time. *I will stand out dressed as I am, and with this hairstyle.*

The most striking difference, however, was my size. I would be unable to disguise that, but I was not so large that I would appear alien. I would stand a good head above most Erretas, though, which was definitely tall enough to be noticed. I would draw attention, which would not be good, but not impossible to deal with.

I was back on Erreta. I was where I needed to be, and I even had my own body back. *Why do I still feel an ominous foreboding feeling?* It was *wrong* to be in this world, but in my own form. I did not belong here like this, but this was the hand I was dealt. Considering all that had happened, it was a pretty good hand too. Since I was here, I hoped Arden would be as well.

I set out determined, but my haircut and wardrobe options were limited at ten-thirty at night. More importantly, I needed to test how much of my former power I had access to.

I took a rubber band from Umbridge's office to hold my hair back. I ripped off what was left of my tattered cloak and armor. My clothes would be misconstrued as a costume if I walked around wearing a cape. My pants, despite the holes, looked fairly normal. Plus, I had on a loose-fitting, tunic-like shirt. I still looked questionable, but I also wouldn't draw too much attention. Hopefully, the darkness would make my odd appearance less obvious.

I couldn't go back to Umbridge's house. He had no friends, and I looked drastically different from him. Umbridge's nosey neighbors would surely notice me pulling his car into the driveway. Besides that, Umbridge's clothes no longer fit me. Not much was open past dinnertime here and definitely not any department stores. I needed to see if passing through the alarms at the school was a fluke or if I could do it anywhere.

I made my way out to Dr. Umbridge's old, beat-up car. It creaked and tilted to the left side when I sat in the driver seat. Earlier today, I comfortably drove this vehicle to the school; now, I could barely fit. I reached under the seat and pulled the lever to make more leg room, but my knees still hit the dash. *I just need to get from point A to point B.*

I drove off, hoping to go unnoticed as I made my way to a quiet shopping plaza. I parked and walked up to a men's clothing store called Scott's. I knew the store didn't have surveillance cameras, only an alarm that would go off if the sensors picked up movement. Again, I bypassed the alarm that apparently couldn't detect me in my true form, easily turned the lock of the front door, and quietly walked in. Scott's was more of a handyman's store. It appeared they had more tools than actual clothes, but most people in this town worked with their hands, so it made sense.

I rummaged through a wall of boxes filled with boots made for outdoor activity until I found the larger sizes. Then, I scanned the wall to the left and saw nothing but overalls in denim, white, black, and tan. *There has to be something better in here.*

I grabbed the biggest shirt I could find and some jeans with large pockets and loops on the side for hanging your tools. *Good enough.* These jeans may not look like they're from this decade, but at least they were from this world.

I changed into my new clothes, and closed the entrance of the store like it was my own. I took my old clothes with me. There was a large disposal bin in the back of the plaza, so I threw my clothes in. I needed to ditch the vehicle too—just not where everyone knew who owned it.

I needed to think about the bigger picture, but how the hell was I going to find Arden? She would have a better understanding of what was happening. I knew she reported the information back to the Council before I had the chance to. She always was so intelligent. She would have figured out what was going on long before the rest of us.

I didn't know for sure that Arden was here, but it just made sense. It clicked in my brain like a puzzle piece. *Just drive*, I thought. I knew where I need to go to test myself.

CHAPTER 12

SENIA

This was my second stop on my long list of destinations to see this week. I spent the last few days sunning on the beach and sipping tropical, frozen drinks in a bikini that I would have never let myself wear before my diagnosis. The suit was black, and gave me thin tan lines where the strings gathered. I had been thin, pale and sickly when I left my life behind, but when I said I was done with it—I meant it. I wasn't going to spend my time on the couch feeling sick. Sure, it might speed up the process to skip the medication, but I didn't care. I didn't have anything or anyone to hold me back, so for the first time in my short life, I decided to live.

I walked with a spring in my step for the first time in longer than I could remember. "Remember." The word came to me like an echo in my head, freezing me in my own tracks for a moment. I made myself snap out of it and continued walking down the cobblestone street lined with shops. No, I couldn't remember anything these days, could I? The brain tumor still made me lose time and control of my mind. Who knows? Maybe this change in my brain was what finally allowed me to not care so much about what would happen and gave me the freedom to be brave.

I felt freer than I ever had. I was always such a nervous person, always wanting to do the right thing and make all the *safe* choices. Look where that got me.

I wasn't as sickly-looking anymore. Sure, I was thinner, but at least I had a healthier color from my time in the sun. It felt wonderful to sit in a beach chair with my toes in the sand, listening to laughter and waves crashing in the middle of the day. On a normal day, I would have spent hours trapped behind a desk with windows so far from me that I never saw the outside world. By the time I would leave work, it was already dark outside, and then it would be dark again in the morning when I left for work. That was no way to live.

I am going to buy whatever I want today, I thought. Maybe I'd buy a new outfit or some high-heeled shoes that I was always too afraid to wear. I stopped in front of a shop that looked very luxurious and stared at a pair of extremely high heels in the window. As I reached for the door handle, I saw my reflection in the window. My hair was in a high pony tail, wisps of it stuck out every which way. I tried my best to flatten them with my hand and straighten my out-of-date sundress before walking in.

Despite my appearance, I was greeted with a smile by a lovely middle-aged woman who was dressed to perfection. Her hair was up high too, but sleek in contrast with my wild mess of hair. Still, the woman treated me nicely and asked if she could help me. She spoke a language so foreign to me that I could barely understand, though. Lacuna famously attracted people from all over the world, so there was no official language. *Boy, could she ever*, I thought. Then I laughed at myself.

"I am interested in trying on those shoes in the window," I said. I felt a little shy still for asking, but I was a woman with money to burn. I deserved those ridiculous shoes.

"Of course, miss. What size would you like? They tend to run a bit small." I concentrated extra hard on the sales woman's words, so I could understand what she was saying.

"I usually wear a size seven where I live," I responded.

"I will be back momentarily. My name is Dee," she said. "I'll bring a few sizes just in case."

I hoped this was what she said—it made enough sense. I browsed through the store as I waited for Dee to return. There was no one else in the store, likely because I was there in the middle of the day, and it was not a very populated area in the first place anymore. *How did I know that?*

"*You* don't know that, but *she* does," entered my mind. I shook my head.

The store was fairly small, so once I browsed, I sat on an upholstered bench in front of a floor-length mirror. In my normal fashion, I not so gracefully plopped down. I hoped Dee hadn't returned yet to see that little slip-up.

As I sat and waited, I wondered what was taking her so long to return. I allowed myself to look at my image in the mirror. My hair stuck out in random places, so I decided to take it down, make it neater, then pull it back into a pony tail again. As I let my hair fall, I noticed how long it had grown. It had been ages since my last haircut, and I had never dyed it before. I let my hair hang for a moment at my shoulders and noticed the wave of my hair and the dull, light-brown color. As a child, I had light golden blonde curls. Over time, I had let it darken. I pulled my hair back into a pony tail and thought back to the dreams I kept having about me lying in a field with my long, blonde hair strewn about me—and the shadow.

Dee returned then with as many boxes as she could carry and dresses on hangers balanced on her forearm.

"I think you should try these on as well," Dee told me with a knowing smile. She laid out several beautiful dresses—most of them black—for me to see in the small sitting area. She then lined the shoe boxes below each dress and opened the lids to show me the gorgeous shoes she had paired with each dress. Dee muttered something to me about needing a change. She pointed to the shoes I had originally asked to try on.

"These first, then I will show you to a dressing room," Dee told me.

For the first time ever, I tried on something that cost more than my first paycheck, and I loved it. I stood looking in the full-length mirror, standing straighter and taller than ever. Whether it was the shoes or my new outlook, I couldn't tell, and I really didn't care.

I smiled at Dee and asked what dress I should wear with them. Dee picked up an elegant black dress to match the sleek shoes on my feet. Dee then escorted me to the small dressing room. I pulled the curtain shut and flung off my old sundress. I slipped into the dress and examined myself in the mirror. It was much too large and hung on me, which made me momentarily sad that I was so frail.

Nope, I thought. Then I called out to Dee, saying. "I need a smaller size!" I smiled a little to myself. I sure did smile more these days. Wasn't that ironic?

Dee returned to me quickly, shoving her hand in the dressing room through the side of the curtain with a dress that looked way too small for me at first glance. I decided to try it on anyway and was astonished at how well it fit me. I stepped back into the high heels and examined myself in the mirror. I slid open the curtain to show Dee, who beamed at me like I was her own little doll to dress up. *This was going to be fun*, I thought.

"Hand me the next one please, Dee!"

I couldn't wipe the smile from my face that day. I walked out of the store, arms filled with bags. I bought everything Dee suggested for me, and even gained a kiss on each cheek for it before leaving. I wore the shoes out that had guided me into the store in the first place. I tried to maneuver my way down the cobblestone street as graceful as possible. I found myself faltering constantly, but I didn't care. I was walking in heels and a new outfit—my head held high. I felt the weight of my ponytail bouncing with my every step, and then I knew where I would go next.

I stopped and turned around. I nearly jogged back to Dee and asked her where to get my hair done. I pointed at my hair and shouted— as one always did when trying to communicate with someone whose language wasn't your own. Dee drew arrows on the street map I had acquired.

I entered a very large and ornately-decorated salon.

I was ready for a new look, but I didn't know what I wanted. I sat in the salon chair, flipping through a magazine, so I could point and translate as best as I could to the man holding my hair. He had the scissors, after all; I had to make sure he knew what I wanted.

I didn't want extremely short hair, though that would be a drastic change. I wanted something that would make me feel different from boring old Senia. I watched him pull out the clasp that held up my hair. He worked his hands through my hair. I watched in the mirror as my hair fell down at my shoulders. I knew exactly what I wanted.

I used my hands to show several inches past my hair's current length, then flipped through the pages of the magazine until I found a woman with the perfect golden blonde color. The dream of long, blonde hair was about to become a reality.

I felt and looked like a new person. Men and women alike stopped and stared at me as I walked by them. I wasn't Senia, who wore mismatched pantsuits and hid behind a desk. I could barely stop myself from tossing my new blonde locks around like I was in some sort of hair commercial.

I needed to drop off all of my shopping bags in my suite. I went for the large suite and spa package when I booked the hotel. I had thoroughly enjoyed the spa already. I glanced down at my freshly manicured hand to my new watch and noticed that I had a mere thirty minutes before my dinner reservation at the hotel's famous rooftop restaurant called Sol. The restaurant was the real reason I chose the hotel in the first place. I hurried to the elevator and pressed the button for the top floor. As I rode the elevator up, a sharp pain hit my head. I pressed my palm to my forehead, dropping my bags.

"Miss. Miss?" A waiter stood above me in a pressed crisp white shirt, looking at me. I sat, menu in hand, twirling my hair in the other. I wore a long dress that could only be described as a gown. I looked around, noting the small table set for only one guest in front of me. It was dark outside, but the city lights shone brightly through the magnificent windows that reached from floor to ceiling of the restaurant.

I continued to glance around, wondering how I made it to the restaurant already. I had lost time again. I didn't remember anything after dropping my bags in the elevator.

"I'm sorry, what did you ask?"

"Sorry, miss. I didn't know if you heard me ask what you wanted to drink."

"I'm sorry. No, I ... I didn't hear you the first time. I will have a glass of wine, something red, whatever you recommend. Thanks." I tried to put a smile on my bewildered face.

"Absolutely, miss. I will be back shortly with that for you." He started to turn away, then stopped himself mid-turn. "Are you alright, miss?"

"Yes, thank you. I'm fine." I was still a little dazed. "Maybe a glass of water too, please." I smiled to try and reassure him.

"Of course, back in a moment."

I stared down at my place setting and tried to focus on what happened. Somehow, I got myself dressed and made my reservation, but I couldn't remember any of it. It wasn't so big of a time gap that something momentous could've happened to me, but the gaps in my memory happened more frequently now. I had done so well today too. I was leaving my old life behind, and this minor hiccup was bringing me down. I started to slouch a bit in my seat, a stark contrast to how I had walked earlier that day through the city. I spun my fork in circles, the prongs digging into the tablecloth.

I noticed a man and woman dining with their two daughters. The mother cut the young girl's food into smaller pieces. "Elbows off the table" is what the mother must have said to the older girl because she made a pouty face before straightening herself up and placing her own hands on top of the cloth napkin lying on her lap.

I watched them and thought back to my own mother and what she must have felt going through a similar situation as mine. No, my mother would never have done anything so wasteful or irresponsible as I was doing now. I wished she was across the table from me.

I thought that was what bothered me most of all. I was still alone, no matter how many exciting and new things I did. There was no one here with me to enjoy them. If I had to accept that I only had a short time left in this world, I wished I could have at least had someone by my side to share it with.

I had never been in love or had a best friend I could call on when I needed them most. Tears welled in my eyes, but I refused to let them fall. I was sitting at an extravagant restaurant I had always wanted to go to, in a city I had never been to, and I felt miserable. I forced myself to look up and not notice all the couples and families dining together while I dined alone. I was going to look over them and through the windows to the magnificent views of the city below and the world I had always dreamed of knowing better.

This would be it for me, so I could sit here moping in a place that most people would never see in their lifetime, or I could appreciate the beauty of my surroundings. I made myself sit up straighter again and adjusted my chair. Then, I smoothed the front of my elegant gown.

The waiter returned with a goblet of water for me, and presented a bottle of wine that he carefully poured before allowing me to taste. I nodded that it was fine, and then ordered the lobster tail and steak.

"They are very large portions, miss," the waiter informed me. "Are you sure you would like both?"

"Yes, I'm sure," I said, "And you can leave that bottle of wine too."

"Yes, miss."

I could tell he thought I was a little crazed.

I ate off each plate, going back and forth between the steak and the lobster until I had enough to fill myself up. The waiter checked in on me several more times and looked at me like I was a barbarian. He asked if I would care for the dessert menu. I pulled the cloth napkin off that I had not so gracefully turned into a lobster bib, and said "yes."

The waiter handed me the menu as he tried his best to not look disgusted, but he failed miserably. I didn't care. I ordered a decadent chocolate cake. As I finished the slice of cake, I knew what I wanted to do next. I wanted to try something else I had never done before.

When the waiter brought the check, I asked him for a place I could go dancing.

Barely containing his eye roll, the waiter politely offered to escort me to the concierge. I was beyond full from the outrageous meal I devoured, but I was carefree Senia now. I wasn't the girl who went to bed after dinner. I was the girl who went out dancing by herself in her new clothes and new look. I even changed my signature and artfully signed the check before letting the waiter pull my chair out for me.

"I know where the concierge desk is, thank you," I said. "I need to go to my room to change first."

Just like that, my dream dinner at Sol was over.

CHAPTER 13

LYRIS

I slept on my cot, curled up in an attempt to ward off the cold, when I felt someone's presence. I sat up straight, forgetting my surroundings at first. As my eyes adjusted, I was able to see through the clear barrier. The new guard was tall and a lot more intimidating than my former escorts.

"On your feet, Suttor," he instructed. His voice was so deep it could've lulled me back to sleep had my heart not been thudding so hard. *What now? More questioning? Is it time for my trial?*

I stood up to clear my brain. I needed to be on my toes for whatever was about to happen—especially if my fate depended on it.

"Hands!" the guard barked.

I held out both hands. He placed restraints on me, then escorted me out of my cell. I looked back to see if Balor had noticed. He was up against the barrier watching me, the sleep still in the corner of his eyes. He appeared to be concerned. That look of fear did little to calm my nerves.

The guard guided me away from Balor and the little cell I had called home, and I tried to calm my own fears. Walking on the cold floors and the rush of adrenaline woke me up. The brighter lighting as I left the cell area helped as well. This new guard moved me along faster than Rhetta and Len had. He didn't speak at all as he led me to a corridor I had not yet seen. I felt too scared to ask him questions. The guard seemed like a no-nonsense sort of person, and I didn't want to chance getting roughed up again.

Once we made it to the end of the hall, the guard used his lambent to open a passage into a larger corridor with warmer lighting. The enormous, golden room seemed to glow from within. I took in the sheer size and magnificence of my surroundings. The length of the hall seemed to go on forever. My eyes could vaguely see that there was an end to the path ahead. When I tried to look up, I noticed the ceilings were so high above that my eyes were momentarily blinded from the bright light. I dropped my head back down and saw dark spots in my field of vision. *Think about your trial and how you will get yourself out of this mess.* It was hard to concentrate on anything other than the grandeur around me.

This guard was unfazed—like he saw this room all the time. Maybe the highborns were used to this setup, but I certainly was not. I found myself gawking at ancient-looking tapestries that seemed illuminated as well. I had to remind myself that I could be walking to my own demise.

As I grew closer to the end of the corridor, I realized there were figures seated at some sort of grand marble dais. They were slightly above my line of sight, so they would be able to look down on me—I assumed. As I got closer, I saw the figures were actually five very judgmental-looking people wearing white robes.

Seated behind the marble dais was a man with dark black hair, his tanned skin a dark golden color—the typical highborn look. The woman seated beside him had a similar look to her, though her much longer jet black hair was braided and worn in front of her shoulder. In the slightly lower seats next to them sat two blondes—one male and the other female—with lighter skin tone. They only added to the glow of the room. These two looked like mirror images of each other. On the end seat was a large man, head shaved, skin much darker than mine; he also had unusual golden eyes.

It was hard to put an age to any of them. It seemed like they glowed right along with our surroundings. They all looked ... *impressive.* That was the only word that came to mind. They also looked pretty intimidating. *This is it. This is my trial with the Council of Five, and I am in deep shit.*

"Greetings, subject. I am Ashala of House E'Theramon, Second of the Council of Five," said the woman with the long braid.

"Our Lead, Tahrell of House E'Trell," she motioned to the dark-haired man beside her, "will declare your sentencing after a brief deliberation between the Council members. You will speak when spoken to. You will answer any of the Council members questions honestly and efficiently. Do you understand?"

"Yes." My throat dried up, and my heart raced.

"Then, let us begin. Lyris Suttor, you stand accused of high treason against the realm of Anatan."

At the mention of my name, the large Council member jerked up his bald head. His golden eyes met my own for a brief moment. They were wide and looked ... shocked? Confused? They were unreadable to me, but some sort of emotion emitted from his vibrant eyes that he didn't want me to notice. Did he know me? I didn't recognize him. He visibly centered himself and looked back down to the report as fast as possible. That was the look of a man who knew something was wrong but didn't want anyone else to know. Whatever he knew did nothing to calm me or my pounding heart.

I didn't have much time to dwell on it as the one called Ashala continued my hearing. "Found in your possession at the time of your arrest was a lambent filled with stolen files and recordings—some from this very Council," Ashala said. "Though you were prompted by enforcements to unlock your lambent and release this stolen property, you denied these requests and even resisted arrest."

Yeah, I was gently prompted by the nice enforcements and tried to run away through the brick wall of a man they sent to rough me up. That's what happened.

"Your report from your questioning session proved ... interesting. You admitted to multiple criminal activities with Severin Eilish," Ashala said.

I did? I don't remember anything from the questioning. This is bad if I have admitted to working with Severin. I wonder how he is being dealt with? He probably went free after giving me up—if I know anything about him.

"However, when asked about the information on the recordings, you—" Ashala looked around to her colleagues. "Is this correct? The report claims she didn't answer."

The other Council members shifted around in their seats and looked down at their own reports. I didn't know what was so shocking about not answering a question, but based on what Rhetta said to me back in my cell—it wasn't good. I still had not been directly asked anything in this trial, so I was forced to remain silent. This much I remembered from the little bit of coaching Balor gave me.

"Whatever you do, don't talk over them," Balor had advised. "They hate that, and it will definitely sway their view of you."

Nothing he said could have prepared me for the amount of intimidation I felt. Maybe I was lucky that they'd not yet asked me anything. My mind jumped from thought to thought. *How could I give them the answers they wanted and save myself? How the hell am I going to get out of this?*

"I saw that in the report, but assumed it was made in error," the blonde female said. "Lead, do we have the questioner available to clarify?"

"The report is accurate. She was somehow able to dodge questioning," the Lead responded.

"Can she be taken in for additional questioning?" The blonde female asked.

I saw the Lead clench his jaw. "She already has ... several times."

I had? I didn't remember any of this. Rhetta and Len, I remembered. Walking through the bright halls, and Balor, and the cell—all that was there. But the questioning and the healing? I had no recollection. I *know* it happened, but I knew nothing about it.

"How can that be?" Ashala questioned. "I've never heard of such an incident in all my time on the Council. Is there anything unusual with her medical records?"

"The only thing unusual about her medical scans was the extensive damage done to her body," the bald man grumbled.

The other members turned their heads toward him—almost in unison—at his interjection. It looked like they tried to glare him into submission. He appeared unmoved by their response. *This one makes me nervous.*

"Why don't you ask her again now?" The bald man suggested.

"She may not answer truthfully, Cade," Ashala said.

"She's just been instructed to do so, and she hasn't been given the chance to speak on her own behalf yet," Cade said.

Tahrell nodded his head as though mulling the suggestion over.

"Lyris, do you know what was on the recordings in question? That is, did you ever view them yourself?" Tahrell asked me.

I cleared my parched throat before responding in a somewhat weaker voice than usual. "No, I did not."

"Easy enough," Cade said.

"We're just going to take her word for it then?" The blonde female asked. "She didn't respond in questioning, but she responds so easily here?"

"I agree with Lyde," chimed in the other light-skinned blonde. "How can she be trusted? She's obviously a slippery criminal, one who has freely admitted her crimes and has somehow avoided questioning."

"Do we have surveillance of any of these crimes? What did the oculi reports show?" Tahrell asked.

Ashala swiped through something in front of her, eyes darting back and forth as she read in silence. "Nothing except for the day in question in which you can see her entering the meeting place with Severin," she stated.

Isn't that convenient ... no surveillance of them beating me into submission? Where was the legal action for that?

As Ashala continued scanning whatever records she'd been given, Lyde got a wide-eyed look on her face.

"Did anyone happen to look at the final conclusion of her medical records? Scroll to the page with her blood results."

The Council members seemed to do just that. I tried to remain standing still as I awaited what they would say. I knew the results. I knew before she spoke again.

"She has the blood."

I don't know what I expected from a trial of that magnitude, but the all-out argument that ensued was not it. I heard many tales of the Council, even knew some of their names and hierarchy, but I had always heard the Council was formal, unwavering, and civil. I learned their names and personalities as I watched them transform from the unified highest law of our kind to a chaotic dispute. Some of them seemed to rapidly unhinge. *This is about more than me. This is the start of a true division within our justice system. I think I am about to become the scapegoat.*

What started as a tight-lipped discussion became a yelling match. The Council started to unravel, and all I could do was look on in disbelief.

"She has a small fraction," Cade said. "I'm not sure this is wise."

"We can discuss that later, Cade," Ashala responded.

"We can discuss it now as she is a citizen of Anatan and has her right to know her sentencing and the reasoning behind it." Cade stood his ground.

"This is a serious crime that demands severe punishment, Cade!" One of the twins interjected.

"She is charged with high treason against the realm. If she is lying and does in fact know what is contained within those recordings, then she forfeits her rights as an Anatani," Ashala stated.

"If she knows what is on those recordings, then she absolutely cannot be released," stated the male blonde.

"That is the entire point of this trial, Latham! I am well aware!" Lyde glared at her twin.

"She has the blood. She should become a Watcher. It's as simple as that," Latham stated.

"We don't know if she has enough of it to travel," Cade interjected. His deep voice broke up the cacophony of the other Council members. "We also don't know if she is guilty of such a severe crime or if she merely took the recording for someone else. If she's the middle man, then we need to know who actually *knows* the information on that recording."

"So question her further," Lyde suggested. "Find out who she was selling the information to."

"We already have the names she gave up in questioning. We need to know if *she* has viewed the recordings or not," Ashala stated.

"Apparently, there's no way of knowing. She's avoided questioning on several occasions, so all we have is her word. If we can't trust her word, then there's only one course of action. She should be sentenced as a Watcher and provide a useful service for her realm," Lyde said.

Clearly fed up with their behavior, Tahrell made a show of clearing his throat to gain the silence he needed to speak. "Since the Council has decided to openly discuss the manner rather than dismiss the subject for a more private deliberation, I see no other choice. The subject has been questioned repeatedly to no avail. There will be no further questioning."

Cade and Ashala both faced Tahrell, and appeared to be on the brink of speaking, but Tahrell held up his hand up to them, letting them know he was done being interrupted.

My heart hammered so hard in my chest that I felt my blood thrumming through my entire body. *My blood, that is the problem, isn't it? They need me as a Watcher, and it doesn't matter if I am truly guilty of it all or not.* I felt light-headed and struggled to control my body.

"The evidence is clear. She is shown on the oculi and had the recordings in possession at the time of her arrest. Whether she has knowledge of the information on the recordings or not, she has admitted to stealing them and working with a known criminal on several occasions. Furthermore, her medical records show she now has the opportunity to fulfill her penance in a working manner. I would caution the Council to think about the severity of her crimes at such a young age and the repercussions of allowing her to return to society without remorse. However, the girl is young, and, therefore, I do not suggest a life-sentencing, but a sentence as a Watcher with completion after a successful ten-span cycle."

No. Ten spans could end up longer than a lifetime, couldn't it? Ten lifespans as someone else, ten full lives rather than my own life here? I struggled to breathe.

Cade opened his mouth to speak again, I hoped on my behalf, but was forced to remain silent as Tahrell spoke right over whatever he was going to say. "Those in favor?"

This is it. This is my life, determined by five people who just met me and need to use me to set an example. I knew this was the best decision for them, but it didn't make it any easier for me. It made sense, so I should've seen it coming. If I *did* know what was on the recording, the process of becoming a Watcher would keep me imprisoned for long enough to keep the information concealed with me. If they were lucky, I would lose it all together. From what Balor told me, it was very hard to regain your own memories as a Watcher, especially when you're first starting out. *If I even made it that far. Cade had argued that I only have a fraction of the blood. What if I am unable to make it as a Watcher? What if I end up like that broken man I saw in the cells?*

I heard the Council members' voices in the background. They sounded far away from me. I vaguely registered the members rising to their feet, some declaring yes and some no.

The energy in the room shifted as the Council sat back down in silence, waiting for their Lead to speak again. Tahrell rose to his feet, looking every inch the highborn Anatani. I'd never felt so different and lesser, looking at that man as he peered down his nose at me.

"The decision has been made by the Council of Five and will be entered into the official records of Anatan. Lyris Suttor, you are hereby sentenced to a ten-span cycle as a Watcher with chance for reevaluation after the completion of six successful cycles. You will be taken for further testing and begin your sentence after the results of your final medical examinations have been cleared. Thank you, Council members. We will reconvene for the next case after a brief recess."

Tahrell motioned for the guard to come forward, and I found myself once again in restraints as I was formally dismissed. The other members of the Council rose and quickly exited, seemingly not wanting to make eye contact with each other after the divided proceedings. Only the one called Cade looked back at me before leaving. He had a strange expression on his face, like he'd lost a battle.

The guard took me back down the long corridor I'd been so in awe of on my way in. I felt a sense of relief when the trial was over, but still had so much dread for what was to come. *Now we will see if my small fraction of the blood that is so highly sought after can save me.*

CHAPTER 14

CARRICK

I drove through the night in the old clunker vehicle and only refueled once before making it to my destination. Dr. Umbridge's memories were still pretty clear to me since I had just been here. He knew of the most remote place to look up into the night sky to study the stars. Dr. Umbridge would drive here by himself to get the best view. Cornfields surrounded me now as they once surrounded him. No one came out here, especially in the middle of the night. If someone did, I looked every inch the farmer in my new clothes.

Here we go, I thought. I clapped my hands together once, blowing my breath into them in the cold night air. I crouched down to the ground and placed my hands on the dirt. Closing my eyes, I tried to feel as I had in times past. I lifted my right hand just a few inches above the ground, letting it hover for a moment before slapping it back to the ground. I felt a slight tremor just beneath the ground. I opened my eyes and took a deep breath before slamming both my palms into the ground. The ground cracked a little and shook beneath me.

I gulped for air, taking in shallow, rapid breaths. Random thoughts passed through my mind. *How is this possible? The Council would surely look for me if they knew that I held the power of the Khassos again. Surely they already were for what I had done back in the Great Corridor. Can I trust myself with this amount of power I possess?*

I was afraid to further test my limits because I did not know the damage I could cause. *Perhaps I have even more control now than I did in my past.* With that thought came another unpleasant one: *My sister is looking for Eirene.* Arden would know that Eirene was a sitting duck with no knowledge of me or our past.

The powers that be wisely kept Arden and me apart somehow. Maybe whatever dispatched us from the Great Corridor knew to send us to opposite places because whenever I met up with my sibling, devastation followed.

A vivid image of Arden flashed before me; rage shown in her colorful eyes, and heavy rain fell down on her. She was soaked. I blinked and the image was gone.

Before I knew what I was doing, I pushed some soil forward with a force that created a small hill. Dr. Umbridge's tiny vehicle sat at the peak of the mound. The car alarm beeped until I reached in my pocket and pressed the keyless entry remote to make it stop.

Control. I must have control. I can't draw too much attention to myself before I accomplish anything.

In an instant, a thought clicked into place. I had thought about it all wrong. I didn't need to camouflage myself. If I truly severed the Council's communication with Erreta, they couldn't detect me. I needed to be visible and let Arden find me. I had the power to shake this world— or crush it—if I wanted to. I surely had the power to find my sister.

Where can I go to get the most attention? Nowhere on this continent—that was certain. *I need to travel to a place where what I could do as a Khassos would be an anomaly. I have to travel as the Erretas do. I can't risk using my power more than needed before I find Arden—especially when I don't have a grasp on my level of control. I don't have the Panoptis to help me move about from place to place. Of course, I would think that after I am finally free of the system.*

The Panoptis had imprisoned me for so long that it had almost become part of me. Now, it was the one thing I could really use.

The Council of Five never answered me when I asked them how long it would be before Erreta came to an end; I knew it must not be long.

I required little sleep in my true form, but I was fatigued from the series of events over the past day. I had to keep going just a little bit longer before I could rest. I could sleep during my travels, but the travel systems in Erreta were lacking compared to what I was used to. *I need to find an airport.*

I marched up the hill and lifted the vehicle so I could set it down on flatter terrain, then drove off.

The structure surrounding me seemed to give off a golden glow. I had not physically been here since before I started serving time as a Watcher. It was the place where the Council of Five sat when they held court or communicated with Watchers. Their images transmitted back to the Great Corridor. This place was always in my vision, but never within reach for me. What I would have given to reach through the barrier to wring Tahrell's neck. This time, it was not the Council of Five who sat in their seats to judge me. It was only Tahrell; that is how I knew I was not truly here.

"You no longer hold a seat on the Council, Tahrell. What are you doing here?"

Tahrell glared at me; his dark eyes stared into mine—just as they always did. His dark hair was pulled back and showed where it had grayed at his temples. Tahrell was wearing a robe similar to what the Council wore, except this one was a dark blue color instead of the white robe he usually donned.

"I have waited a long time to speak with you like this again, Carrick. Just you and I, no other interlopers," Tahrell said. His smile told me he was up to something. "Tell me, how fairs your partner?"

"If you are trying to anger me, you should know that I have had lifetimes of experience in controlling my hatred toward you. There is little you can say that will have any effect on me now. What can you say to me that could possibly be worse than what you have done to me?"

Tahrell sat up straighter, adjusting himself on the seat that was once so familiar to him. "I suppose you are right. What could I possibly say to hurt the man who has nothing to live for? The man forced to relive his punishment over and over throughout all of our time? Death would just be a sweet release for you, wouldn't it, Carrick? You are just as untouchable as you have always been." Tahrell stopped. "Or so you think. That has always been your biggest flaw. You think you are above punishment—above us. You think you can make decisions for all Anatani—for an entire race of people. The effects of your crimes can never be undone, but I can and will prevent you from causing further damage to our kind. I know nothing I do to *you* will matter, Watcher. But what I do to *her* is another matter. Isn't it?"

A slight panic built inside of me. I thought back to the last time I watched Tahrell and the other Council members decide our fates. He had the same look on his face then as he did now.

"She is bound to the Erretas world, which *your* own Council decided," I replied. "You cannot touch their world. It is law, one not even you can change."

"Not directly, no," Tahrell said. "But she is not an Erretas, nor are you. Even worse, the Erretas world is ending—as you know. So, I wonder. What will become of her then?"

I raised my arm, fist clenched, but chains suddenly appeared and stopped me mid-air. *This is not really happening. We aren't really here. How is Tahrell speaking with me?*

"You are still a Watcher, Carrick," Tahrell said, "among other things, and so you are linked to us still. You may have found a way to take your true form, but we still have a connection to you."

It was as if he was reading my mind.

This was not how any Anatani communicated with me. I was always sent to the Great Corridor, and I only spoke with the Council of Five to report findings. I thought back to the damage I caused in the Great Corridor. They must had been unable to repair it yet, or surely I would be dispatched in a much less threatening form by now.

It could have something to do with those orbs. They were shattered, but two remained. *That must be it.* They had no way to pull me back to them now. The thought was so freeing; I grinned wider than I had in a very long time. *Time to wake up*, I thought.

"Get out of my head, Tahrell. You control me no longer."

My surroundings started to fade.

"You are never out of our reach, Carrick. We will find a way."

I woke with a jolt. I looked around, but found I was in my seat on a large jet. It was not the dream that jolted me. I saw lightning flashing out the window; the jet bounced back and forth. An oxygen mask appeared in front of my face; and the other passengers cried out in fear. *They cannot do this, no matter how hard they try. They cannot harm Erretas simply to get to me.* Most Anatani could not even be present in this world; the Sators made sure of that.

I thought back to the first time I was dispatched and the explanation I received. Only the Watchers could walk among the Erretas, interact with them, and be physically present in their world. Tahrell wasn't the one causing the storm, he couldn't.

The cabin lights flickered, then went out. The jet dropped, then hovered, as if weightless. I panicked again. The plane had lost power. *Will I permanently perish since I am in my true form, or will I regenerate all over again?* I thought back to the words Tahrell said about my death being a release. Would it be a release to finally end my penance, to stop my suffering, once and for all? *No, this is not how it will end for me.*

I unlatched my safety belt when the lights flickered, then remain lit. The jet woke up from its sleep like a great beast. I heard the engines again and no longer felt the floating sensation. A voice came on the intercom to reassure passengers. They all breathed a collective sigh of relief. The tension in the jet began to ease, but outside, the storm still raged. I would make it to my destination, but I had my work cut out for me. Hopefully, there would be little Tahrell or the Council could do to stop me.

CHAPTER 15

SENIA

What started as a clear sky abruptly turned into a stormy night. The rain came down, but I made it to my destination and under the overhang before it began to pour. I had never been to a nightclub before, but that is what I stood outside of now. In my excitement to change into my shorter dress, I forgot a jacket. The cool night air gave me goose bumps. Luckily, I didn't have to wait long before I showed my passport to the doorman and entered the club.

I didn't know what I expected, but it wasn't *this*. The club was dark and crowded—and extremely loud. I got a few looks as I made my way toward the large bar opposite the dance floor. I ordered a fruity drink that looked like something I saw on television and had always wanted to try. I almost walked away from the bar, drink in hand, but realized that wouldn't work in my sky-high heels. Instead, I leaned against the bar, trying not to concentrate on the fact that my dress was short enough for my rear end to stick out if I leaned over. I sipped my drink and nodded my head to the music a little. *I'm not brave enough to do this on my own, after all*, I thought.

"Can I get a shot of tequila?" I yelled over the music to the bartender.

"What kind?"

Hell if I knew what kind. I was only doing what I saw actresses do in movies. The bartender finally made eye contact with me; he must have appraised my expensive attire. "Top shelf?" He asked.

"Yes!"

He poured my tequila and slid it across the bar. I tossed the liquid down; it burned my throat and I squinted a little as I set the shot glass back on the bar.

"You like to party, huh?" asked a man with dark short hair. He eyed me up and down before waving the bartender back over toward him and his friends.

"No, not really," I nervously laughed. Then I remembered I was not going to be shy, boring Senia anymore. I was not too afraid to talk to strangers.

"Actually, yeah. Yeah, I do now," I said. The man was good-looking.

"Good, let me buy you a drink then."

"Oh, no, that's okay."

He looked down at his shoes, clearly discouraged, which, gratefully, I picked up on. I obviously didn't know how any of this worked.

"Do you dance?" I shouted.

He smiled at me then and instantly looked even more attractive. Without responding, the man grabbed my hand and pulled me toward the dance floor. My heart beat so hard as I began to move with him. The alcohol started to kick in, and before I knew it, I was tossing my new hair extensions around and moving with the music like no one else was watching.

I changed dance partners several times on the crowded floor, not caring what anyone else thought of me and not really caring who I danced with. Surprisingly, I didn't feel embarrassed. I felt happy as I swayed in time to the beat.

I decided to call it quits when one of my dance partners got a little too handsy as he whispered in my ear.

I had worked up quite a sweat by the time I reached the bar again. Another drink and a breather would do me some good. Not being used to walking in heels—let alone dancing in them—I had to lean my weight onto the bar to give my feet a little relief. I wound my hair up to get it off my neck and fanned myself with my other hand as I waited to be served. Just as I reached for my freshly-poured drink, someone knocked into me, causing me to spill the drink all over my arm and the bar.

"Shit, I'm so sorry!" A woman said.

"Don't worry about it." I tried to wipe the sticky drink off my arm as I turned around to see a striking woman looking at me. She was tall for a woman, and big—not overweight. She had muscles like an athlete. Her presence was overwhelming. If I hadn't had heels on, the woman would've towered over me.

"Let me buy you another one," she offered. The tall woman flagged the bartender down and asked him to wipe up the spill on the bar and replace my drink.

"Sorry about that," she offered again. "It's really crowded in here tonight, more than usual."

"Oh, you come here a lot?" I asked. Then I thought it could be misconstrued as a pick-up line.

The woman laughed. "Yeah, I've been looking for someone. I just tend to pick the wrong someones lately."

The music got louder and muffled whatever she said next.

"What?" I shouted, feeling like an old woman who was hard of hearing.

The woman's mouth moved again, but I still couldn't make out what she said. I shook my head no, communicating that I still didn't hear her this time. As I looked into the woman's eyes, I noticed how vibrant they were. Maybe it was the lights moving back and forth on the dance floor, but they seemed to change from color to color. It mesmerized me for a second. There was something familiar and almost reassuring about this woman; she felt like an old friend.

"What's your name?" The woman shouted.

"Oh! Seni—" I stopped myself. I wasn't Senia anymore. I was someone brave and new. I was ... Sen. "My name's Sen," I shouted back to her. It was a small change, but it felt good.

"I'm Paige," she replied as she stuck her hand out for me to shake.

"Nice to meet you, Paige." I beamed a huge smile, and Paige returned it in kind.

Since I could barely hear when we were shouting at each other only mere inches from each other's faces, I stopped talking and awkwardly sipped my new drink. I assumed Paige would eventually leave—or maybe I should. But neither of us did. I bobbed my head to the music and tried to observe my new companion without being obvious.

She was quite beautiful, but in a strange way. Her eyes—beneath long lashes—sparkled with a vibrant color I couldn't put my finger on. Her hair was a reddish auburn color, but it was hard to tell with the flashing lights. It was thick and curled like how you would imagine a medieval princess's hair to be. Her skin was smooth and golden —the kind of skin that was accomplished from getting just the right amount of sun.

Paige caught me staring, and I tried to quickly turn my head away. Paige stopped me and motioned for me to come closer. Paige tucked a tendril of hair behind my ear and leaned in. "You want to get out of here?" she whispered.

"Sure," I responded, completely naïve, yet again.

The bad weather had cleared up before we left the club. It wasn't until we walked several blocks that it dawned on me it wasn't such a great idea to go somewhere with a total stranger. Someone wanting to spend time with me—whatever the reason—had excited me so much that I left without thinking it through. I was Sen though, and Sen was adventurous. Sen could make new friends. Sen wasn't afraid to leave with strangers.

Well, I am still a little afraid. No. There is nothing to be afraid of now that I am no longer Senia.

It was exciting to be in a new city with new people. I was supposed to have a fun night, I reminded myself, and my spirits lifted.

I walked with a spring in my step, well as much as I could with aching feet. The cool night air felt wonderful after the sweaty, overcrowded club. It was getting late.

"See that street sign up there that says 44?" Paige pointed out. "Where we are going is just around that corner."

I squinted, looking for what Paige was talking about. It took a moment to find the small green sign.

"You can see that far in the dark?" I asked. "I can barely see that there's a sign at all."

We made it a few more blocks, and once we rounded the corner, I sighed with relief as we walked up to a building with a sign that read "Pizza," lit up in neon lights.

"This is the best pizza in town," Paige said.

I didn't think I could ever eat again after the decadent meal I devoured a few hours ago, but I enjoyed Paige's company. We stood in a line that was out the door and down the street, which was surprising at that time of night.

"It must be good if this many people are willing to wait."

"You've never been here?" Paige asked. "Everyone comes here, especially after a night out."

"I never saw it recommended on any of my travel sites," I replied.

Paige laughed. "On your travel sites, huh? So you don't live here? Just visiting?" Paige asked. "For how long?"

"I'm not sure yet. I'm trying to see several places before my *uh* ... holiday ends. I'm just sort of playing it by ear and going to the places on my list."

"I see, taking it day by day, then?"

"Something like that."

We took a few steps forward.

"Where are you staying while you're here?" Paige asked.

"At the Diamanta."

"Well then, I guess you're buying."

"Oh, sure!"

"I am only teasing you."

We got far enough that I could actually see food behind a glass partition. It smelled amazing, and I realized my stomach was rumbling a bit. It was so nice to have my appetite back after quitting my medications.

"What do you usually get here?" I asked Paige.

"You *really* like recommendations, don't you?"

"Yeah, I suppose I do."

I felt that warm reassurance from Paige again.

"Everyone asks for the special, but I'm not everyone." Something about her statement made my head spin for a moment. *No, not now. I don't want to lose time again, especially not when I finally have someone to talk to. Focus.* I take another step closer to ordering. *Focus.*

"What can I get you?" asked the man behind the counter.

"I'll have a slice of the spicy supreme," Paige said. "And she'll have the special." She pointed in my direction.

"No, I won't," I interject. "I will have a slice of *uh—*"

I don't actually know what I want, but I know I don't want to be the person who only gets what is recommended to her anymore.

"I'll have the pepperoni," I said. I turned to Paige. "I'm not everyone else either."

"Here, sir, I'm buying." I handed him my credit card, and Paige and I shared a smile. We walked over to the sitting area with trays in hand. The scent of hot pizza wafted through the air. Paige motioned with her head to sit over toward the windows at the entrance.

"Much better-people watching if we sit where we can see the street," she explained.

We sat down at a wobbly table stained and sticky with grease. I felt a strange sort of happiness overcome me. It was a foreign feeling. Who knew something as simple as meeting a new friend could have such an effect?

I was supremely proud of myself for everything I accomplished in one day. I was learning to be brave enough to leave the old Senia behind. I was finally living a little, and it felt wonderful.

People moved in and out of the busy pizza shop, creating a buzzing background noise around us. I took a bite of pizza, and it didn't disappoint.

"It is really nice of you to show me this place. I don't think I ever would have found anything as good as this on my own."

"No problem," Paige said. "I can show you a lot of places that definitely won't be on your travel websites. What are you doing tomorrow?"

I was so thrilled to be asked that question. I could barely contain my excitement. "I have nothing planned for tomorrow. Well, I really have nothing planned period, so if you wouldn't mind showing me around, that would be great. I'm really glad I met you, Paige."

"I'm really glad I bumped into you. Why don't we meet at a café down the road from your fancy hotel tomorrow morning? Let's say ... ten?"

"Sure! That would be great. What's the café called?"

Paige gawked up at the television screen behind my head.

"What is it? What's wrong?" I asked.

Paige didn't answer. She continued to stare, so I turned around in my chair to look up at the screen for myself. "Breaking News" flashed at the top of the screen. Images of a huge fault in the ground followed by video coverage of a massive earthquake that hit halfway across the world had Paige's attention.

"Shit!" Paige stood up, knocking her chair halfway to the next table. "I've got to go."

"Is everything alright?"

Paige looked down at me. "Shit," she said again.

Paige placed her hands on the table, letting her head hang down as if she wasn't sure what to do. "Where are you going next?" Paige asked. Her strange behavior made me a little anxious.

"I don't know. I haven't decided yet." I exercised caution.

"Don't leave the city yet," Paige advised. "At least not until I come back. Okay?"

"I thought we were going to meet up tomorrow?"

"I can't now, but I will be back. Just don't leave until I come back. It's important."

The man from behind the counter approached our table, momentarily breaking up our odd conversation. "Is one of you Senia Ska-lee-skee?" He only slightly mispronounced my name.

"Yes, that's me." I anxiously looked back and forth from Paige to the man.

"You left your credit card at the counter." He set it on the table in front of me.

Paige grabbed my hand as I reached for the card.

"Look at me," Paige said.

I saw that her eyes were in fact different colors of green, blue, and a golden brown. One color fading into the next as I studied her.

"No, you're not," she said to me.

CHAPTER 16

CARRICK

I traveled to the most remote and uninhabitable place I knew of, but when I finally arrived at my destination, I found I couldn't make myself do what needed to be done. The population was so small in Claudere that I scarcely saw a living creature in my travels here, let alone an Erretas since I left the airport. *I must do this*, I repeated often to myself. I knew it was the only way—no matter how dangerous it would be. My time was limited, and this was the best way to grab my sister's attention.

I knew it would work, but I still stood unable to make the first move.

"Now or never," I said aloud. I clasped my hands together and breathed into them as if giving them life. I jumped off the ground—as high as I could—then slammed the full weight of my body onto the ground. I let the impact reverberate within my body as I remained in the same position. I concentrated on every nerve in my body, allowing myself to become one with my surroundings. The sensation started like a sweet caress that began at my fingers and made its way from my head to my toes. The caress became a thrumming warmth that coursed through me, causing the ground beneath me to tremble.

It no longer felt as if the ground was beneath me; it felt part of me. Though my body rested on top of the ground, I was mentally imbedded in the earth. I felt my world begin to shake. It had been millennia since I had done this. I could not allow myself to release the whole of my strength; I had to contain it. I had done it before. I could do it now.

The power within me built up to a roaring heat of glorious sensation. I allowed myself to feel the bliss of what was once lost to me. I felt my head fall back almost in rapture as the power surged through me. I almost lost control, but I forced myself to think of my own body and remember it was separate from the earth. *How can I let go of this power?* Tears streamed down my face from the frustration of holding back and the ecstasy of holding on. I could not describe the depths to which I felt that of the Khassos inside myself, when I had thought it lost to me forever. Letting go was a misery I felt not just in my body but in my soul. The power of the Khassos was what I was—my reason for existence. *How do you tell yourself to stop breathing?* That was what I faced now.

Stop. But I could not let go. "Stop!" I shouted aloud this time, or I thought I did. But the sensation was too great. Everything around me shook from the force I held. I had the power to demolish my surroundings. If I didn't let go soon, I could completely destroy this world. *Remember why you are doing this, Carrick. It's because she can't remember.*

The last time I did this, Eirene's eyes glistened with tears. Eirene, the name that could always sober me and bring me back when I was lost. That is what helped me stop. I slowly severed my connection, then all at once and far too fast. I collapsed face-first into the ground and felt as shattered as the ground I laid across. If ecstasy is what I felt before, a deep sorrow is what I felt now. The pain of letting go before I decimated this world hit me like I had run into a brick wall. Silent sobs racked me as I clutched the ground for support, but it would not support me for I was its destruction. I made myself lift my head. As I did, I saw the fault line begin to take form in the distance. It was similar to the first crack in a piece of glass. My surroundings shook as the plates beneath the ground shifted. I had to leave. *Arden will come now. She will come, and if she destroys me—well then that is what I deserve.*

Some hours later, I sat on a motel bed, my weight caused the flimsy mattress to sink to the ground. All I could do now was wait for Arden. I had traveled to the next closest area that showed any sign of life. Since it was sparsely populated, my lodging options were limited.

Everything inside my tiny room was old and dirty. The heater was broken, and the television reception constantly cut in and out, but I sat, waiting and watching for the news to change. I occasionally tapped the side of the television in an attempt to better the reception. I was all too aware of how gentle I would have to tap the television. Truthfully, it was difficult for me to move in my present state. The events of this afternoon still haunted me, and using any sort of force was a struggle, but I need to have a connection to the outside world that wasn't too far from what I had done. The dusty old television was all I had right now.

Once the effects of my actions were picked up by the news, Arden would see. I now knew how much harder it would be to contain my power, and I didn't dare test the limits in a place where I could endanger the inhabitants. It was too painful to dwell on what I once was and the millions who had perished because of me. Memories of past destruction kept me from losing control now. The feeling of sheer euphoria had overcome me as I manipulated this land's topography to my own liking. I shook the earth using only my hands. I couldn't even think back to it.

That kind of power was crippling. Before you knew what you were doing, you would be lost to it.

At one point, Arden told me it felt much the same for her in lifetimes past. That was when we were still partners. The ecstasy the Khassos felt was indescribable to others who could never experience what it was to hold that much power. It was the sort of power that could manipulate the world around you. That was why it was so difficult to let go once I started, but I had learned this was how the Khassos were designed. Once you allowed yourself that first slip of letting go, it became an unstoppable force. The Anatani couldn't have the Khassos develop a conscience halfway through demolishing a world.

That was exactly what I had done, though; I had developed a conscience. Well, Eirene had developed one for me, I suppose. I read poems about moving heaven and earth for the one you loved, but I was the only one who truly knew what it meant to do so.

I knew it was only a matter of time before Arden would see what I had done and track me down. That was step one of my plan, but then what? Would Arden have any information that could help me, or would she fight me every step of the way, just as she had since we were first created?

I hadn't seen my sibling and partner since the day I was sentenced. But she was sentenced too, I had to remind myself. *Could she ever forgive me?* I remembered the look on her face as the Council convicted her for a crime I had committed. That was not the worst of it, though. What I had done to her was far worse in her eyes than the eternal punishment she shared with me. We shared everything with each other before, so Arden was guilty by association. She was sentenced to the same penance, but was kept separate for my own safety. At least, that's what the Council had said. I knew they were right. If given the chance, Arden would do what we both did best—destroy.

No matter how many lives I lived, I would never forget Arden's last words to me. The hurt in her voice was deeper than I had ever heard. She knew then that it would be the last time we would be able to speak freely to each other.

"I loved him," she said to me. Arden was calm at first, but when I did not respond, she raised her voice. "I loved him, Carrick!"

"He would never have loved you back." I was truthful with her.

If she had slapped me, it would have eased the tension between us. Instead, she let her anger subside. In its place came despair and tears.

"When did you become so cruel, Car?" she asked.

I hung my head and let out a short laugh. "How could I *not* become cruel? How are you not cruel yourself, Sister? Does it not pain you to watch them die? Even if you feel nothing for them, does it not pain you to watch their creations fail at our own hands?"

"They do not fail because of us," she interrupted. "This is who we are, Carrick, who we must always be. It is our duty as part of our people. It is our contribution to the realm. It is our gift. No one else knows what it is to hold such power."

"If you can still view what we do as a gift, then you are not who I thought you were, Sister. You know now what Eirene and I know. We do not have to keep up this pattern any longer. They refused to listen and so did he—"

"Don't," she stopped me. "Don't you dare speak of him to me." She bowed her head in sorrow, visibly gathering herself. "They will surely kill you in kind for what you have done."

"Yes," I replied. I let the inevitability of my situation sink in.

"Did you think of us at all, Carrick?"

She was unable to control herself any longer. Tears streamed down her face, and she choked back the sobs she had desperately tried to hold in. It broke my heart to watch her, but there was nothing to be done and nothing I could say to ease her pain. So, I watched on in silence.

Arden seemed to calm herself long enough to look up into my eyes. I watched my sister's face transform as the shock faded. I saw it sink in that she was losing more than the man she had loved. She would lose her brother too. She would lose her people, the world she lived in, and the life she led. I watched as the hysteria visibly stretched across her face. Arden shook with the grief of it all, tears leaving tracks down her face, though she was no longer crying. Her eyes were swollen; her complexion so pale as if what had occurred had aged her and started taking her life from her. Arden's eyes, like my own, drilled into me. What I witnessed then was much worse than watching her sob in pain. I watched her break. Her entire being transformed before my eyes, and I saw her become something different. She was no longer my sister. She was no longer angry at me. She was utterly broken, and I had done it to her.

"What have you done, Carrick? Oh, what have you done?" She wailed. It was like taking a knife to my heart.

I heard a loud rumble of thunder in the distance, which brought me back to the present. I let the tears well in my eyes, but refused to let them fall. The past could not be undone, but maybe, somehow, I could make it right.

Another crack of thunder; it was louder this time. I stood to pull the drapes back. Outside, the rain created a massive wall of water, and lightning flashed. She was close now.

The memory of the last encounter with my sister was still so fresh, even after all this time. I was sure the wound was still fresh to her as well, I thought. How would I ever face her? Even worse, what if she fought me—which she deserved to—and I couldn't stop her?

CHAPTER 17

LYRIS

I tossed and turned, unable to fall asleep due to the looming threat of my final medical examination. It was the last step for me before my penance would begin. *Will I become a Watcher? Will my blood fail me?* I saw with my own eyes what could happen if it did. The exact science behind it all was never divulged to me, and yet my mind raced with the little I did know from the Council and what Balor had told me about becoming a Watcher.

Any time I got exhausted enough to rest, I remembered the wild eyes of the man who passed my cell. A shiver ran through my body as I brushed dark wisps of hair from my face. I forced myself to sit up straight on my cot. I could not let myself sleep again if those were the thoughts I was to be haunted with. *What if that isn't the worst that can happen? What if death is a possibility?*

I squinted toward Balor's cell, letting my eyes adjust in the dark. He seemed to be asleep. I could barely make out his dark form and the steady rise and fall of his ribs. Who knew when I'd get to see a familiar face again—not that I was that familiar with the criminal I'd begun to consider a reassuring presence. That's how desperate I'd become in here; I needed Balor's ridiculous talks to put me at ease.

Whatever I thought I knew about this world, Balor turned upside down. He'd lived as a Watcher for a long time, so who knew how much of his memory was accurate. He'd made being a Watcher sound almost appealing, but then why had he tried to take down the Panoptis? I had so many questions for him and so little time left before I would take my own journey. Would I be able to remember anything he told me? Would I even remember myself?

Balor said no one remembered themselves at first. As a Watcher, you became another entity, and only realized once your time was up and you returned to yourself who you truly were. This concept seemed implausible to me, like a myth passed down to scare Anatani from committing infractions. Yet, here I was, stuck in a cell, after believing my entire life that there was no violence and little repercussion for crime in Anatan. I was on the brink of losing the *real* me.

The real me? What does that even mean? I had run from a background I didn't fully understand. The only real family I'd ever known was Suttor, but she wasn't my blood, so who was responsible for this? Who gave me this genetic factor that now determined my fate? Was it my father? Though I'd known exactly where he was my entire life, he had never much cared to know where I was. He already had one child. Someone of our station couldn't be caught with another. He'd be in one of these cells, too, had he claimed me as his own.

And my mother ...well, those answers died with her. If anyone would know, it would be Suttor. My mother told Suttor everything when I was a child. If it wasn't for Suttor, I wouldn't be here today. The dark thought hit me that if it wasn't for Suttor, I probably wouldn't be here in this cell today either.

One dark thought led to another; before I knew it, I worried again about my most imminent threat. Absentmindedly, I twirled the ends of my hair as I had since I was a child. There were so many unanswered questions and no time or freedom left to ask them. I suppose it now mattered little how I came to have the blood. It was in me, and there was nothing I could do to change that. *I am who I am—or at least I will be until my penance begins.* How would I remember who I was? What should I commit to memory of myself?

What am I truly? A thief, a criminal in a place where there is no crime. Hell, my name isn't even mine—it belongs to Suttor. I don't belong here in Anatan, not like the other law-abiding citizens and highborns do. Maybe Balor was right ... maybe there was something for me to seek on the other side. Maybe there would be something better for me in a different life. It was the only hope I had, so I clung to it as I finally let myself drift to sleep.

They came for me the next day, and fear, like I'd never known, coursed through me like a liquid jolt to the body. Feeling both numb and alight with dread, my feet moved one after the other through the dimly lit halls. My mind went into a strange state of panic.

Thoughts flickered in and left before I had time to grasp them. One was of Balor and how I didn't get to say goodbye. The next thought was about my anger toward Severin and his betrayal that landed me here in the first place. My heart ached at the thought of Suttor and my mother, so I made myself concentrate on the floor and my steps. *This test won't be death for me; this is just the unknown. It is natural to be afraid of the unknown.* Yet my heart raced and my body still felt stiff as Rhetta and Len guided me toward the bright lights of the medical examination room.

As we entered the room, I expected to see Garron, but instead, we were greeted by a woman with dark hair tightly pinned back. She was much smaller in stature than my two guards.

"Please have a seat." She motioned me toward the bed-like device that previously scanned my body and collected that fateful blood sample that got me here. I went through the motions, trying to maintain my composure; on the inside, however, I screamed. I was ensnared. As the bed enveloped around me to rescan my body, I felt trapped.

"Her heart rate and breathing are rapid, but other than that, everything looks good," the medical examiner addressed Rhetta and

Len instead of me. "Guardian, could you step out and ask my assistant for the sedative?"

With a slight bow of her head, Rhetta used her lambent to open the door and stepped out. Len remained; he looked rather uneasy. Any time we accidentally made eye contact, he immediately looked away from me.

Great, even he doesn't want to see whatever is going to happen to me, and he sees this all the time!

The faint noise of granted access alerted us that Rhetta and the assistant returned. Rather than Rhetta's stoned-faced expression, I looked at the large form of Council member Cade.

The medical examiner appeared confused. The sheer size of him was jarring. Cade stood next to Len, towering over him. Cade was surely twice the size of the medical examiner.

"Councilman, I—" the medical examiner stammered.

Does a Council member always attend a Watcher's sentence? This seems ... odd.

"I meant to say ... I ... how can I help you?" The medical examiner was still clearly shocked by Cade's presence. She looked like she was the one being sentenced.

Not normal, then. What is going on?

"I am here to administer this Watcher's sedative," Cade said.

His statement wasn't an explanation to the medical examiner, and he clearly didn't plan on giving her one. An even more confused look crossed her face. She opened and closed her mouth, unsure of what to say to next.

Len shifted his weight back and forth and glanced at Cade every so often, then back toward the door. Len needed Rhetta; he didn't do anything without her as far as I could tell. He was clearly lost without her direction. Everyone remained silent, waiting for what would happen next.

Finally, Cade stepped toward me.

Yes, I could use that sedative right about now. Thank you.

No one challenged Cade's authority. "You may leave us," he informed the others.

When neither Len nor the medical examiner made a move, Cade spoke again. "Now." It wasn't said in anger. Actually, there was no emotion in his voice. It was merely a command.

Len and the medical examiner gave me one last worried glance, then made their way to the door. I was left to fend for myself against Cade.

Every word he spoke was calculated. He didn't waste a breath on unnecessary words. He conveyed his arguments during my trial that way too.

The scanner beeped, grabbing my attention. My heart pounded as Cade drew nearer.

Reaching up to the scanner, Cade stopped the beeping while keeping eye contact with me. He appeared to be studying me, taking in my features and truly looking at me rather than my medical chart. It was extremely unsettling. I wanted to look away from his golden eyes, but I couldn't. Cade's presence demanded my full attention, and for the first time since I had been here, I wasn't thinking about my sentence or what would happen to me. I needed to figure out what this man was about.

"There's no need to be afraid of *me*." He emphasized the word "me" like it was ridiculous that I'd fear the imposing figure in front of me rather than my terrible fate as a Watcher. "I truly am here to give you the sedative and calm you before your first cycle begins."

"Is it normal for the Council of Five to swing the ax themselves? You always come down here to start a new Watcher's penance?"

He laughed, but it sounded like a deep, grumbly sound. The smile reached his golden eyes, and he grunted deep in his throat to cover it up. He wasn't supposed to be amused by a prisoner.

"No." He removed the seal from the sedative and prepared my arm. He swiped something on the screen of my medical chart, and the scanner reshaped to hover over my arm, waiting for the liquid of the sedative to be inserted. Cade's presence was soothing compared to the guards and medical examiners. Perhaps soothing was the wrong word to use to explain this man, but it took my mind off of my impending doom for whatever reason.

Cade inserted a small vial of liquid into the arm of the scanner, and without warning, pressed the screen above to give the command for the scanner to inject it into my arm. I felt a sharp pinch of pain then immediate calm.

"That was quick," I quipped. My head started to swim. *Is this it? Will this be my last coherent memory of my true self before I lose it?* I panicked, then no sooner than I thought it, the panic faded into a calm melting feeling. My eyes felt heavy. My entire body did. It was smart to drug us so we didn't have time to lose it before being transformed.

Cade studied me, but I didn't feel scared. His eyes gave off a trace of pity. As he should, I thought.

"It will be difficult for you to remember yourself, especially on your first cycle as a Watcher, but some find it helpful to try and tether themselves by concentrating on one specific memory or word. It can serve to anchor your mind to your true self. It will also help you remain calm leading up to the transfer. Whatever thought or memory of your life soothes you, try to cling to that in the time just before you leave yourself."

This was the most Cade had spoken. I knew it was important to remember, but wasn't that the problem? I was about to forget myself to become another. Anchor myself, I thought.

I almost laughed. A happy memory, something important to remember about myself so I didn't forget myself entirely. Did I have any of those? My mother ... Suttor ... in the days before ... when we could just live ... before worry ... before struggling ... when I was still a child. *Mmm,* I could almost feel the happiness I had felt with them ... with my family.

I felt another slight pinch. From the corner of my eye, I saw another injection go into my arm. This liquid was crimson rather than the clear blue of the sedative. *Is this it? Am I becoming a Watcher?*

As if trying to cover up that there was another injection, Cade looked into my eyes. "It's time now," he said.

Cade moved his hand on the display above, and the bed began to move. We were leaving the medical room. I wouldn't just go into oblivion from the injection, there was more to come. I felt like the bed floated through the air as we made our way into the halls. Cade walked alongside me. I saw another flash in my mind of the man dragged past Balor and I.

No, don't let that be your last thought. Stay calm. Think of your family. Remember to anchor yourself. Give me another sedative.

We entered a large room filled with strange machinery. I was unable to take everything in while sedated and with my body secured to the scanner. I vaguely registered that there were translucent orbs taking up most of the space in the room. Cade locked my scanner into a slot of what looked like a large, glass tube. I watched him motion on the display of the operating system just out of my line of vision. Restraints appeared from the scanner and wrapped themselves around my arms, legs, waist, and finally, my head. I felt little fear, except that I would forget to do as he had instructed me—to anchor myself. I was unable to move my head due to the restraints, but saw Cade's outline operating the machine I was trapped in.

White light illuminated around me, and a humming noise reverberated through the glass tube. *This is it.* If it worked and I became a Watcher instead of whatever that screaming man had become, I would need to do as Cade instructed.

Remember Mom. Remember Suttor.

White light blazed around me, forcing my eyes to shoot open. The thrumming of the machines vibrated through my body. I didn't know what moment would be my last. Panic welled up inside me again, despite the sedative. I tried to close my eyes again in concentration. I had to remember myself before it was too late.

The vibrations grew deafening, but I closed my eyes and clung to memories of my family and what we once were. I saw Suttor holding my hand, looking down at me with her kind eyes. I saw my mother smiling while holding my other hand. I felt a slow, warm breeze brush the dark tendrils away from my face, then my mother tucked my hair back behind my ear.

I felt happy, almost content. I felt that memory. I knew myself and who I truly was because of them. I had my anchor. I felt myself smile, my eyes still tightly closed as the machine and everything around me seemed to ignite into one thrumming, bright light. I clung to my memory, and just as I let go, I heard his deep voice. "Remember."

CHAPTER 18

SENIA

I played detective for two days, looking for a clue as to what happened to my new friend, Paige. Maybe she had family where the earthquakes hit and needed to get to them. That, however, didn't seem plausible. I looked up every last bit of information I could find about the earthquake. From what I found, it appeared all the damage happened in an uninhabitable place. The closest town, Claudere, was some place I had never even heard of.

Perhaps Paige was an environmentalist or worked in some other area that would require her to go to the site of the earthquake. I concocted all sorts of reasons why that news clip had upset Paige so much, but nothing seemed right. Even the earthquake itself was strange. Every news article I read said scientists were baffled by the incident in what they called "a most unlikely area" for the fault lines to shift.

The whole thing seemed strange. Had I dreamed up our entire meeting? I had more than my share of gaps in memory lately, but this would be new. I never made up a person before. No, that couldn't have been what happened, but just to make sure, I went back to the pizza shop.

The place looked even dirtier than it had at night, but still smelled delicious. I waited in line like everyone else and ordered my pizza. I hoped to see anyone who was there from the other night. The man who worked the register when I had first come in wasn't there for the day shift, but I described what he looked like to another employee, and he told me the guy was due back in for work later that night. I could wait that long, I thought. After all, Paige told me to wait. But why?

"Stay in the city until I come back," she said.

The last words she said were even more puzzling. I couldn't get Paige's eyes out of my head as I replayed the scene in my mind. "No, you're not," Paige had said.

"I'm not what?" I should've replied. Instead, I froze, unable to respond or move. Her eyes hypnotized me; I even dreamed of them that night.

The night I met Paige, I walked back to the hotel alone and in a stupor. I hadn't bothered to call for a car. I wished I would have had the presence of mind to chase after her. All of these strange things happening to me had to be linked to my illness, but I didn't want to dwell on that. I couldn't explain it, but I had faith that I hadn't imagined this. For some reason, my encounter with Paige was important.

No. It's not important. Your mind is just playing tricks on you. Get a grip and move on. You're a new woman, not the kind of woman who waits around for some stranger just because she was nice to you.

I didn't have much time left, so why waste it waiting around for something I didn't understand. It was foolish. Yet, I found myself walking down the street my hotel was on, looking down every side street for the café Paige originally suggested for us to meet.

I searched the area in another new outfit, but flat shoes this time. Just because I was a new woman who wore heels didn't mean I was going to wear them when my feet hurt. My new flats looked just as chic. I looked into windows, telling myself I was only window shopping and looking for a place to have some coffee. I passed several coffee shops that were far too commercial to be a place Paige would take me. As if I knew her well.

When I was about to give up and make my way back to the Diamanta, I took a moment to dig through my purse for my street map. As I pulled the map out, a passerby hit my elbow and knocked some of the contents of my purse to the ground. The old Senia might have apologized as if it were my fault, but that wasn't me now. As Sen, I looked around for the rude man who hadn't bothered to apologize, and upon finding him promptly yelled out, "Excuse you!"

It was a small victory and really not *that* rude, but it felt liberating. As I bent down to pick up my lipstick and wallet from the street, I saw it. Sitting in the trash bin was a white paper cup with a curved artistic-looking handle. I had never rummaged through the trash before, but I found myself doing just that. I pulled the cup from the trash bin. Armistice, it was called, and the address printed at the bottom of the cup displayed the street that I was on. I looked up to see where I was. Then, I looked at the surrounding street numbers and used my map to find the right direction. I walked block after block, constantly checking the street map to make sure I was going in the right direction until I finally made it to Armistice.

The entryway way to the café looked so small that I didn't think there was room enough for people to sit inside. Upon entering, I saw a flight of stairs with a sign pointing up. I took the steep stairs one at a time; each stair creaked and groaned. I turned right when I made it to the top and saw a register and tiny area to order. When I turned further, I saw a sitting area and the reason this place was so charming. A rooftop garden with tiny lanterns and orbs lit up my vision. It looked like something out of a children's fairytale. Bright flowers were everywhere, and rustic white furniture seemed to glow. It was a vision.

"Can I help you?" a girl asked from behind the counter.

"*Umm*, yes," I smiled. " A friend of mine recommended you. This place is beautiful."

"Yeah, we like it," she smiled back. "Would you like to wait for your friend or go ahead and order something now?"

"Oh, no. I mean, no, my friend isn't meeting me here. I can go ahead and order. What do you rec—" I caught myself. "I mean, what are my options?"

The girl rattled off a list of beverages and then pointed to the cases of sweets. I ordered then; while I waited, I tried my best to describe Paige to the Armistice employee.

"She has auburn wavy hair and she's very tall," I explained. "And her eyes," I started, but stopped myself. *How could I describe her transfixing eyes?* I couldn't. "She's someone you would notice if you saw her."

"Nope, I haven't seen anyone like that here before, but I'm pretty new. Jason is probably a better bet. He's on break right now, but if you stick around for another ten minutes, he should be back by then."

"Okay, sure," I replied. "I've got time. I'll just sit outside."

"I will let you know when he gets back," she answered. "*Um*, I'm sorry, what is your name?"

"Sen. My name is Sen," I responded, but it still didn't feel right when I said it.

"I'm Lexi."

"Thanks, Lexi." I walked out to the rooftop garden.

I looked for a place to sit, but instead, found myself exploring with coffee in hand. There was only one other couple in the garden, and they didn't notice me. I studied a large flower I had never seen before. It was an effervescent blue at the tips and electric lime green color in the center. Its shape made it look like a small doll wearing a gown. I strolled further beneath a trellis covered in white flowers that grew on the arch like coral rather than twisting like flowers typically would around a trellis. Everything past the trellis glowed, but as I got closer to what I previously thought were tiny lights, I noticed they were flowers. I looked closer, examining the flowers for tiny lights hidden in them or even for glowing insects, but I found neither. What I did find were glowing droplets of dew on each petal and light coming from the core of the flower itself. *How in the world?*

"Hi, are you Sen?" A man's voice cut through my thoughts.

"No," I instinctually replied. "Sorry. Yes, I'm Sen. That's me."

His brow furrowed a bit, clearly confused as to why I didn't know my own name. "I'm Jason. Lexi told me that you were asking about another customer that comes in sometimes?"

"Yes!" I said. "I'm sorry, I'm just so distracted here in this beautiful garden. All of these lights and flowers are just spectacular. What kind of flowers are these?" I pointed to ones I had thoroughly examined. "I've never seen anything like them. How do you get them to glow like that?"

This time, Jason couldn't hide his confusion. "What lights?"

I looked around me again. *What does he mean "What lights?" The whole rooftop is aglow.* "The lights coming from the flowers. How do you make them look like that?"

Jason continued to look at me as if I told him the sky was pink.

"Ma'am, there are no lights out here. It's actually getting pretty dark out. Maybe we should step back into the café."

My mind was starting to play tricks on me too. As if dying wasn't enough, did I have to lose my mind? I looked back down at the flowers and they seemed to shine even brighter. I could see them. I was staring right at them. It all looked so real to me, but I knew by the look on Jason's face that my mind was wrong.

"There are no lights in the flowers, then," I said.

"No, ma'am. Why don't we go inside and I'll get you some water."

Water, I laughed to myself. Why is everyone always trying to get me to drink water as if that will somehow magically fix me? I followed Jason back inside. I stared at the floorboards, trying to hold back tears. How much of what I saw and did was real? Oh no. *Paige.* I knew it was too strange and too good to be true to encounter someone I connected with so well.

Jason returned from through the door behind the counter with a large cup of water and a large cookie. "On the house." He smiled.

I tried my best to smile back, but I couldn't do that and hold my tears in at the same time. "Thank you, but I can pay for it."

"Oh no, I insist!" Jason tells me. "From the owner."

"You're the owner? That's wonderful that you are doing so well for yourself. You look so young."

Jason appeared to be at least ten years older than me. He looked confused again. First, I was seeing things; now, I spoke to him like an old lady.

"If you don't mind me saying so," I added, feeling even more embarrassed.

He laughed and told me he was definitely old enough to own his own business and that he inherited it from the original owners. They had passed away.

"I actually started coming here when I was still a boy," he said. "I came in with my mother every week. The owner took a liking to my mother when she worked here. I think my mother must have reminded the owner of her own daughter—or grandchild. She took my mother under her wing and helped her out when she was still a little too young to have me."

I could see Jason was reminiscing now.

"The owner's name was Ruthie, and she was the sweetest lady. She would give me sweets and tell me stories when I was little, and then when my mother passed—" he stopped and looked at me. "Well, when my mother passed away, Ruthie passed this place on to me. She said this place brought her peace, and it would do the same for me. That's why Ruthie named it Armistice. She said it was a fancy word for peace, and that some day, it would lead someone very important to her peace as well."

I listened to Jason as I sipped my water. His story soothed me.

"Ruthie must have been quite a person to give her business over to someone who wasn't related to her."

"She was." Jason got a little glimmer in his eye before clearing his throat. "But yes, after that big long story that you clearly didn't ask for, I am, in fact, the owner. I feel a little over my head sometimes, truth be told."

He looked into my sad eyes and attempted to make me smile. "Hey, you shouldn't be accusing me of being young though. You look much younger than me."

"No, I'm not," I replied instinctually. I heard Paige's voice saying again, "No, you're not." My head spun, throbbing pain came out of nowhere. *Stop it.* I took another big gulp of water and felt the pain subside a bit.

"You've never seen a woman come in here with long, wavy auburn hair, have you? She's very tall and has really unusual eyes," I said.

"You mean Paige?"

My eyes grew wide as I looked back to Jason. He had my full attention. "You know her? You know Paige?" I couldn't hide the excitement in my voice.

"Sure. She comes in here almost every day, or she has since she first came in about a month ago. She's really friendly. She said one of her friends told her about us. Paige always sits back by the trellis where I first saw you."

That's weird. She came in and said the same thing I said, and then she sat in the same place I did. What does this all mean?

"Do you know anything else about her?" I prodded. "Where does she live?"

"I don't really know her that well," Jason replied. "She just chats with me every once in a while when she's here. I thought you said that you were her friend. Don't *you* know where she lives?"

I started to tell him that I didn't really know Paige that well myself, but then the lie came to me, one that will be believable because it had a shade of truth to it.

"Actually, I've been having trouble remembering things lately. I was just trying to track her down, and the only thing I could remember was that she told me to come here. You see, I have a brain tumor." Saying those words forced tears to well up in my eyes. "And I need to tell her, but it's getting so difficult to remember. I lost my phone somewhere. I can't remember when, so I can't call her."

Lies mixed with the truth really were the easiest to spin. If Jason had any information, I was determined to make him feel guilty enough to spill it.

Jason studied my face. *Oh, come on*, I thought. He met me not ten minutes ago before realizing how much I had already felt for Paige, who I had just met as well. I let a tear fall, but before it could trickle down my face, Jason caught it with his thumb.

"I'm so sorry, I don't have any more information for you. I wish there was anything more I could do for you. Anything at all," he said. "You seem like a very lovely person."

"No, I'm not." My response was a reflex. *Why did I say that? I am a very lovely person. I always do the right thing. I am kind and honest.* Perhaps that's why I said it. I was not Senia anymore. I was lying, crazy Sen now.

"*Ahh!*" I clutched my head. The sharp pain was back with a vengeance. I needed to get out of here.

"Are you alright?" Jason asked.

"I'm fine. I just need—*ah!*" The pain was too sharp to finish.

"Do you need me to get you to a hospital?" Jason was clearly worried.

"No, I just need a car." I nearly reached for my phone to call for one, then remembered my lie. I felt another searing pain and nearly reached for it anyways.

"I'll call you a car. Just sit tight, I'll be right back." Jason strode back toward the door he had come through earlier.

I tried to take my mind off the pain, but watching the door waiting for Jason to return wasn't helping. I turned to face the garden again. The lights I had seen before still burned brightly, contrasting with the sky that had darkened even more since I walked inside. *It isn't really there.* I stared at the trellis, trying to take my mind off the pain. I tried to think of Paige and how she stood in that same spot beneath the trellis. It meant something. I knew it did, but I couldn't put my finger on it.

I saw each tiny, brilliant light that illuminated the garden. I couldn't tell if my vision was blurring or not, but the lights seemed to sway back and forth like they were dancing in the dark. I allowed my eyes to relax and felt my head sway as I watched. Suddenly, I saw the club from the other night.

I swayed to the music, the colored lights moving all around the dark setting. My pain began to dull. I saw Paige's eyes and the way those same lights seemed to dance in them, calling me in like a siren. All I could see were her eyes, so familiar and captivating.

"No, you're not," I heard Paige's last words to me. At first, they were in a whisper, then grew louder until it felt as though I could *see* the words.

"No, you're not." This time I heard my own voice say it. *No, I'm not what?*

"Sen? Sen!" Jason returned and shook my shoulder, but I just stood there staring as if paralyzed.

I heard a voice somewhere in the distance as the lights continued to flash before my eyes. The sky was pink and the lights made it sparkle. I reached for a lock of my golden blonde hair and sighed. I loved color and light. It was so beautiful.

"Sen!" Jason screamed.

I still stared with unseeing eyes.

"Sen!" He said one last time. Like a reflex I replied, "No, I'm not. I am not Sen."

Jason moved in front of me, blocking my view of the garden. As he did, I collapsed in his arms.

CHAPTER 19

SENIA

I drifted in and out of consciousness, letting my mind relax. *Why does it feel so good to finally let go and rest?* I floated through a world of lights and color. *Beautiful.*

"Don't you think so, Brother?"

"Don't I think what?" he replies.

"Don't you think it's beautiful?"

"It needs something. I can't put my finger on it."

My brother always ruins my fun. I want my creations to be pretty and happy. He wants them to be sensible and sustaining. It is a good thing he is there to balance me out—or so he constantly told me. I know it to be true, though. I only let myself be so carefree because he is serious all the time. I know he would make sure that everything that needed to be there would be. Truthfully, though, I am more than capable and only act nonchalant to drive him crazy.

"Why did you add this one again?" He holds a tiny, pink flower in his hand.

"Because it's pretty." We saunter down the slopes of hills covered in green blades of grass that gave life to the area I am working on.

"Why truly, Sister?" He asks, using that exasperated tone he always does.

"The last time I added that particular flower, a colorful insect species rose up around it to use it for shelter. Then another came along and used it for food, and everything around it continued thriving, and then—"

"Okay, okay, but why don't we try to make it white this time? That way the light it absorbs—"

"No, it should be pink," I said.

"Just because you enjoy your bright colors does not mean they are always right for a place."

"I know, Brother, but in this place, it is right. I can tell this will be a place that will thrive from color."

"And how exactly can you tell that, Sister?"

"Well, because you keep trying to make it so gloomy. I mean, a people called the Ire? Seems to me like people who are named after anger and rage will need a little cheer around them. If they are surrounded by darkness and grays all the time, they are bound to fail. They need color."

My brother laughs a full throaty laugh, finally smiling for the first time since we got here. I grin back at him in triumph.

"Oh, Sister, what shall we do with you?"

We stroll through the rolling hills, studying our surroundings as we go. For me, it is like making an enormous painting, adding to it little by little until the perfect details are revealed. I walk inside that painting now, though, adding the finishing touches and admiring the architecture my brother and I so painstakingly created together.

I am quite a distance ahead of him now, I realize. I stop walking as I hear dripping water. The only noises we should be hearing at this point in the process are the sounds of our own voices and footsteps. I close my eyes in concentration. Silence. I open my eyes and look back at my brother; he is crouched down over a large, leafy green plant I had decided on. I walk a little further, but hear it again. It is a dripping noise, like water falling, droplet by droplet. I turn back to my brother.

"Do you hear that, Kallan?" I ask. "You didn't start the water without me, did you?"

I wait for him to pop up out of the brush, but see nothing but green as far as I could see. I can't do this without him; where has he gone?

"Kallan?" I call out again.

Fear rises through me, gently at first, and then in a rush throughout my body. It rises in a frenzy before I can stop it. I walk back toward where I have last seen him, trying to track his steps.

"Kallan?"

I panic and move faster. The dripping gets louder. *How can that be?* I break out into a sprint, swatting away the thick brush I had just put there.

"Kallan!"

The dripping is faster now and sounds like the clanging of metal. The faster I run, the louder it becomes. I am frantic, and the clanging becomes a rapid beeping noise as I run.

Suddenly, I am hit by something that knocks me down mid-stride. Searing pain in my head overwhelms me, and I lay on the ground momentarily paralyzed before rolling onto my back. I stare up at a pink sky, the three moons aligned flawlessly above. They are aligned perfectly, I think. Then I see only white light and bolt upright, gasping for breath.

Nurses surrounded me and a nearby heart monitor beeped at a rapid pace.

"I can't breathe! I can't breathe!" was all I could say between gasps.

A female nurse took my hand, then tried to put something into the IV that was already attached to me. *I don't know why I am here.* The nurse spoke to me in a language I didn't understand, but her soothing tones attempted to calm me. A man approached my bed and spoke to the nurse before roughly grabbing my other arm. He tried to communicate with her too, but the nurse didn't understand him. He used the restraints to still my arms so the female nurse could inject medication into my IV. Almost immediately, I began to calm down. I let the beeping noise lull me back to sleep.

"Don't you think it's beautiful?" I ask, turning toward him. When I do, I find his eyes are already fixed on me.

"Yes," he replies, without taking his eyes off me.

"You're not even looking, Carrick!" I scold.

I nudge his large arm and smile, then I take his chin in my hand and force him to look at our surroundings.

I look up to the light-blue sky above and large white shapes floating slowly through it. What is the purpose of those, I think. Kallan will surely know. I will have to bring him here. But how has this place come to be? My ears fill with unfamiliar noises of creatures I know nothing about. I smell fragrances from the ground beneath. Everything around me seems so alive, and my senses are filled.

"How can this be?" I ask in awe.

Carrick bends down, his hand digging into the ground before I can stop him. "Carrick, don't!" I cry out in horror.

"Don't worry, my love. I'm only checking for similarities," he assures me.

My heart races in my chest. I know all too well what he can do, and I cannot bear for him to harm this place. It fascinates me. Whoever designed it certainly knew far more than my brother and I. It is so ornate and delicate—so intricate—as if it had happened slowly and perfectly over a great amount of time.

Carrick holds up a hand of ground to me, allowing me to study it closer. The blades of grass stick up at the top and then root themselves into a rich dark soil filled with moisture.

"Carrick, it is similar to our own designs, but even more delicate."

How is it that life here can survive? I continue studying a clump of soil and plant life, trying to note every detail. I have never thought to make something so fragile. I have always thought to make everything as sturdy and strong as possible to ensure its survival. This is different. This whole place is so different and yet so like what Kallan and I work on. *We need to find Kallan. We need to bring him here so that he can see.* The light fades above me, and my surroundings grow dark. A shadow seems to form above, and when I look up to study it, the world around me seems to fade away.

I opened my eyes, seeing nothing but white and then spots until my vision cleared. I saw a fluorescent light above and heard the dripping of my IV along with the beeping monitor. I vaguely noticed movement toward me from the corner of my eye, then was lost again.

The tears I refuse to let fall cloud my vision. I blink my eyes open, trying to focus on the task at hand. My heart sinks; I know what I must do. Without looking, I reach out for his hand. As always, it is there for me to hold. His large hand envelops my own. I look up into his deep, colorful eyes. I have grown to love them so much. But no, I suppose I haven't grown to love Carrick. I loved him from the beginning as if I always had and always would. Carrick always feels so warm and reassuring, like no matter what I face, he will be there to protect me. Even now, with the full knowledge of what must be done, he looks at me so adoringly. My heart lurches as we lock eyes, lost in each other as we always are. It will be our undoing, though. I know it. I feel it like an ominous warning inside my mind, but yet I cannot unlock my eyes from his. I am lost to anyone but him, and he to me, so nothing else should matter to us now.

I take a deep breath and make myself look away from him before squeezing his hand to let him know it is time. We stride hand in hand, looking straight ahead, as we make our way down the corridor to speak of a place called Erreta with the other members of the Council.

My heart beats faster with each step, then it begins to beep faster. *No, that isn't right.* My mind wanders. A beeping noise rings in my ears as my heart races to match its noise. My surroundings blur around me as if trapped in a memory that I can no longer recall. I know what the corridor looks like, but when I try to look forward and walk further, I can't imagine it. I have forgotten where I am. When I turn to look at the man holding me up, he is faceless. I know he is there. I know he has always been there, but I don't know him anymore.

Panic arises again. For some reason, I can recall the feeling of panic and know I have felt it often. It is the only thing I can say feels familiar to me. I try to squeeze his hand again and find that I feel nothing. I release his hand and look down at my own. To my horror, I find that I can no longer see myself or imagine what I look like. I try to recall what I look like, who I am, and where I am. I can't focus on anything. I dig deep, trying to force myself to remember something, anything that I can focus on. I lose everything. It is as if I have lost my sight. My vision blurs, but I don't see darkness. I can't focus on or see anything around me. I close my eyes, trying to concentrate with all my might. Everything around me seems to race; it is as if I am moving at a rapid pace, but nothing stirs.

"We're losing her. We're losing her!" I heard noises all around me, but looked with unseeing eyes as my body jolted up and down. It felt like I was being pulled up by some invisible force yanking at my chest. I could not see, but I could feel the panic around me. Why did I not feel the same? I felt so calm. I had done this before, after all. *What a ridiculous thought*, I chided myself. Then, oblivion claimed me.

Everything stopped with a jolt, jarring me. There was no sound and nothing to see. There was nothing, and I, too, was becoming nothing. It felt good to me, this nothingness, as if I had longed for it. I didn't float. I didn't land. I could no longer see, but it wasn't the blackness of closing my eyes; it was the blur of unseeing eyes. It was as if I no longer existed, but I had consciousness of my nonexistence. It was the strangest sensation. I felt both frightened and at peace, and I had longed for this, I thought. I had longed for an ending. My mind had been so full for so long, unable to use any of it. I remembered knowing I possessed the knowledge and power, but could never quite reach either. How frustrating life had been for me, this last life and all those before it.

This poor dying girl, I thought. *But she isn't me*, I remembered. *She remembered.* This thought jolted me like a lightning strike through my body. Instead of nothingness, I felt a shock of life coursing through me as thoughts came rushing in like a flood. I remembered, and the nothingness turned into memories rushing at me, returning my senses. I was not her. I was not this dying girl.

My ears rang as hearing returned to me, beeping and ringing like the echo of an old familiar voice. And *I* heard it ring in my ears over and over. Not her ears, but my own. No, you're not. No. You are not this girl.

Open your eyes, whoever you are, I thought. But I could no longer see. I tried to close my eyes. "Close your eyes and remember," I told the girl. Where I came from, the sky sparkled with stars as far as the eye could see—like prisms reflecting lights of every color. I never could duplicate it, but when I closed my eyes, it's what I saw. I knew now it was what I had dreamed of. I saw the sky that once was—the sky filled with color. And when I thought of it, I could see it in my mind as if it was there before me—my home forever lost to me.

"Open your eyes, Senia," I said.

I knew when the girl did, I would no longer be there. I would go back to being a memory just out of reach, just like my home. I would return to the prison of that full mind trapped inside a dying girl. *Open your eyes* was the last thought of my own, and then I was gone.

CHAPTER 20

CARRICK

I watched out my window for hours, the rain pounded at the windowpane until I thought the glass would break from the sheer force of the water. The storm raged on, but still no Arden. I didn't know if I was ready for her, but I had to make myself ready for whatever would happen.

Would she try to kill me on the spot? More importantly, *could* she kill me if she wanted? Arden's power, though somewhat different from my own, was designed to match me. If we fought with our powers unbridled, we would obliterate our surroundings. We knew no other way. As Khassos, our power lay in destruction. I needed Arden's help, but I worried about how to reason with her. Surely Arden felt the same way toward Eirene as she did toward me and would not feel obliged to save her. All I truly hoped for was to speak with her and gain information that might help me save her and somehow find a way to bargain for Eirene's life. I had to get Arden talking—it was the only way. But how could I reason with someone who felt they had nothing to live for?

The wind howled, and then I heard a change. It was slight at first, and then grew louder, like the noise of this world's trains. The sky turned from a dark gray to a sickly green color. I'd seen it in other worlds past, but a green sky was unnatural here. The power flickered and then went out, leaving only a short buzzing noise. I grabbed my large coat and threw it on, hoping to shield myself a little before making my way to the motel door. I slid the chain and twisted the lock to open the door, but the door slammed into my body as the wind blew it open. It would have easily broken bones in an Erretas' body — and it did hurt mine—but I was able to move out from behind it and leave the room. Abnormally large hail fell in chunks, pelting the roof and smashing windshields of a few vehicles parked in the lot. A chorus of car alarms sang as the wind howled angrily.

I used my coat to shield my face as I ran toward the motel's front lobby. I grasped for the door handle, but it was blocked by something the front desk clerk had apparently used to keep it shut. I banged on the door as softly as I could without breaking it and shouted for the clerk to let me in. I doubted anyone could hear me, but just as I was about to break down the door, I heard a voice call back to me.

"Are ya crazy?" I heard an older man shout.

"I need to get in!" The hail came down sideways now, hitting me and soaking through my coat.

"Go back to your room. It's not safe."

I knew I could easily break through the barrier and the door, but that would just put them in more danger.

"Yeah, well it's not safe for you in there either, buddy. Is there anyone else staying here?"

"What?" he yelled back at me.

"Is there anyone else staying here?"

"No. Just go back to your room."

"I know there are other people here. I can hear their car alarms going off. Tell me where. I want to help, and if you don't open this door I'm going to break through your window and come in that way."

I knew he heard me, but he let the silence stretch out, perhaps contemplating if I really could break in. A round face with overgrown, dark gray eyebrows popped out through the curtains of the window.

As he took in my size, the clerk apparently decided I was capable of breaking the window—and the door, for that matter.

"I have the door blocked with a book case so it might take us a minute to move it. There's a family of four in here with me. That's their car making all the noise," the clerk said. "And there's a couple in 105."

"What's your name?" I asked.

"Name's Tom," he replied.

"Okay, Tom, you work on the bookcase, and I will be back in a minute."

The wind blew so hard I could barely walk, but room 105 was close by, and I didn't waste time. I kicked the door to room 105 in and heard a woman squeal in fright.

"It's alright." I raised my hands in the air. "I'm here to help. We need to get you both out of here. We are all going to stay in the main building. These walls are not going to hold up. So, we need to make our way over to the front lobby."

The woman, and I assume her husband, both nodded in unison.

"Is there power in the office?" The man asked me.

"Don't think so, but trust me, we are better off there. It's not safe here." As the last word made its way out of my mouth, I heard a loud crack. As if in slow motion, a tree headed right toward us. I looked at the couple who stood frozen—just waiting for the impact. I knew I wouldn't be able to move them in time without injuring them.

I broke the rules. I did what I could not in all my time as a Watcher. I moved with my Khassos strength beneath the tree and caught it before it could land. I shoved the tree back toward an empty parking space where I let it land with a thud; the impact of the tree created a small crack in the pavement.

I interfered in the lives of Erretas. Did it matter that I had done so because of another Khassos? All the rules I had known in my time as a Watcher had changed. My sister and I here, in our true forms, affected this world. It all felt wrong, but I didn't have time to think about it.

All I knew was I felt like I was meant to be here. I got the same feeling as a Watcher when my purpose for being somewhere clicked into place. For some reason, though, my conscious was still aware of a wrongness in the back of my mind. I returned my attention to the storm and hoped Arden knew more than I did. I hoped she could be bargained with.

I was soaked to the bone from the rain and hail. My hair hung in my eyes, and when I pushed it away, I realized the couple had their eyes locked on me with unbelieving eyes. It was as if the raging storm around them no longer existed, and I was much more shocking to them than the storm.

"Come on!" I shouted. I reached for the woman's hand.

She looked back to her husband as if asking for some sort of reassurance.

"We don't have time for this." I took a step toward her and picked her up in one fluid motion, then turned to walk back to the front desk entrance.

"What do you think you're doing?" The man shouted at me, trying to grab for his wife.

"I will pick you up too if you don't move. Now!"

A chair from a nearby picnic table flew behind us and crashed in to a window a few rooms down. The man instantly swallowed whatever he was going to say next.

As we hustled toward the lobby, the man fell several times. I took his arm and dragged him behind me; his wife, all the while, silently bounced on my shoulder.

When we finally made it, I hoped the clerk had moved everything away from the door. I placed the woman back on her feet and tried to use my body to block the hail from pummeling the couple.

"Tom!" I shouted. The tension rose in my body, and I didn't trust myself to knock on the door. Any time I had been in a storm of Arden's making, I had been a Khassos and helped her in the destruction. I was losing control. I staggered, trying to contain the Khassos within me.

"Bang on the windows," I told the couple.

"Tom! Tom!" We all shouted. I turned for just a moment and saw it in the distance—a whirlwind. It towered from the ground to the sky, and its width stretched wider than the building we clung to. The couple noticed I stopped yelling and turned to see what I was so awestruck by. They stood motionless, looking at the beast we now faced.

"Tom! Let us in!" They screamed.

I turned to them, knowing I would again have to break the rules in front of them.

"It's alright," I assured them. They exchanged a panicked look before continuing to beat on the window and door.

"Move aside," I told them calmly.

I yelled to Tom again. Still no response.

"Move away from the door if you're still there," I shouted.

I waited a moment, and after hearing nothing, I kicked open the door. As a result, a large bookshelf and sofa were sent flying through the counter at the front desk area. The couple regained their look of horror once again before scrambling over the shattered bookcase and sofa. Tom emerged then, furiously waving his hands in the air over the damage I'd caused. Then, he stopped mid-sentence as his gaze assessed the gigantic whirlwind.

"We don't have much time." I tried to break Tom's trance as he stared on in horror. "Is there a cellar or a basement below?"

Tom gathered himself again. "Yes, a basement."

"Let's go then, quickly," I commanded.

I followed behind Tom and the couple toward what looked like a storage closet filled with games and books to rent. Tom opened a door at the back of the closet and motioned for the family he spoke of earlier to follow the rest of us as well. I looked down the small flight of stairs and saw a dark stone cellar that clearly hadn't been used much. It looked like the sturdiest bet the group had, but it wouldn't be enough.

A whirlwind that size would crush everything in its path. It seemed Arden was keen on breaking the rules as well. She would let this storm rage to weed me out and evidently did not care for the others whom she would hurt in the process. I saw one of the small children look up, tears shining in her young eyes. She was terrified. As I looked at the little Erretas girl, all I could see was my sister—a frightened little girl who watched as the world around her crumbled.

I grabbed Tom's arm, stopping him before he continued down the stairs. "Don't open this door no matter what you hear. Understand me?"

The man who I had saved earlier made his way back up the stairs and grabbed my hand. "I understand you," he said. "We won't open the door, no matter what."

He reached for Tom and led the clerk the rest of the way down the small flight of stairs before looking back up at me one last time. He smiled as if telling me he was in on my secret and no one else would ever know. I nodded to him in appreciation and closed the door behind me.

I had watched millions die in my time as a Khassos, but to watch these Erretas who I had lived amongst for so long perish would be my breaking point. I had to find a way to keep them safe. If I had to fight my sister, then so be it, but I would find a way to save this world. They were the only people who still accepted me, and this was the only place I could now call home. *If Eirene is in this world, then I will be in it too*, I thought.

I slammed the slanted door shut, locking the others in, and looked around the damaged front desk area for something to bar it shut. I found a sitting area and snapped off a metal chair leg, then slid it beneath the door handles.

I went back into the whirling fury of wind. I had to move forward. I couldn't afford to look back any longer; what I did had haunted me through eternity. More determined with each stride I took, I resolved myself to do what must be done. It was time for an ending. I was promised long ago that I would never find release from what I had done, that I would go on living forever, without my other half. My other half ... that could mean many different things to me.

Was my other half my sister, the one I had been a partner to as a Khassos? She rained obliteration from above while I tore the ground up from below. We were the perfect pair of annihilation, but without each other, what could we possibly be? I no longer had that part of myself—the part of me that demolished worlds. We held more power than any other beings. We four: Arden, Eirene, Kallan, and I made life possible for so many.

No, I corrected myself. Kallan and Eirene made life; Arden and I ended it. Leaving a path of death and destruction was all I was made for—all I could ever do. Was it even a wonder what I had done?

I ruined the perfect balance we achieved for ourselves and for our people. How could I ever be whole when I had dissolved that balance?

It was almost difficult to breathe now as I got closer to the whirlwind. I threw my weight toward the air as if it were a wall I needed to break through.

I knew it was time to start. I let the wind and rain beat me down to the ground, and I let my hands sink into the ground beneath me to brace myself. *I will control myself this time. I can skim the surface without losing my resolve.* I had to, or I would lose this world and Eirene with it.

I felt myself connect, and the energy surged through me, but this time, I didn't let it spread past my hands. A cold sweat broke out on my brow despite the weather around me. I held my power in check, using it to crawl my way into the center of the storm. I had to keep my mind elsewhere or I would lose the battle with myself. I continued crawling on the ground, half of me afraid to dig deeper and the other half afraid to rise to my feet and leave the power. I knew the storm would crush me if I did.

My other half. Was that Eirene? She was the one I loved enough to betray my people and my very way of life. No, she was my life. She was the other half of our balance. The creator to my destroyer, and I took that away from her too. I thought back to all the times I watched the light go out from her eyes, and all the times I watched it return as she remembered for a few brief moments before I lost her again. If she had held on longer, would I see the memory of more than who I once was in her eyes? Would I see her remember that I had taken her other half too? Would it break her to have that knowledge as it did my sister? Either way, Eirene lost me and her brother, Kallan, that day. I ended Eirene's other half just as I end all things.

I would have my ending now too. I struggled to crawl further while holding on to a mere sliver of power. *No more*, I thought. *I must make it to the center of the whirlwind.* If I could make it there, I could let go and stand in the eye where it was calm.

I pushed myself through, nearly losing my grip on the ground several times before I finally allowed myself to let the power surge up further into my forearms. The ground began to tremble as I delved deeper. I clenched my teeth, struggling to not release the power I held, struggling to hold on to the ground as my surroundings transformed around me and the whirlwind tried to engulf me. *No more*, I thought.

"No more, Arden!" I shouted into the wind, but even I couldn't hear my own voice.

Arden, if you can hear me, I'm sorry. I'm so sorry, Arden. Please, my sister.

I could hardly tell which direction was up and which was down. I was losing my grip, and I didn't know which would win out—my resolve to hold on or to unleash destruction.

"My sister," I whispered.

I let my grip on the ground go and my hold on the power with it, knowing that the storm would take me. As I let go, I waited for the wrath of the storm to hit me, but felt nothing. I laid flat on my back and looked up, stunned to see the sky. The wind howled around me, but I made it to the eye. I knew I hadn't made it that far on my own. I had only just reached the surface of the whirlwind. I remained on my back, gasping for breath. I didn't think I had the strength to make it to my feet, not yet. I turned my head and saw that I was not alone.

"Hello, Brother."

CHAPTER 21

CARRICK

I didn't know if I should try to show strength or remain on the ground in a submissive position. I suppose after begging Arden to stop, it would be foolish to try and show any sign of strength now. I waited, willing her to speak again, trying to gauge where I stood with my sister. The thought crossed my mind that had she wanted to, she could've started the destruction of this world without me. No, my sister likely wanted to treat me in kind and do to me what I had done to her. She wanted Eirene, and though I could not blame her, I could not stand for it either.

I continued to wait, the fear of what was to come built up. I let the stretch of silence between us go on. The only sound was the howl of the winds around us. I made myself look up at her, allowing myself to look into her eyes for the first time since that terrible day so long ago. No matter how much time passed, I was still unprepared to face Arden. In some ways, it was almost worse than all the times I had met Eirene's eyes. When Eirene looked at me, the pain was only my own. The memories lost to her were not lost to my sister. She remembered all that happened.

The guilt I had tried so hard to forget lifetime after lifetime felt fresh and new when I looked at Arden. I planned on letting her speak first, to remain submissive to her for all the pain I caused her, but when I met her eyes something compelled me to speak. Whatever she felt toward me, I still loved my sister, and seeing her overwhelmed me.

"Arden," I began. My voice cracked with emotion. "I..." but Arden stopped me. She held her hand out and turned her head away from me.

"Don't," she said. Evidently, she also struggled with facing me.

When she turned to face me again, I could see the tears in her colorful eyes. Her expression seemed to jump from hatred to sadness as she looked down on me.

"How much do you know?" she asked me. I noticed a sense of urgency in her voice.

I was astounded that this was her first thought. I didn't quite know where to begin. She kept her distance from me, standing with arms crossed as the whirlwind spun around us. She made a gesture with her head as if granting me permission to stand. I put my weight on my right arm before pushing myself to my feet. Arden was tall by Erretas standards, but I still stood above her. It all still felt wrong. The two of us here, in our true forms, but in Erretas clothing, harnessing our power rather than unleashing it fully as we used to. I cocked my head, realizing how well Arden controlled her power. I had nearly lost myself to it, but she held hers casually. *How did she manage to learn such control in such a short time?*

"I know I have not gained the control over my power as well as you have, Sister. I know that our time is limited because though our communications have been severed. Tahrell was able to reach me somehow."

Arden's eyes widened. "He was able to speak to you?" she asked. "In this realm? How is that possible?"

"I don't know. He told me that I was still a Watcher and a connection remained between us and our true realm. I can only assume they are working on repairing the Great Corridor and will resume our typical process as soon as they can."

Arden's brow furrowed. "What do you mean repair the Great Corridor? What happened to it?"

"Oh, so you don't know about that?" I asked. "I—well, for lack of a better phrase, I destroyed it."

"What? How?" Arden seemed taken aback. "If that is possible, don't you think a Watcher would've tried it long ago?"

"To be honest, I don't know how I was able to accomplish it myself. Something happened. I don't know what, but there was something wrong with my last Watcher form. To start with, I arrived late, then once I returned to relay my information to the Council, they already knew what I came to report."

She looked at me, trying to assess if I was still the brother she once knew or the brother who betrayed her. "What was your information?" she asked.

I took a deep breath. "This world cannot go on much longer. The Council plans on letting the Erretas die out." I paused for a moment, allowing her time for that knowledge to sink in and try and gauge my sister's reaction. This clearly was not new information to her. I had suspected as much. "You already knew."

"I did," she replied.

"There is another land, however; one I thought they could inhabit—" I stopped, remembering the jubilation I felt as Dr. Umbridge came to that conclusion, "but the Council will not allow it. Our people will inhabit it instead."

Arden's eyes widened. That was new to her.

"The Council has rationalized this decision based on the notion that the Erretas will destroy their world on their own before they can fully inhabit the new one. The Council of Five told me they will inhabit it and name it Kallan, as a memorial of some sort."

At the mention of his name, Arden's eyes and nostrils flared. I expected Arden to tell me to stop. I expected her to get angry at me for saying his name. Instead, she said, "They will pay for what they have done."

"Arden, how did you know about the Erretas?"

"My last time here as a Watcher allowed me to learn of their fate, but not of this new land you speak of. I assume that is something you learned as a Watcher?"

I nodded yes.

"I reported to them and was transported back shortly afterward, but before I could get very far with my next form, something strange happened," Arden said. "I saw a blur in my vision, then a burst of colors so vibrant I could not see anything else. It was as if I was hypnotized by the colors. Then I was blinded by a bright white light, and just like that, I was myself again—still here, but not as a Watcher, as a Khassos."

Arden had been through a similar experience to my own.

"I suspected you might be the one who told them about the remaining lifespan of the Erretas. The Council was aware of the information before I relayed it to them," I said. "I knew another Watcher must have told them before me, but how were we both dispatched to learn the same information in the first place? And how was I able to destroy the Great Corridor? I did not possess my Khassos power there. I had my physical strength, maybe, but not Khassos power. I was able to topple over the pillars of the Great Corridor into the barrier as if it was merely the wall of a building. There was no resistance, it just ... shattered."

"I do not know, Brother, but something is amiss," Arden replied. "However it happened, our connection as Watchers has been severed for now, and we must act fast, for they will surely do everything in their power to regain their leash on us."

I had nearly forgotten the whirlwind that howled around us. It felt good to speak with my sister, as if on a mission, as we had so many times long ago.

"You must teach me, Arden." I gestured to our surroundings. "I struggled with holding onto a sliver of my full strength, but you stand here discussing plans with me, barely breaking concentration as you hold twice the power I was able to possess here."

"Concentration and patience were never your strong suits, and that is precisely how I am able to manipulate the power of the Khassos so well here. It is more difficult to harness the elements than it is to smash the ground below," she chided. A hint of a smile appeared on her face.

A smile from my sister was more than I could have ever hoped for. It was a drink of water after wandering through a wasteland.

"You have always been the stronger of the two of us, but you never were quite as canny," Arden said. "You don't have the patience to acquire the knowledge I possess, Brother."

Something clicked in my mind then. "Arden, we still have our knowledge from all the Erretas we interacted with before. We can warn them of what is to come and help them make their way to the new planet before the Council can stop them. We can interact with them as we never were able to as Watchers!" I felt a surge of relief as the plan unfolded in my mind.

"There is no time for that," Arden said. "Don't you think the Erretas who helped us gain this knowledge have gone into a state of panic doing everything they can to save themselves? They know it's too late. The Council told me as much. There is nothing the Erretas can do now but wait."

But why does that plan feel so right? It feels like the idea isn't even my own, like I should be going through those very motions as a Watcher in order to save the Erretas, and yet Arden said it could not be.

"So that's it, Sister? We leave them to their fate? Have you thought about what will happen to us in our current state? We are in this world now too. We may not survive it."

"That would be a welcome blessing to us both. Would it not, Carrick?"

Anger arose within me. "No! It would not be welcome to me. I will not let them win. I will not let all that we've done be for nothing. I will not go quietly and let my sacrifice mean nothing."

"Your sacrifice? This was your decision, Carrick—not mine, not hers, and surely not Kallan's! Or have you forgotten? No, of course not. You haven't forgotten, but she has. She remembers nothing of your betrayal. Is that why, after all this time, you still search for her? Because when you look into her vapid eyes, you see her, but she can't see you?"

Arden looked at me then as if remembering how much she hated me. Her expression seemed to say she chastised herself for acting as my sibling rather than my enemy. I waited for her anger to erupt. I reminded myself that she was not on my side. She did not want the Erretas to live; it was better for her if they were wiped out of existence. She served a penance for a crime she didn't commit because of this place. This place, and Eirene's dreams, were to blame just as much—if not more than me— and Arden wanted Eirene dead.

"After all that happened, you still think of them rather than us," Arden spat at me. "You still think *only* of her!" Thunder and lightning cracked in the distance. "After all this time, do you still show no remorse for what you did? Do you still fail to see not only what you've done to me, but also to all of our kind?"

She stared at me, waiting for my response. I glared back at her. As if knowing what I was thinking, Arden spat on the ground in front me.

"I, too, held onto hope that our penance would not be in vain; that maybe you would learn from your mistake, but I see now that it has all been for nothing. You still think you made the right decision, Brother. I think you would make the same decision again today even knowing what it cost me and your precious Eirene. Well, I will not allow you to make the same mistakes again, Carrick. You do not have the right to choose my fate a second time."

She straightened her stance, and at the same time, studied me like an enemy about to charge into battle. I braced myself and dug my heels in.

"I think I've found her, Carrick," she said. "I think I've found Eirene, and it's time you two were reunited."

Chapter 22

Senia

"Senia?"

I sensed the presence of a man standing to the right of my bed. My eyes cracked open then squinted to block the harsh fluorescent lighting of the hospital room. I noticed the ache in my head first; it was a constant throbbing that I fear I would live with for the rest of my short life. The next thing I noticed was the numbness of my body—as if I were hit by a car and they gave me something to numb the pain. My throat was dry and sore, like I had been screaming. I opened my eyes further, trying to take in more of my surroundings. *What happened to me? I am in a hospital, monitors beep steadily next to me. I am constrained to my bed, wearing a paper thin hospital gown.* A shiver ran through me.

"Oh, Senia! You're alright." A man hugged me. *My father is here.* He held me and the familiarity of him, or rather the familiarity of anything, brought me to tears.

"Dad," I tried to cry, but no noise came out. I let the sobs rack through my body, not caring about the further pain it created.

There were no tears in my father's eyes, but I don't ever remember him crying. This was as much emotion as I had ever seen him display, but it was so good to have him here. It was like I traveled a long journey and came home again. I feel like I left my body here, and though it sounded ridiculous, it seemed so true to me. *I am dying, and now my father knows it. Now I have to face that I am dying.*

I once thought to protect my father from my illness, but now I knew I needed his support. I looked up into my father's sad eyes and tried to speak, but found that I still couldn't. I tried to get the words out to my father, tried to say anything, but again—nothing. Tears welled up in my eyes, and the only noise that escaped me were moans deep in my throat.

I had no words. Before, I hadn't wanted to speak to my father about my illness; now I may never get the chance. I looked up at him and watched as realization filled my father. His eyes widened just a fraction, then he pressed the alert button for the nurse. The strength of the father I always knew returned in his expression. He reassuringly placed his hand on my shoulder.

"It's alright, we're going to figure this out," he said. "Let's get someone in here and see what's going on." He pressed the button again, growing impatient.

An older woman, short and round of stature, appeared and asked something in a foreign language. After piecing together that we didn't understand her, the nurse left and returned with another female. She was still slight, but slender and younger. She greeted my father and I with a thick accent, then came to my side.

"You gave us quite a scare, miss," she stated. "The doctor will be in to speak with you soon—"

"My daughter, she can't," my father interrupted. "That is, she's having trouble speaking."

The nurse hesitated for a moment, glancing at me then back at her chart.

"I will bring some water and ice chips for her in a moment, Mr. Schaleski." The nurse turned to walk out of the room.

"Wait, wait a minute," my dad said. "My daughter has had what they told me was a near-death experience and now she cannot talk. I want to know what's going on. If you don't know, then get a doctor who does in here now."

The nurse was seemingly unfazed by these orders and calmly told my dad to wait a moment, then she exited the room anyways. I watched my father pace back and forth, his hand constantly running through his dark hair as he always did when he was stressed.

We waited in silence for what felt like hours, but in reality, it was only a few minutes.

A female doctor appeared in the doorway, files in hand, and greeted my father with yet another extremely thick accent.

"Mr. Schaleski," she shook his hand.

"Ray," he told her.

Then the doctor faced me. "I'm Dr. Alaric. I'm going to examine you, and then we will go over a few things with you both, alright? Now, first thing's first, can you tell me your name, miss?"

I tried to speak again, but only a soft groan of air escaped me. As if on cue, the nurse walked back in with my water and ice chips. She set up a table across my bed.

"The nurse told me you are having some trouble speaking."

Dr. Alaric examined me and encouraged me to drink. Hand shaking, I reached for the cup, nearly knocking it over; the nurse assisted me. The water felt cool and revitalizing before it became painful to swallow. The doctor said something to the nurse in their language, and the nurse set down a pen and paper.

"Let's try this again, shall we?" Dr. Alaric said.

I glanced at my father before reaching for the pen, hand still shaking. Dr. Alaric held the paper on the table for me and encouraged me to write.

"Now, can you tell me your name?"

I nodded my head as if to tell her I knew the answer even if I couldn't communicate it.

"And please take your time," Dr. Alaric said. "I know this might be difficult for you."

I gripped the pen as forcefully as I was able, then began to make a mark. Halfway through the struggle of writing a single letter, I realized I started to write an "E." That's not right, I coached myself. *Try again.* I scribbled over the letter and started again. A swirling zig-zag of the letter "S" appeared, then a vertical line with three not so straight horizontal lines intersecting it, which ended up through both the S and my attempt at the letter E. Then, I finally etched out a very haphazard "N."

Dr. Alaric stopped me. "Alright, no need to struggle any further; you know who you are."

Her words seemed wrong somehow.

"Now, do you know where you are?" she asked.

I shook my head no. Obviously, I was in a foreign hospital, but I couldn't remember how I got here.

Dr. Alaric gestured toward my father. "Do you know who this is, Senia?"

I nodded yes, but my doctor's expression seemed to say that she doesn't believe me, so I began to write out "Dad." This time, I was able to write with less of a struggle. My father smiled down at me, relief on his face.

"Can you tell me if you are in pain, Senia?"

I held the front of my head to indicate where I felt pain.

"On a scale of one to ten, what is your level of pain now, Senia?"

I hesitated for a moment. The throbbing pain was back in my head, but it wasn't the worst I had experienced. I held up seven fingers.

"Alright, we are going to give you something to manage that here soon."

I nodded to show that I understood.

"We are going to need to run further tests. I have Senia scheduled for a scan this afternoon," Dr. Alaric told my father.

I forced myself to sit up as straight as possible to show I was paying attention and that I understood what the doctor was saying about me.

"I understand you have been filled in on Senia's tumor to some extent, but it seems to be growing quickly. We did some bloodwork, and it appears Senia has not been taking any medications. Now, some of what has happened to her in this recent episode could be due to her lack of medication; however, we need to see how permanent her lack of speech is. She seems to have comprehension, and her ability to write, however shakily, is a good sign."

Dr. Alaric turned on a screen on the wall, then touched a file to display the image of my tumor so my father could see it for himself. He stared as Dr. Alaric continued.

"Now, you can see here, the mass is in the frontal lobe." She pointed to the tumor. "This is the problem."

My father gulped, continuing to stare at the screen.

"It is not uncommon for a tumor in the left frontal lobe to affect speech, memory, and motor control," Dr. Alaric stated. "What we are seeing with Senia now could be the start of her losing those functions. I'm not sure how much further this loss will progress, or regress, with the time that she has left—"

"The time she has left?" My father interjected. "What about operating? What about treatment?"

Guilt and shame built in my chest. I felt very much like the small child I was being treated as. My father studied my face; the hurt showing on his own was almost unbearable for me to see. Even if I had the ability to speak now, what could I possibly say to make this better? I was granted the small mercy of not having to tell my father, after all. I deserved that at least, didn't I?

Dr. Alaric paused, looking back and forth from my father to me, gauging my somber and guilty-looking expression.

"I'm sorry, Mr. Schaleski, I assumed you were up-to-date with the progression of Senia's illness."

"Ray," he interjected. "It's Ray."

"At this point, we are unable to operate," Dr. Alaric said. "Our goal now is to make Senia as comfortable as possible."

At that, I began to cry. No noise escaped me, but the tears streamed down my face. Yes, I knew how bad my condition was, but my father knowing made it more real. I had tried to ignore my condition and enjoy what time I had left, so hearing my diagnosis again was like watching another nail get driven into my coffin.

"How long does she have?" My father asked.

"It's difficult to say, but I would estimate a few weeks at least—a few months at best."

What little color was left to my father's face immediately drained at Dr. Alaric's response.

He said nothing.

Dr. Alaric gathered her files to leave. "I'm going to give you two some time, and I will have your pain medication administered shortly. We will know more once we do another scan, but for now, just try to relax. If you can, continue to write things out as you are able, this will help solidify your thoughts in your brain."

Upon Dr. Alaric's departure, tension built in the room. My father ran his hands through his dark hair again, this time, breathing heavily but saying nothing. *I don't know what I can do. It's not like I can say anything.* I picked up the pen and scribbled out the word "Sorry." It was all I could really say at this point anyway. He just stared at me.

Finally sitting down in the chair beside my bed, he opened his mouth to speak, but the first nurse walked back into the room. She added to the strained silence since she did not speak our language. I watched her attach a large bag to my IV. She held up a button connected to its cord and demonstrated how I was to use it. Then she smiled and left the room.

As the medication started to kick in, the pain began to subside. I felt drowsy. *How long could my father and I sit in silence?* My eyes drooped into a sleepy state just as my father began to talk.

"How long have you known?" he asked. Strangely though, it didn't seem like he was speaking to me. He was facing me, but not talking *to* me. My mind played tricks on me again. He knew I couldn't tell him.

Was he hoping to spark something within me that brought back my ability to speak? He never was a very caring or compassionate father, but I expected this news—his only child dying of a brain tumor—would force him to show a *little* emotion. He seemed angry—not sad—when Dr. Alaric gave him the news. He had hugged me earlier, though, when I first woke up. He was compassionate, wasn't he?

I blinked, struggling to keep my eyes open, and tried to focus on my father's face.

"How long have you known?" he asked again.

My father studied me, waiting for me to miraculously speak. *Is that it? Is he hoping for a miracle?*

I held up three fingers to show I knew I was sick for three months.

He shook his head as if disappointed. "No," was all he said.

My father moved so his face was only inches away from my own. He stared into my eyes. His eyes were so dark they almost appeared black; then it was as if all I could see were his eyes. My head throbbed, but I had no desire to break eye contact, no drive to move at all.

"How long have you known?" he asked a third time.

I began to feel a bit panicked. I heard my heart monitor begin to beep a little faster as I continued to look into my father's dark eyes.

I saw movement out of the corner of my eyes, and I thought he was touching my IV. I closed my eyes, trying to figure out what was happening. My heart monitor beeped more rapidly still, and I blindly reached to push the call button. I didn't know why I was panicking, but I was. I felt my father's hand grasp my wrist, then the other forced my chin up so I was face-to-face with my father, but I refused to open my eyes.

"Don't be afraid," he calmly said, "just answer me. How long have you known?"

I was confused. I answered him already. I told him I knew I was ill for three months. I answered him the only way I could. Why did I suddenly feel so frightened by the man who raised me? *He's your father.*

He's only trying to help you. A strange thought crossed my fading mind. *No, he's not.* Then I let deep sleep claim me.

When I woke again, I was enclosed in a tube, and a faint light spun around me. I stared up at the light above me, not knowing if I could move or what was happening. I attempted to lift my head, but found that it was strapped to whatever I was lying on. I winced at the pain from the effort it took to move, and noticed my hands were free from restraint. I lifted my hand and wondered what was causing a pinching pain. Then I noticed bruising and several puncture marks on my hand. A voice came over the intercom, speaking a language I couldn't understand. I was in a hospital in a foreign place, I reminded myself. *I am getting a head scan. I am dying.*

Someone entered the room then and bent down to where I could see him. He motioned to me while speaking. Though I couldn't understand the man's words, I gathered from his hand motions that I was not supposed to move. I attempted to nod but was held back by the restraints on my head and ended up giving the man a thumbs up to show that I understood. He nodded back to me. Shortly after, I heard the machine that was surrounding my body start to thrum again.

I waited, trying to lay as still as possible until the man finally returned and removed my head and chest restraints. Another man entered the room with a wheelchair for me; he assisted me in getting out of the scanner. I was astonished at how weak I felt. I needed all the help I could get, making my way from the machine to a sitting position. The orderly rolled me through the hospital halls back to my room. I stared up in a daze at the fluorescent lights. The longer I looked at them, the more my eyes played tricks on me.

My father smiled as we entered the room, but his smile didn't reach his dark eyes. Once I was situated back in my bed, I made a writing motion to ask for the pad and pen. I had questions of my own and wanted to write them down. Though I felt weak, my writing skills were much improved—almost normal. "What happened?" I wrote, then turned the paper toward my father.

"You had another episode," he responded.

A large binder was on the floor next to his chair. I pointed to it to ask him what it was.

"That is information about you."

My brows furrowed in confusion, but I couldn't think of what else to ask about the binder. Perhaps it was my medical records. I thought for a moment about what I wanted to ask next.

"Home?" I wrote.

"Do you want to go home?" he asked.

I thought for a moment, and then shook my head no.

"I thought you might say that," he said. "I've planned a trip for us."

I raised my head to look at him; my questioning eyes prompted him to go on.

"We need to get you cleared by your doctor before you can leave, but I don't see her doing that," he said. "I've looked at your charts while you were getting your scan, and I don't think you have much more time."

I didn't know whether to be more surprised at his candor or at his hidden knowledge to decipher medical records so well.

"I think we should wait to hear more about your scan and get your medication," my father said. "Then we take off. No point lying around in a hospital bed miserable, right? What do you say?"

I nodded once in agreement. My father had always been very logical. He was a scientist, after all, and so this didn't seem *that* out of character. I truly thought he'd be the one person to offer me some compassion. It was better this way though. What good would it do to dwell on the sadness of my situation? My father was right. I put the best smile I could muster on my face and wrote, "Let's go."

CHAPTER 23

CARRICK

"How can you be sure it was her?" I asked.

"I can't be sure, Carrick, but—" Arden stopped herself, as if unsure how to continue.

"What?" I prompted.

"I felt a connection to her, one that is difficult to put into words. It wasn't like anything I had ever felt between myself and an Erretas. I just felt as though ... I knew her."

Arden let her voice trail off as she looked at the raging storm around us.

"Suppose you should call all this off now," I gestured to the whirlwind.

She gave me a sheepish look. "I wish it were that easy. I'm still trying to figure out how to control the Khassos within myself as well, Brother."

"What exactly does that mean, Arden?"

"Well, I've figured out how to gather the strength to use the power again and not let it get out of control, but I haven't quite figured out how to release it to make it stop." Arden sounded a bit ashamed of herself.

"I see. So ... not so superior to me, after all? We can work it out together, Sister."

Before I realized what I was doing, I gently placed my hand on Arden's shoulder, touching her for the first time since the day we parted. It was a natural reaction, I realized, an instinct to comfort my sibling, even after all we'd been through. She slightly recoiled at the touch, then made herself relax under my hand. She allowed me to touch her only for a few brief moments before stepping away from me. She looked up into my eyes, her own colorfully shining with grief.

"You realize what it will mean to take them on, don't you, Carrick? We could lose everything all over again, including what little we have left of our people." Arden hesitated. "You know you could lose her too?"

"If anyone would know, it would be me."

Even as I looked into my sister's eyes, I couldn't shake the feeling that I was unsure I could trust her, but I *had* to trust her. She was the only one left to me.

"She has been lost to me many times, Sister. I have to at least try. If I lose her this time, at least I will still have you—I hope."

"I cannot be certain it was Eirene, but if it was, her memories were still lost to her. She didn't recognize me. I saw what you did on the broadcasts and suddenly left her. I knew I would never be able to take her with me on such a far journey without enforcements getting involved. It was too great a risk since I was so unsure of her identity. I left her in the coastal city, Lacuna, and told her to wait for me. We had only just met though. I don't think she would necessarily stay there just for me. She told me that she didn't live in Lacuna, that she was only on holiday, but I know her hotel, so that is where we should begin our search. Oh, and a name, I have her name!" she said triumphantly. "It's Senia. Senia Schaleski."

I became flooded with hope and excitement. She had a location and a name; that was good enough for me.

"We will find her," I stated.

"And if it isn't her, Carrick?" Arden asked. "Hell, even if it is her, what will we do next? If it is her, she doesn't have her true form returned to her as we do."

Arden was right. Eirene wasn't in her true form and couldn't create without Kallan, but she still had to have some value to our people. She was, after all, the last Sator. Would they not want her to survive? The Council made it clear when last I spoke with them that Eirene was lost to me. Furthermore, she was lost to them because of me and what I had done to Kallan, so why couldn't I make a trade of sorts? Eirene's protection in exchange for my return. I was so caught up in my own thoughts that it took me a minute to register that Arden, too, seemed lost in thought; her brow furrowed as she paced back and forth.

"What is it, Arden?" I tried to read my sister's mind as we had once been able to.

"It's a question that has always tugged at me. If Eirene was the most powerful being after—well, after all that happened, why would she *allow* them to do it, Carrick? Why didn't she stop them?" Arden waited for my response, gauging if I comprehended what she *really* asked me.

Arden's question cut like a knife. Was Eirene capable of such a thing?

"You mean, did Eirene allow them to erase her memory and punish me because she knew the atrocity she and I committed? You think she knew and allowed us to be punished?"

"The answer lies in what you two did. If she could betray her own people; if she could knowingly aid you in the destruction of our world—of her own brother—for what you believed was right, then yes. Of course she could allow herself to be punished."

"She couldn't have known what she was doing, Arden. She couldn't know they would drag you into this too. She couldn't know what I would suffer."

"I think you are mistaken," Arden said. "Was she not there when we were sentenced? Did she not watch them drag us away?"

I could sense Arden's anger begin to rise again.

I tried to remember how Eirene reacted. She hadn't known Kallan would be a casualty. Eirene sat on the ground, cradling her brother's lifeless head, crying over him as though she would die right along with him. I never forgot the look in her beautiful violet eyes as she glanced up at me. I never saw that look of hatred in her eyes before.

That hadn't been part of the plan. Eirene and I planned to meet as a Council and hash out a strategy with Arden and Kallan. We planned to address our people to reveal there was a world we had no part in planning. The world of the Erretas was not so unlike ours, but it was unique and made entirely by some other force we didn't understand. We had to study it. Kallan and Eirene had to try and replicate it. We couldn't let it to be destroyed; that's what led us to our next thought.

If there was another life force that could create better than we could, that could succeed where we failed, why should we continue to destroy worlds that did not succeed as well as we hoped?

We were told by the Anatani scholars of our time that there was a finite amount of energy that must be reused. My purpose was to destroy what they made so the Sators could recollect the energy and create again. If that was no longer true, then we could stop destroying. I no longer had to watch as populations screamed for mercy while I crushed their failed world. Eirene and I approached Kallan to tell him of this happy news, but he did not view the news of the Erretas as we did. He agreed their world was not to be touched until we could piece together how they formed it, but the Khassos would not be relieved of our duties; Kallan wouldn't stand for it.

Eirene and I approached the rest of the Council of Five, hoping to change our history, and we succeeded in that. We pleaded with the others to understand, but it was ultimately Tahrell's decision in the end. He stepped in as a new Council Lead when everything was done. Looking back now, I realized Tahrell viewed our idea as a threat to his power all along. He would not stand for the system the Sators and Khassos worked out for the gain of their people, and what he viewed as his empire, to change. Truly, Kallan and Eirene held the highest power as the Sators, but Kallan was not on our side, and that turned the tide of what was to come. Eirene and I decided to take matters into our own hands, but Kallan stood in our path and changed everything.

Arden knew nothing of Eirene and my plans. She was blindsided by what happened. The turn of events crumbled our world and her life with it. What pained Arden most was the loss of Kallan. She loved him as I loved Eirene, though he never returned the feelings. Kallan was a good man, and I killed him. It was the worst thing I ever did, even after crushing all those millions of lives as a Khassos.

Nothing ever shook the memory of the glaring eyes of the ones I loved most. I envied Eirene because she didn't live with the memory of those eyes burned into her mind wherever she went. I did. She didn't remember everyone's eyes watching on with hatred as we were sentenced. She didn't remember my own eyes or my sister's—so colorful and expressive— showing every emotion as plain as we felt them. Perhaps most painful of all, Eirene didn't remember Kallan's eyes, as determined as my own, as he fought me. His eyes seared into my memory—into my soul—and I was unable to do anything about it. Kallan was my friend; he may have become my brother by law had Eirene and I gone on as we were.

Whatever I had done, I felt it more deeply than anyone I affected by it. What if Arden was right and Eirene had allowed us to be punished? If Eirene thought this punishment fit the crime, she was wrong. I would have been punished every day without it, knowing I hurt those I loved the most. Their eyes followed me everywhere I went. I could escape the people I wronged, but I would never escape the memory of them. Maybe Arden was right, maybe those eyes haunted Eirene and it was more than she could bear. Maybe it was more than I could bear too.

The ground began to reverberate beneath us, my anger poured out of me before I knew what I was doing.

Shame seeped through me, and I let my gaze drift to the ground below us before meeting Arden's eyes again. I saw she had grown angry too. She matched my glare as if in challenge. She had always thought I had no right to be angry. I was the reason for Kallan's death and our punishment, and Arden was right. It was time I realized that. It was time I realized that Arden should be the one to take her vengeance. I let my anger drain away.

"I am sorry, Arden, truly."

I watched Arden's eyes shine brighter, tears glistened in them. Her eyes changed to a vibrant mix of violet, blue, and green, much like the rolling seas of the Erretas world we stood in.

"I know my words cannot bring Kallan back, or change what I did, but you are wrong. Had I known what they would do to you, my sister, I would not have acted as I did. Not for Eirene's sake, but for yours, I would have acted differently. It was not your fight; it was hers." I extended my hand out to Arden, taking a cautious step forward. "I mean that, Arden. I would."

She appraised me further, allowing a single tear to roll down her face. With her auburn hair flowing in the wind, her eyes shined so brightly with the colors only the Khassos held. I almost forgot where we were and all that had transpired between us.

For a moment, I was lost to all the other lives but my own, remembering what life was before. It was a time when I did what I was designed to do. I wished what I had told Arden was true, that I could go back to that time with her, a time before I allowed my conscience to intervene.

Arden clasped my hand, squeezing and smiling at me.

"Help me, Arden. Help me this one last time and let me see her again. Then you can have your revenge on me and whoever else stands in your path. You deserve to have your vengeance. Let me see Eirene one last time as herself. Help me make her remember, and maybe they can give her another chance to be part of our people again."

Arden pulled her hand out of my grasp.

"I know you think Eirene should be punished for the part that she played, but believe me when I say she did not know how I would act. Had she known, she would have never allowed me to kill Kallan. I acted alone, and you both should have the revenge you are owed on me. If you will be my partner one last time, Arden, I will not resist or fight you. If you wish to kill me or return me to the Council," I choked at the very thought. "Whatever you decide, my sister, I will quietly go with you if you help me save her."

"I am not you, Brother. I—"

Whatever Arden was going to tell me stuck with her; she could not say she was not a murderer. She was.

I don't know if she still hated me and agreed that she should kill me. I don't know if she decided I had suffered enough or Eirene hadn't. I don't know what she thought in that moment, and I refused to ask her.

Arden swallowed whatever she was going to say to me, and decided instead to nod in agreement. "I will help you, Carrick, one last time."

CHAPTER 24

SENIA

"Your hair is lighter," my father said as we made our way down the bustling street.

I nodded in response.

"You look more like her now—more like your mother."

I smiled at that, but felt sad as soon as I did. I could remember a little of my mother, but not really what she looked like. I more so remembered the feeling of what it was like to be a child in my mother's presence than the details of my mother's appearance. It frustrated me to no end that some memories were so distinct in my mind while others were out of reach. I wondered where we were going, but I couldn't write my question down as we walked—not at the pace he moved. *I will find out soon enough, I suppose.* I couldn't recall how we got out of the hospital. I lost time again. It was freeing not having to ask questions all the time, but it was also frustrating. I would have to be patient with the time left to me.

"You remember her, don't you? Your mother?" he asked.

I didn't want to upset him further, so I nodded—slightly lying that I did. He looked perplexed rather than pleased. My father's dark hair bounced slightly with every stride he took, dark eyes determined. That is what struck me most about his current state. He no longer seemed upset that he was losing his only daughter. He just seemed determined; but to do what, I did not know.

I matched him stride for stride, but that became difficult after a while. I became winded so easily now. If I had my voice, I would've asked him to stop, but he was winding his way through the crowds in front of me. I concentrated on my breathing and keeping up with him. One foot in front of the other, I coached myself. *Breathe.* Pain coursed through me from my forehead down to my toes, causing me to stop in my tracks. I couldn't concentrate on anything. The searing pain crippled me. My head throbbed like a second heartbeat. I could only hope my father would notice I was no longer behind him. I had no voice.

Others rushed by, bumping into me as I tried to remain standing. It was no use. I dropped to my knees, clasping my head, feeling like it might explode with pain. My head fell back and I glanced up into the light above, which only made the pain worse. I closed my eyes, and when I opened them again my father stood over me. There was no sympathy in his dark eyes. He reached down to help me stand. It was odd that I would notice that while in so much pain.

"Come on, Senia," he barked. "We're running short on time." He grasped my hand in his own, then supported my elbow with the other before pulling me back to my feet. "I'm sorry. I know this is difficult in your condition," he said, "but we need to keep moving."

My father guided me through the crowds again, this time maintaining a hold on my arm so he wouldn't lose me.

What is so urgent? Am I supposed to know and forgot? Had my father already explained his plans to me or the need for expedience? The lines were blurred between what I forgot and what I remembered.

My thoughts jumped from one to the next without much rhyme or reason. *Where are we headed and why? I am sick, dying even, so why can't my father let her enjoy her final days relaxing? Wait. Her? That is wrong. Why can't my father let me enjoy my final days relaxing.*

For whatever reason, I found myself dragged through a crowded city by my father as if I was a small child he was afraid would get lost. For some reason, I thought we were in a different city than the hospital, but I couldn't be sure. This place looked different; it was much more confined and populated.

The pain in my head was never-ending, and I fought to keep moving despite it. I noticed the crowd thickened and formed a queue in front of a large, gated building. We didn't stop at the end of the queue to wait our turn though. My father led me past the line and straight up to the door. Ignoring the complaints around us, he pressed on.

My father turned back to me. "Stay close."

With his grip still locked on my hand, I had no choice but to go where he went. I had no voice and was so weak I could barely walk. Once at the entrance of the gigantic building, a security guard stopped us. He spoke a language I could not understand. Maybe I *could* understand it, but my mind wouldn't let me. *Do I know this language?* It didn't matter. I couldn't speak.

I tried to free my hand, bracing myself to fall as fatigue overwhelmed me, but my father caught me. In a flash, I saw him remove something from his pocket. I couldn't see what it was; my vision was fuzzy, and the pain in my head continued. My father raised his hand, palm facing toward the guard. The guard momentarily flared his eyes. *Was that shock on his face?* No, it seemed to be fear. The guard ushered us inside the large building.

He disregarded the angry voices protesting our entrance and escorted us to the side before roping off the entrance. A moment later, several other large men pushed closed the enormous entrance doors. The crowd's cry rose in protest.

What is happening? Everything was going by so fast it was hard to focus.

Guards rushed others out of the building through a small side door marked "Exit."

I had only a few moments to catch my breath and glance at the ancient-looking building. It was built of huge stones placed in a circular pattern. When I tried to look up, I became dizzy trying to see where it ended. Banners hung from each level, and large, red, glass lanterns dangled from chains underneath wooden sconces. When I looked to the back of the first level, I saw blue candles lining all sides and a great altar of some kind in the middle. Clearly, this building was very old. It looked as though it was made by hand.

I wasn't allowed much time to commit the details to memory. Another man came up to my father. The man gestured to me as he spoke to my father. The man was of a similar build to my father, and also had black hair and the same dark eyes, but their similarities ended there. This man had a full black beard and wide nose. His nostrils flared as he spoke, but his eyes remained on me. He studied me—as if waiting to see if I understood him. But I remained leaning against the stone wall for support. Whatever the two men said led my father to grab my hand before assessing my current condition and asking if I could walk.

"I can have you carried if you cannot go any further," he said.

I didn't want to be carried by a stranger, or by my own father, for that matter, but I didn't think I could make it another step. I shook my head no, and with a wave of his hand, my father had one of the larger security guards sweep me from my feet. We walked behind a large tapestry framing the altar. I noticed the altar was in the center of the building, but everything behind it was roped off. The noise of the other guests exiting seemed to die down the further away we got from the front.

My body ached as I swayed back and forth in the arms of the large stranger. He also had black hair and a beard, but was a full head taller than my father and the other man he walked beside. My transporter and I trailed behind them as ropes were removed for us.

My concentration on the enormity of the building and its décor was broken by the screeching of wood across the floor.

My father threw his weight into a large bench, sliding it across the floor until it was far enough to allow the other man to roll up the textile beneath it. Doing so revealed a floor of colorful tiles. They created a pattern of one large circle with six smaller circles inside of it, each a different color. The six smaller circles appeared to glisten and shine—as if they moved. I saw it before, but had no idea where. My mind wandered again, making it difficult to focus. I gazed at the floor longer. *There should only be five.* Then my gaze was broken as my father lifted the large circle from the ground like a door.

Where am I? I had to think it through again. *This is my father; I am following him.* I jumped with a start, realizing my feet were not on the ground. I forgot I was in the arms of a very large and unfamiliar man.

I grimaced, clutching my head. I watched as my father motioned the others forward and began descending a spiral stairway. It was dark, but my eyes quickly adjusted as I was carried down behind my father. There was nothing to see except stone. Eventually, we hit another small door marked "Exit." We did not go through the door though. My father found another circle in the floor. This time, he twisted the circle to unlatch another door.

We took an even tighter path that wound downward. I feared I would be sick. At the end of the stairway my father abruptly turned toward me. He did not speak, he only gestured with his head for me to be put down. Apparently my transporter was not allowed to go further. Without a word, the guard turned on his heel to leave us. Why did my father not feel the need to explain? Or had he already told me and I just couldn't remember?

The other guard placed something in my father's hand, then pointed to his right before leaving as well. I realized it was pitch black, but I could see clearly. My father grasped my hand, nearly missing it at first. He led me to what appeared to be a wall. I watched him feel around the wall, and I realized he could not see like I could. He found what he was looking for on the wall—a circular disc of some sort. Then he stomped on the ground, which loosened the stones below.

He released my hand and told me not to move. He dropped to his knees and felt around on the floor for the loose stones, lifting them as he went. He fumbled several times before I bent down to assist him. I could see, and he couldn't. He didn't stop picking up stones, but I saw him smile when I began to help. I didn't hide how well I could see, but maybe I should have. *Why did that thought cross my mind?*

We removed several large stones. Some were too heavy for me to lift so I guided my father's hand to them so he could lift them. He cast each stone aside with a loud clunk until a pile formed.

He lifted a particularly large stone, and I saw another circle made of colorful tiles that were about the width of a large person. I placed his hand on it, knowing he couldn't see it. He smiled at me again, then felt around until he found where he could pull up. He motioned for me to stand back, so I did. He revealed yet another level we would have to descend to. I glanced down at it, not wanting to struggle down another flight of stairs. I knew, however, that if I let my father carry me, we would both fall. So, I took his hand and guided him for the first time. I stopped several times to catch my breath, and my vision blurred from the exertion. Luckily, the steps were straight rather than spiral, which allowed me to scoot my way down the last few until I saw light. It wasn't the light of a flame that you might expect in an ancient-looking place like this. The light was blue and faint at first, but grew stronger as we walked toward it. We walked toward what looked like another wall; blue light flickered as if taunting us, but my father could see now. So, he withdrew the disc he had retrieved from the wall from his pocket.

I could not clearly see due to the angle I was at. Somehow, I managed to stay coherent on the journey here, but if I had to go back up, I didn't think I would make it. *That better be the last flight of stairs.*

My father placed the disc into a slot beneath the blue light, then placed his palm flat against the wall. There was another object in his hand, and the stone wall slid open. Light flooded through the opening in the wall. My father motioned for me to make my way inside.

The doorway in the wall was so small that we would have to crouch down to walk through it. We stepped into the room. I hesitated as I realized the room was enormous behind that tiny door. It seemed to glow a golden hue as if light shone through it from windows above. But there were no windows, only light that emanated from within. Table after table lined the room, each stacked with papers and large books. The hair on the back of my neck stood on end.

My father barely spoke to me since we entered this strange building. I waited for some sort of explanation now that we made it to our destination. Instead, he acted as though nothing was out of the ordinary.

My father sat down at one of the tables and opened a thick book, flipping through it as if I wasn't there. My loud gasp for air brought my father's attention back to me. He looked across to me and studied my expression.

I searched my surroundings for some way to communicate, but saw nothing. I had many questions, but my first would be: What is this place? I made a writing motion with my hand, gesturing toward my father.

"Your pen is in your pocket, remember?" he said.

I winced at the word "remember." I didn't remember, and I was hardly aware of anything but my breathing and the pain in my head. My father certainly made it more difficult to communicate when he barely spoke himself. I slowly stood up and found a pen and paper in my pocket. I set the small pad on the table and flipped it open. The word "Why" had already been written. I couldn't recall what led me to ask "why" at some point, but wasn't that the most important question I *could* ask? I turned the page back, knowing I would need the answer to that question more than once. My hand was shaky, but my writing was still legible. I turned the pad toward my father.

He glanced at the paper. "What is this place and why are we here?" He read my questions aloud. "Those are both excellent questions, but not so simple to answer." He seemed to pause to think of an answer.

"This place," he said, gesturing with his hand at the surroundings, "houses the oldest records that survived in the only areas that remained untouched by devastation. They were excavated over the course of Erretas' history, and gathered here in order to piece together the true origins of this world. As to your second question, we are here so you can learn from them."

I stared back at him, more confused than ever.

"Do you understand what I've just told you or are you having trouble because of your," he hesitated. "Well, because of your illness."

I didn't quite know how to answer. On one hand, yes, I heard what he said. On the other hand, I definitely didn't understand it, and I didn't think it was because my mind wasn't properly working. What he said simply didn't make sense. We stood in the surviving ruins of some place that held the world's oldest records, and somehow, my father had access to them. What did any of this have to do with me or my father? What devastation had he referred to? What was I supposed to learn from these ancient records?

His words had been "so that you can learn from them." Did that mean he already knew? There were so many questions, and I didn't know where to begin. So I sat for a moment and collected my thoughts.

I thought my father could see I was confused. As if testing me, he asked if I could write down his name and my own. I rolled my eyes and jotted down Raymond Schaleski and then Senia Schaleksi. I turned the paper to face him. I wanted him to know I still had my wits about me.

He glanced at my writing. "No."

My brow furrowed in confusion. I turned the pad around so I could study it. Had I misspelled something? Was I truly losing my mind and could no longer remember my name? I studied my words over and over, but I couldn't figure out why it was wrong. I tapped my hand on the table, making noise to gain my father's attention. I pointed at the names on the pad, trying to tell him "Yes, these are our names."

"No," he firmly stated again.

Panic set in. I flipped to the next page and wrote, "What is my name?"

He chuckled. "If you can't tell me, then I'm not certain I know."

What the hell does that mean? Is he intentionally being cruel? That isn't like him. My father wasn't always the warmest man, but he did care for me. He was never cruel. I remembered him teaching me to play catch in our backyard and hugging me before he sent me off to college. I remembered this man, but somehow, it still wasn't right. He didn't *feel* like my father. I hesitated to ask the next question, but I knew I had to.

"Are you my father?" I wrote, then faced the notepad toward him. I anxiously waited for his response. He squinted his dark eyes.

"I suppose that I was Senia's father," he replied.

I felt a chill run through my body. *What is he trying to tell me?* What does he mean he *was* Senia's father?

He reached across the table for my hand as if trying to steady me. "I can see you are confused. Let me read you an excerpt from the histories, then you may ask me more."

I nodded as a dreadful feeling came over me.

He cleared his throat. "The Sators had become stagnant, unable to make new the world around them. And so, the Khassos were created as a means of balance for our kind—a way to collect the energy and very life force around us. What was old could be made new again, and thus life could remain unending. With the creation of the Khassos came the birth of a new age—an age with boundless ideas and creations unknown to us before."

He stopped reading then, and waited for me. I didn't know how to react. I gathered from how he spoke that I should know this information. He read the words to me as if helping me study for a test, reciting them as if that should trigger a memory for me. I knew I should know what he was talking about, but I couldn't remember.

"You do not remember the histories, I see," he said.

I couldn't tell if he was mad or not.

I shook my head no. I had no idea where he was going with this information or what he meant by saying he "was *Senia's* father." Those words kept reentering my thoughts. My unease intensified the more I thought about what it might mean. I had no choice but to listen and hope that he could somehow make sense of all this information for me.

"With the Khassos came destruction, but with it a new way of life for our people," he went on. "The power held by the Sators was unmatched, but beyond that, we were descendants of them. Our very world was made from their own vision, and so we were bound to their decisions. We were all but helpless to succumb to their every whim."

I realized he was no longer reading from the book. He referred to the people in the histories as "we." He shared straight from his own memories. I cleared my throat out of habit. My mind struggled to grasp what my father was trying to tell me. My father spoke of other worlds, of gods, and powers. How could any of it be real?

I stood up and looked away from him, trying to think of something, anything else that I knew to be true. Up until a few minutes ago, I knew this man to be my father. I thought that was real. There was no way for me to tell what was and wasn't real anymore. This illness stole everything from me, even my own family. My father was the only person left, and now this had happened. What a cruel joke.

I had to pull myself together. *Treat what he says as truth. Choose to believe it, however ridiculous it might sound. Maybe this will get me somewhere.* I had to give it a try.

I picked up my pen and paper, and this time, sat directly across from my father at his table. I studied him, taking in every detail of his looks and mannerisms. It all appeared the same as I had always remembered from the time I was a child. He was my father. I knew that he was, so why did that feel incorrect now? Why had he asked if I knew my name and then acted like my answer was wrong? Why had he told me he was Senia's father—as if I wasn't her?

I thought for a moment.

"What is your name?" I wrote. Then, I added "real" before "name" on the paper. He smiled at me. Did I finally catch on to his little game? I glared back at him, angered that he was toying with me.

"Know that I am not trying to frustrate you on purpose. I need to find out how much you know, and the only way for me to do so is to test you. I cannot give you all the information. You need to give some to me," he said.

I jabbed the pen at the pad, pointing to my question again.

"I'm sorry," he said. "Yes, you did ask me a question—and a good one. My *real* name is Tahrell."

The name meant nothing to me. Why did my father go by Ray if his name was Tahrell? When he didn't speak further, I scribbled "EXPLAIN!"

He stood up from our table and motioned toward a span of shelves that extended to the ceiling. Each book was thick and contained writing or symbols of some sort on them. However, I could not decipher anything.

My father, or Tahrell, that is, searched for a few moments before finding the book he needed. He thumbed through the pages until he made it almost to the end. I saw the print within the book was faintly aglow. It was as though the words were displayed on a computer screen, flashing like a living document rather than the dull print or handwriting of a typical book.

I blinked a few times to see if the text really *did* glow.

A memory hit me. I saw myself standing in front of a trellis that was lit up. I saw the entire glowing garden, sensing a familiarity with it and the words I saw now. There was a connection between the two, but it was just out of my mind's reach. I searched for the connection, but grew frustrated. I had to force myself to concentrate, no matter how much it pained me to do so.

Tahrell searched another page with his index finger.

"Ah, here it is. Tahrell of the house E'Trell. Son of Trell. High Seat of Anatan. First Position of the Council of the Five. Fourth Age-Year 3015 of the Fifth Age. Ruler of Justice in the six Realms. Fifth Age Year 3015–present. Successor Rahm of the house E'Trell. Son of Tahrell. High Seat of Anatan. First Position of the Council of Five. Fifth Age Year 3,016–Present. I also *created* the High Seat, but I don't suppose they could put that in here."

Something about the word "Anatan," triggered a memory. I *knew* that word. My mind searched for the attached memory. As if by habit, I closed my eyes. An explosion of color filled my vision. Those colors changed to details—skies and stars moved in a rapid motion. I saw every blade of grass, every living being. They were smaller than specs in a land set amongst a vibrant sky that sparkled like a prism reflecting every light and color imaginable. I saw this all in the span of a heartbeat. As I opened my eyes, I grasped the side of a shelf to steady myself.

My father bent down so his face was at the same level as mine. "What is it?" He asked. "You are not in pain. It's not the illness, then. You remember something. Something in what I read is familiar to you?" He grasped my face in his hands. "You don't move away from my touch, so it isn't *me* you remember."

What does that mean?

"I saw a place. It was colorful," I wrote down. That poor, quickly-scribbled description was nothing compared to what I actually saw, but how could I even put into words what I witnessed? It was like seeing everything all at once—things I hadn't known existed, and yet I somehow knew them. It felt like I had painted them in a portrait from my own thoughts.

"You saw Anatan," he said. A smile formed on his face.

"I want to show you something else now." He spoke to me in a different tone. "Follow me."

I took a deep breath and forced myself to follow. I had to stop and catch my breath twice, but I finally found him even further into the room. He appeared to be holding scrolls. This area of the room looked very different from the ancient-looking library Tahrell rifled through before. He unrolled the first scroll but rather than paper, a translucent material similar to a film revealed itself. The scroll hung in the air, displaying its information without any support. The paper was also lit by a light within it. The scroll had writing on it that I couldn't decipher, but it also displayed images and outlines of a body.

"These documents are from a time that most beings do not know ever existed. This was recorded in an age of the Erretas that was lost—even to *them*."

Did he stress the word "them" just now? I don't think my father and I were part of them. However ridiculous this all seemed, I was stuck. I didn't know where I was or how I would begin to leave this enormous building. I had no choice but to listen.

"If you were to remember our history, you would know the Sators created all that we know—every planet, every universe, every realm. It was well known that the Sators were the only beings who could create. So all things originated from them. However, I am here to explain to you that what we thought to be true is incorrect. Here, in these very documents, you will find quite a different story. Here, you will find a tale of a people so advanced that they developed the power to create life—seemingly from nothing—themselves. These people were not Sators; they had no *real* power. They were like everyone else, except they thirsted for the knowledge and understanding of where they came from. They pushed the boundaries on what most people thought to be reality. They made a new reality as they expanded, and made discoveries outside of their own world. Perhaps most shocking of all, the Erretas who accomplished all that lived long before the Sators existed."

Tahrell opened scroll after scroll and showed me—on a technology I had never seen—dates that didn't make sense. He attempted to explain what Erreta once was.

The experiments and findings the Erretas made were so far past what I knew from my own world. Yet, somehow, I began to grasp what had happened. I followed Tahrell's story, and even more exciting to me was that my mind let me. After each scroll, and each statement Tahrell made about these unknown histories, he looked to me for any sign of recognition on my face.

I listened to Tahrell as if he were the professor of some ludicrous class. He stopped my lesson abruptly as if he had finished with the end of the story and I had not held up my end of the bargain.

"You see, it plagued my thoughts," Tahrell said. "Where had this world come from that was not made by the Sators? I needed answers, so I made sacrifices for ages to gain the knowledge I now have. I studied Erreta, trying to decipher how it came to be without our help. I was mystified by the discovery of this place, but what I found of its origins was too shocking to ever repeat. The knowledge that the Erretas preceded us would change things for our people, but the knowledge that we came *from* them—that changes *everything*."

Tahrell looked at me again, expecting to see this information register in my mind. It didn't.

"It seemed impossible that they created *us*, but it was all documented—in plain speech—within these books and scrolls. I could not accept that our origin was due to the Erretas, so I combed this world over, searching for the truth until I knew for certain. Now, after all this time, I know it to be true." Tahrell stopped to look at me with true emotion for the first time since he showed up at the hospital. "And I will protect our people from that truth until my dying breath. My son after me, and his son after that—and so on—will do the same until we are no more. We will protect our people just as you tried to protect these Erretas."

Me? How could I know this? I don't remember any of this ridiculous tale he speaks of. None of this made sense to me, and yet ... somehow it *felt* true. My head throbbed again.

Tahrell stood face-to-face with me again. My heart pounded in fear. I knew for certain, as he looked into my eyes, that I had known him in a different life, and it frightened me. My body fought me now, and it wasn't the illness. My body fought to remember as I tried to forget. The battle raged within me.

"You knew this information," Tahrell pressed on. "You nearly died to protect it."

"No!" I wanted to shout, but I still could not speak. I didn't understand why, but I knew I couldn't listen to Tahrell continue. I tried to block it out.

"Search within yourself and remember," Tahrell said.

The word "remember" echoed in my mind again.

"Remember what you sacrificed to keep this from all of us," Tahrell said. "Remember all that you did to the Khassos—to your own kin— in order to keep this knowledge a secret. Remember, Sator."

I wanted to scream, to do anything to stop him. I knew there was truth to what he said, but I didn't know what it meant. I only understood the gravity of it all. *No. No. No.* I blocked him out. Whatever truth there was in what Tahrell had to say, I would not allow it.

I shook my head, and when I did, it was all gone.

I was Senia, and my father stared at me for some reason. Had I lost more time?

Looking defeated, my father seemed to collect himself. "Imagine if all you knew to be true was turned upside down," he said.

I shot him a look.

He chuckled a little. "Yes, I suppose that is exactly what I am doing to you now, Senia."

I noticed that he called me Senia for the first time since this wild encounter had started.

"I can see you do not remember. If you only knew how much this information would affect the real you. And to think, you are the reason we came to discover this planet in the first place. You brought me here again now. Did you not realize you were drawn to this place? Something inside you knows this is where you needed to be. Something told you to come here and pick up the clues you left behind long ago."

Had I come here for some reason besides escape? What had drawn me to this specific city that is so far from my home? At the time, there didn't seem to be a reason. It was just that—an escape—but why here? Maybe my father was right. Maybe something within me had drawn me here. I thought back to the events of the past week, and my head began to ache.

My father shook his head. "I don't know if you will ever remember," he said. "I don't know if you will ever truly return or if it's even possible, but I had to try."

He hesitated then, trying to gauge my reaction to his words. "It seems only you can do that now, or perhaps one other. Still, there is much yet to be done before your death."

Another truth became certain to me. This man was not my true father. I realized I hadn't asked the man what was on my mind most. If any of what he said was true, he obviously thought I was someone else. Even more frightening than that was the realization that I began to think I was someone else too.

Obviously, I couldn't trust this man, but I had to ask. I wrote down "Who am I?"

"Apparently, you are Senia. Now, let's see how well *your* memory is holding up. We need to retrace your steps."

Chapter 25

CARRICK

I arrived in Lacuna as the mid-morning sun crept higher in the sky. It had been lifetimes since I last came to Lacuna. It looked much the same, just more people. I agreed to meet Arden at the hotel she claimed Eirene had been staying at later in the afternoon. It was a good starting point. I had Eirene's Erretas name and her last known location. That could be enough, I thought; it had to be. My anticipation built because I could bump into her on the street at any moment.

Calm down, Carrick. I had to keep reminding myself that I needed to remain as inconspicuous as possible. While I looked for her, the Council could be looking for me. It was hard for me to remember just how much was at stake when all I could think of was Eirene. She was all I could ever think about.

I slowed my stride as I passed small shops. Tall as I was, some people still stared at me. I tried to disguise my build with a large, dark coat, and I kept my head down and shoulders slumped to appear smaller.

I still had a few hours before I needed to meet Arden, so I continued my own search. I didn't know if it was smart to make myself so visible, but the desire to find Eirene was much stronger than my desire for caution. I lived among the Erretas as a Watcher for so long in my past lifetimes; surely, I could blend in for another day. Every

Erretas that crossed my path sent me into high alert. Arden had given me Eirene's description, but it wasn't much to go on. She described her as fairly young, much smaller than us, with long golden hair similar to Eirene's. But Arden clarified that the young woman didn't look like Eirene. Unfortunately, that happened to describe most of the Lacuna population.

I walked the cobblestone streets for hours and studied every Erretas I passed. Sometimes, I failed to be discreet. Some of them glared at me as if I invaded their privacy. Others moved away from me as if I frightened them. To my surprise, a few gave me a coy smile as I studied them. My heightened sense of alert faded the longer I walked. Doubt crept in. *How will I ever find her in a place like this?* I decided to walk toward the hotel, hoping that would prove more successful.

I wondered about them. All the Erretas hustled along, clearly not knowing what would soon happen to their world. *Is this what my people felt on the day I sent them to their doom? Had they been blindsided and so unaware of the battles behind the scenes?*

Erretas of every shape and size passed me blissfully unaware of the fate of their home. I thought again about the question that brought me here in the first place. *How had they come to be?* The Erretas were a marvel, and no matter how much time I spent among them, they always would be. They were everything my people had hoped to be. Their very world is what we had strived to accomplish. Now, it could end for the Erretas—just as it had for my people—and I would also have to bear the weight of that loss. My punishment was truly unending. *No. I will find a way to end my punishment.*

I walked among the Erretas and felt like I was part of them. How could they know they would bring about the end of their home? Their world would naturally die out, the Council had said. But it wasn't the Erretas' fault. Their only sin was living, and living here had worn the place out. It was depleted—much like my own home had been before. Well, before I took matters into my own hands. How much longer would Anatan—the true Anatan, not that bio-dome they called Anatan—have survived if I had not destroyed it? Would my people still be in the same position now—just without me? Would they still be searching for a new home, or was I truly to blame for the loss of the one we had?

Of course, I was to blame. I knew I was. No matter how much I could try to rationalize it, deep down, I knew I was to blame for all of it. There was no use trying to think about what could have been different. It was too late for that now. I couldn't change my past, but for the first time since it happened, I could try to move beyond it.

I couldn't change what I did, but perhaps I could find a way for Arden and Eirene to make it better. That was the best I could offer both of them—a chance to make things new.

I told Arden I would return to my home again and continue my penance, but I knew in my heart that I could no longer go on this way. I had no intention of letting anyone take me back. One way or another, this would be the end for me as a Watcher. I would rather die here among the Erretas if I could not find another way. I felt a sense of pride as I walked with the Erretas. Whether they knew it or not, they accepted me when my own people did not. It was fitting for me to end with them, and in many ways, it could be a relief.

The crowds died down around me as the normal lunch hour grew near. I was nearly to the hotel, only a few more streets to go. My senses were more intense in my true form. I could see nearly every detail around me. I felt every rush of air, from the wind to the small bursts as people passed me. I could smell food wafting from restaurants, and I noticed the strong aroma of coffee.

I had to wait to cross the street, so I allowed the fresh scent to fill my nostrils. The Erretas were so fond of the stuff, but now I noticed how strong the smell of it was. It was pleasant. As I crossed the street, I noticed where the scent came from. It seemed strange to me that the storefront the aroma wafted from looked to be closed. I almost walked right by it, but as I did, I noticed the smell came from above.

I stopped walking and looked up, taking in the coffee smell one last time before moving on to meet Arden. In the last moment, I saw it. Among the brightness of the sky above, it would've been hard for most Erretas' eyes to make out. This was a light I had known all too well but hadn't seen in lifetimes. At the top of the building with that strong coffee smell, I saw the glow of a thousand tiny lights. They were different than those I saw in any other world. They were different because they were *hers*.

I took the stairs two at a time; each board creaked beneath my weight. When I reached the top, I nearly toppled over someone holding a cup of coffee. I apologized, then turned the corner at the top of the stairs. The rooftop had a whole garden of vibrant lights sparkling among flowers that never existed in this world. They were Eirene's flowers, brightly colored and glowing from within. The light emanating from them was so bright that I had to blink several times to make sure the lights were real. For a moment, I was entranced by the sheer beauty of it. It was the beauty only a Sator could produce—only *my* Sator.

I gently touched one of the flowers, and the light sparkled like a prism hitting sunlight. *She remembers. She has to remember or how else could this be?* Furthermore, Eirene was, in fact, here. She was close by. My heart raced and urgency built within me. I turned back toward the cashier.

"Sir, you cannot just cut in line," the cashier scolded me. "There are others here who have been waiting."

"Who did that?" I pointed toward the garden outside.

"Who did what, sir?" Her voice was much more sheepish than before; she was clearly frightened by me.

"Outside!" I barked. "Who made the gardens outside? It's very important. I need to know."

"Sir, I don't know." She looked frightened.

I saw the other patrons looked terrified as well. I placed my hand on the counter, which was the equivalent of an Erretas slamming his hand. The counter cracked in two. The girl jumped.

"I'm sure the owner would know," she confessed. "Just a moment. Let me get him for you."

The girl ran from me, practically barreling through a door into the back.

I said nothing, but heard panting from two people next to me. They looked on in terror at the cracked counter. A man rushed through the swinging door, looking ready to fight, but upon sizing me up, his expression changed.

"*Uh*, can I help you, sir?" He asked.

"You're the owner?" My voice sounded huskier than I intended. These people were already scared enough.

"Yes," he replied. "Is something wrong?"

"I need to know who made that." I pointed toward the garden.

I saw the cashier's head pop up by the window of the swinging door. She took one look at me still standing near her register and darted away.

"Sir, why don't we walk out to the rooftop so Lexi can take care of these customers?" The owner extended his hand to guide me outside. "Would that be okay?"

"Yes." I walked toward the lights again. I tried to stay focused on gaining information, but the lights transfixed me when I was so close to them.

"I need to know who made this garden." I gestured to our surroundings.

He was still uneasy, but seemed to calm a little. He let out a brief sigh—almost like a laugh—but he was too nervous to *truly* laugh in my presence. "You know, you're the second person to ask me that this week."

Without thinking, I grabbed the front of his shirt. "I am? Who else? Who else asked about the garden? A woman?"

I felt the man panic as I grabbed him. He was still for a moment, looking into my eyes a little too long for my comfort. I tightened my grip on his shirt, pulling his face closer to mine.

"Answer me," I growled.

"Paige? Is it Paige? Is that who you're looking for?"

Paige? The name that Arden gave me was Senia. I released my grip on the owner's shirt, realizing time was of the essence. I needed to get information, and I needed it fast. Scaring this guy wouldn't help.

"Listen, I'm sorry. I'm not trying to threaten or frighten you. I just need information and I need it fast," I said. "Please, *uh* ... sir."

"It's Jason. Listen, I don't know what to tell you. Paige was a customer. She used to come in here a lot up until recently, and, well, she looked ... she looked a lot like you."

My eyes widened. "Like me?" I asked.

"Yes, sir. She was tall and you both have those really unusual eyes. It's like they change colors or something."

"What else can you tell me about this Paige?"

"Like I said, she came in here a lot and she was friendly. She had long, reddish hair and eyes like yours. She was very, *um,* large I guess is the best word. She had an overwhelming presence. Sort of like you do." Jason paused. "She was looking for someone too. I think that's why she came in here so often. But sir, she's a very nice woman. I'm sure whatever she did, she didn't mean any harm. Please don't," Jason stopped, not knowing how to finish.

Oh yes, she's a very nice woman indeed. Arden failed to mention this one very important detail of her encounter with Eirene. She knew all along. Eirene created *here.* Arden knew, and yet she kept it from me. *I need to leave, and quickly, before someone finds out I am here.*

"Is there anything else you can tell me about her? Anything at all?"

Jason hung his head. "I'm sorry. I really didn't know her. I only saw her as a customer. She asked me a few questions, and I haven't seen her in nearly a week now. That's all I know."

Arden had known. I let that thought sink in until my chest hurt with the truth of it. This changed how our plan would progress.

"Let me ask you something ..."

"Jason," he added.

"Jason. Can you see those lights on the rooftop? Do you see a garden?"

Jason's eyes widened. "No, sir. I can't, but you're not the first person to ask me that either."

"Yes, I'm sure Paige asked you about the lights as well."

"No, not Paige; there was another woman. She was ill, and she was very disappointed I couldn't see lights out here. She was ... beautiful."

My heart leapt. I listened to Jason nervously rattle on about a woman who collapsed here a few days ago. As he continued, panic built inside me. *She is here. Eirene is here, and I need to find her.*

"I'm sorry, sir. I forgot in all the commotion of taking her to the hospital that there was a connection with the other woman. The other woman, Sen, was looking for Paige when she came here. She asked to speak with me about Paige—just as you are now. Well, maybe not *just* as you are now." He obviously meant my rough demeanor.

Sen ... Arden said the girl's name was Senia. This had to be her.

"Sen was really worked up about the rooftop being a garden full of light and then she collapsed in my arms." He seemed to recall a memory before continuing. "And then we had to take her to the hospital."

The hospital? Why had she collapsed? I had to hurry, but I needed more information, and this seemed like the perfect place to get it. I felt as though I was pulled here—like I typically experienced as a Watcher—to gain this precise information and return my findings to the Council of Five. That thought left a sour taste in my mouth and a knot in the pit of my stomach.

"Can you tell me what she looked like? Please?" I asked.

Jason considered my plea. "You won't hurt her, will you?"

Jason was terrified of me, yet he was willing to show bravery for a woman he barely knew. I had to respect him for that. "I would never hurt her. I love her."

Jason looked confused. "How can you love her if you don't know what she looks like?" He asked.

I almost laughed. He was right. How absurd this must all sound. I didn't quite know how to answer him. "There are some things that can't be explained, but I promise you, I am trying to help her. I am trying to help her and Paige."

He studied me further, still shaken by our encounter but growing braver right before my eyes. I would have to talk him down a little.

"The Eir—" I stopped. Jason didn't know her as Eirene. "The Sen I knew had long, golden hair and the most startlingly beautiful violet eyes you would ever see. She was slight of build, but strong on the inside. You could tell by speaking with her that she was kind and brilliant. Everything about her made you feel at ease, but at the same time tense because you were in the presence of such power and beauty. It is possible she may look different from when last I saw her, but she is her all the same. If you have met her, I think you know exactly what I am talking about."

I searched Jason's face, waiting for him to crack. Time was not on my side, so I needed to act fast.

He smiled. "You are right. Some things just cannot be explained, but somehow, I think we have met the same woman."

Relief coursed through me. Arden told me Senia didn't look like Eirene. Perhaps she lied about that as well.

"Sen did have blonde hair when I saw her, but I suspect she dyed it. She had blue eyes though, and they were kind—like you said— and beautiful. Though," he paused, "her eyes are beautiful to be sure, but the lids around them were heavy and darkened underneath. Her coloring when she was here was a strange, yellowish pale—like she had been in the sun, but it couldn't quite cover up her peaked appearance. She is sick, as I said, so I think that must be why."

"Anything else you can tell me? I prompted. What about her height?"

"She's definitely not tall like you or Paige. She is shorter than me, but a bit taller than, say, Lexi over there." He pointed toward the cashier. "I think you'll be able to find her. She is striking."

Obviously, Eirene had quite the effect on this young man. "Jason, I need you to tell me where this hospital is. I need to know where you took her."

"I don't know if I should be divulging her personal information."

He took a step back toward the inside of the building, but I stopped him in his tracks. I grabbed the back of his shirt this time and turned him to face me again.

I leaned my face down to his. "Jason, I wasn't asking."

On my way out of the coffee shop, I made sure the cashier would not contact enforcements by having Jason reassure her that we were old friends and my little episode at the counter had been a practical joke. The girl was young and scared. She would keep quiet, and hopefully, so would Jason. I thought I had invoked enough fear in him.

I rushed through the hospital entrance. I was supposed to meet Arden soon, and she would definitely notice my absence. I needed answers. *What would I do as a Watcher?* This was so different than that experience though. As a Watcher, I was always in the right place at the right time. Now, I needed to make it the right time and place.

I started in the emergency room area. *Surely Jason would have taken Eirene here.* Jason kept telling me Sen was ill. *Think, Carrick; you need to find her.*

Arden told me her name was Senia Schaleski, and she was staying at the Diamanta hotel. *What else?* She was staying at a hotel. She didn't live here; she was vacationing. Arden hadn't said where Senia was from, but perhaps I had enough information to get some clues. I walked up to the large center desk, several Erretas nurses stood around the podium.

"Can I help you?" one of the nurses asked.

Here goes, I thought. "Yes, my name is Jason. I brought a young woman in a few days ago after she collapsed in my coffee shop. I was wondering if I could just check up on her, that is, if visiting hours are still open. Her name is Senia Schaleski." I smiled my most charming smile, but I received a scowl in return.

"How are you related to the patient?" she asked. The nurse went on high alert at the mention of Senia's name.

"I'm not. I just brought her here. As I said, she collapsed in my coffee shop and I brought her in for treatment. I just want to make sure she is alright," I said. "She is alright, isn't she?" I didn't have to feign my concern.

"Sir, I'm very sorry, but there's an investigation underway. Unless you are immediate family, I'm not able to give out any information about Miss Schaleski."

"An investigation?"

"Yes, and I'm sorry, but I really can't say more."

How am I supposed to get around this? Furthermore, why is she being investigated? What had happened to her? Inspiration struck me.

"Listen, I really don't know her that well," I said in my best Erretas voice. "I just wanted to check up on her, but now you've got me a little concerned. She *did* end up here after taking a dive in my coffee shop. This doesn't have anything to do with me, does it? I mean, I'm not getting sued here, am I? If that's the case, I can see why you wouldn't want me speaking to her. I just could use a heads up if that's the case and—"

"Sir, I can tell you it's nothing like that," the nurse interrupted. "And you couldn't see her even if she wanted you to because she's no longer here. She's gone missing."

The nurse startled herself, realizing she'd said too much. *She isn't here anymore. Well, that wasn't what I expected to hear.* We both looked at each other, still a little stunned at what the nurse said. You would think the enforcements would've started their investigation with the person who had brought her in here, I thought, annoyed, but Jason hadn't mentioned being contacted by anyone. I found myself in quite a predicament.

"I'll be leaving now, but could you tell me the time, please?"

"Twenty til four," the nurse responded, clearly anxious for me to leave after her gaffe.

I needed to meet Arden in twenty minutes, and I was clear across town from the Diamanta. Before the nurse had time to say anything further, I was out of her hair and out the door.

I ran through the events of the day in my head as I tried to calm myself and prepare to meet Arden. I strode through the revolving doors of the Diamanta hotel. It was a very ornate hotel, lavishly decorated. After today, I knew Eirene had, in fact, been in this city— even if Arden omitted some of the details of their meeting. I needed to act as if nothing was out of the ordinary. I couldn't let on that I knew of Arden's betrayal yet, not before we found Eirene.

The lobby was somewhat empty as I walked toward the front desk for my third interrogation of the day.

I heard the ding of the elevator bell and caught *her* movement out of the corner of my eye. It was not the long stride of Arden, but the soft sway of a smaller woman.

I didn't know who she was, only that it was *her*. My heart leapt in my chest, drowning out everything but the sight of her. Time stood still. I studied her as if in a dream. I soaked her in, knowing she did not know me. I gazed at the toss of her hair, the sway of her body as she walked, and the gentle movements of her hands—so delicate. She stopped moving away from me, as if she could feel my observation of her. As she turned toward me, taking in the stranger watching her, she politely smiled and tilted her head to the side as if to question what I was doing. When she smiled, I was certain she was Eirene. She didn't look like *her*, but she was mine.

I remembered my promise to Eirene from ages ago: Whenever she lost herself, I would find a way to bring her back. So, I smiled back at her as a stranger, hoping to become the memory.

CHAPTER 26

SENIA

I retraced my steps at the Diamanta hotel, trying to create distance between myself and my father—or Tahrell. I told Tahrell I would meet him downstairs and then left our room before he had the chance to protest. I felt almost compelled to tell him every detail I could recall of my diagnosis and impromptu vacation on our journey back to Lacuna. I hadn't wanted to, but I felt like I had little control to stop myself when he questioned me. My hand was still tired and cramped from all the writing I did. After all, he was my father even if I didn't know the real him. *Is he truly my father though?* My mind had enough trouble grasping things I knew to be true.

My father was the only person I had left to me. I couldn't speak, and as wild as the last few days had been, at least he could take care of me in my final days. I had so much new information in my head—stories he went over with me in that mysterious library. Tahrell showed me document after document, revealing a civilization well before our time but so much more advanced. I felt like my head swam just thinking about it. None of it made sense. I may have trouble with my mind, but I *did* remember most of my lessons growing up and into adulthood, and I never saw or heard anything like it. It all seemed preposterous, and yet something about it all rang true too.

I was supposed to be concentrating on helping my father retrace my steps for some reason. I couldn't quite recall why, but I knew that was why we came back to Lacuna.

It became more difficult for me to understand what I was doing. I lost time more frequently and had trouble hanging on to consecutive thoughts that might help me piece out what happened. I had to repeat things to myself like a mantra. *I am with my father retracing my steps. I am sick. I am dying.* I told myself all these things over and over, even if they lost their meaning to me at times.

The elevator passed floor after floor, a faint dinging noise rang in my ears as it went. When I heard the final chime letting me know I reached the first floor, the doors opened. I glanced at the front desk as I made my way past it; I couldn't help but notice a very large man leaning against it. He looked like someone out of an action movie: muscular, very tall, and had long hair. Still, I couldn't stop myself from taking him in. He had a presence about him that couldn't go unnoticed. He turned toward me and then watched—as if appraising me. I didn't know what to do in response, so I opted for the polite route and smiled. I felt foolish under his observance, but when I made eye contact with him, it was as if my surroundings changed. Everything moved in slow motion. The tall man's eyes remained focused on me. *Those eyes ... I know them.* They were so colorful and bright. His eyes entranced me, and I felt like they had entranced me like this before. His eyes were just like ... they were just like Paige's! It was my last thought before the elevator chimed; that is when all hell broke loose.

It all happened so fast. One minute I locked eyes with a stranger, the next, my father emerged from the elevator and rushed toward the stranger. I watched on in horror as my father charged toward the large man. To my shock, rather than remaining there to square up with my father, the stranger rushed toward me. It only took him two long strides to make it to me. He scooped me up as my vision blurred again. *What is happening?* I knew I would black out again, and my panic rose as I realized I had no control. *No, not now! Please!* This large man took me away from my father—the one familiarity I had left—and there was nothing I could do to stop it.

CHAPTER 27

CARRICK

I only had a fraction of a second to think. My eyes and emotions transitioned from drinking in Eirene to the shock of seeing Tahrell. The two of us barely had time to recognize one another before we moved—Tahrell toward me, and I toward Eirene.

I rushed to grasp her small body before Tahrell could reach us. As much as it pained me, I made a decision in that split second to think nothing of the Erretas' lives surrounding me. They would all perish if I did nothing, so I would sacrifice a few for the sake of many.

With Eirene draped over my left shoulder, I momentarily dropped to one knee and slammed my fist into the hotel lobby floor, causing the ground beneath to crack and tremble. I glanced to see the look on Tahrell's face before bolting away from him.

Screams rose around me, but I made myself drown them out as I had done so many times as a Khassos. *He had her. Tahrell had Eirene! No, I have her now.* I felt Eirene in my arms, but forced myself not to look at her. I couldn't think of her now, I could only think of Tahrell. As I rushed toward the doors of the Diamanta, I refused to look back. I knew many would be crushed. I had no time. I had to get Eirene away from Tahrell. My mind and heart raced.

How was he here? How had he done this, and in his true form? As soon as we made it to the street, chaos swallowed us. Eirene felt weightless on my shoulder. I vaguely registered she was unconscious now, but had to concentrate on the task at hand.

I made my way to the closest vehicle I could find and pulled the driver out of it. I also told him to run because the building was going to come down. My heart dropped as that realization hit me. *Arden.* Was she still inside, or had she not yet made it? She betrayed me. I knew it, and yet my heart still clenched at the thought. *What would happen to us here since we were in our true forms? Would we go back as Watchers again, or could we meet a more final end?* This was unprecedented, so there was no way of knowing. In our true forms, we would not succumb to something as frail as an Erretas building. Surely Arden and Tahrell would survive. I had merely slowed them, so I needed to create some distance between us.

I all but threw Eirene into the vehicle and took off, speeding down the cobblestone streets as I tried to remain focused on the road ahead of me. Panic arose all around Lacuna. Erretas ran in the streets; the Diamanta slowly collapsed behind me, and the reason for all of this madness lay unconscious in the seat next to me. My heart ached at the nearness of her.

I had so many questions rushing through my mind; The most pressing one was, *now what?* As I continued to speed out of the city to a more open area, I focused on my worry. Why was Eirene still unconscious? She is ill, I reminded myself. *I'm sure her illness has something to do with all of this as well.*

Once again, I needed to make a hasty decision. I couldn't leave Eirene to whatever Tahrell and Arden had planned for her. Perhaps I was lucky that Eirene was still unconscious; it gave me a little extra time to think. No sooner than I finished my thought, my luck ran out. I felt eyes on me, wide with shock and fear. Again, I thought to myself, *now what?*

CHAPTER 28

SENIA

I felt the odd sensation, without seeing, that I was moving fast. Darkness surrounded me, and it was as if I was falling and also rushing forward at a breakneck pace. Just when I thought I would be sick from the strange motion, a burst of color clouded my vision and my eyes shot open. I was afraid to make any movements. I had no idea where I was. Surveying my surroundings, I took note that I was in a speeding car. I tried to squelch the panic already rising within me. *I don't know where I am or who I am.*

Think, Senia. My name is Senia. That was a start. I adjusted my head and noticed the blonde hair resting on my shoulder, but it didn't seem right. *Am I blonde?* Before I could dwell too much on the thought, my eyes widened further as I looked past my shoulder. An extremely large man sat in the driver's seat beside me. Adrenaline surged through me at the sight of him. I had no idea who the menacing-looking man was, but he appeared to be increasingly uneasy. He drove like a maniac.

I needed to ask him exactly what was going on. I opened my mouth to speak to the man, but nothing came out. I turned away from him, closing my eyes, and saw a blinding array of colors when I did.

Remember. The word echoed in my mind, but in another woman's voice. Something in her voice scared me even more than my present situation. It was something I knew but wasn't ready for yet.

Breathe in. Breathe out. As I slowed my thoughts, I began to piece together events. *I cannot speak. Why can't I speak?* The memory came back to me then, and I recalled my mantra. *I was with my father. I am sick. I am dying.*

The throbbing pain returned to my head as if on cue. I was with my father, but clearly, he wasn't here now. Then my last memories flooded back in. The man next to me took me from my father. Back at the hotel, my father had a look of shock on his face when he saw the tall man at the front desk. I watched my father go after the man next to me. But the man next to me ran toward me and scooped me up. Pangs of fear arose within me. I opened my mouth to question the man about what he wanted with me, but nothing came out.

I tried to take in the world outside of the vehicle; we were on an open road, not much around us, but fields and an occasional building. I had been in Lacuna, but we must have been a good distance outside the city now.

The man beside me remained silent. Maybe he wasn't sure how to start a conversation with the woman he kidnapped. I thought about opening the door and rolling out, but at this speed, I would likely be seriously injured. *That doesn't matter much at this point; I am dying, after all.* Maybe it was best to go out on my own terms rather than my kidnapper's terms.

I reached for the door handle, but the man's gigantic hand shot out to me.

"No!" he shouted. "Please don't."

It wasn't *what* he said, but the way he said it that made me stop. He sounded like he was pleading with someone he truly cared about. His voice wasn't menacing like I'd imagined a kidnapper's to be. As ridiculous as it seemed, his voice had the tone of someone who loved me. I felt an overwhelming feeling of warmth toward him.

Think back to the hotel. Think back to how you got here and maybe you can figure out where to go from there. My memory took me back to a strange minute I had with this man before all the chaos ensued. This man had stared at me, and I smiled at him. I actually smiled at him! His colorful eyes looked so familiar to me. Once again, I was left with the feeling that I couldn't quite put my finger on something. I had an untapped memory just out of reach.

With one statement from him, I changed from terrified to reassured, and I couldn't explain why. Thoughts of a woman I met— she had those same eyes—surfaced in my mind.

A vision came to me. I saw those same colorful eyes, then explosions and destruction all around them. All that was mine had been destroyed. I had to grab the door handle to brace myself. I felt a bit faint, and the all too familiar nauseous feeling returned. This brought the kidnapper's attention back to me again.

"Are you alright?" he asked me.

I noticed, even among the panic I was feeling, that he had concern etched on his face. I shook my head no. I knew I wasn't alright, but what could be done? It wasn't like a doctor could help me at this point, and what could this man do to help me? As I continued taking deep breaths through the pain, I held my focus on the man's face. His eyes darted back and forth between me and the road. He had yet to slow down, so we were still on a race through the countryside.

"I'm sorry, Ei—*uh* Sen," he said. "I can tell something is wrong, but I can't stop now. We have to keep moving. I know you don't understand, but we need to create some distance between us and ... them." This man said the word "them" like he wasn't quite sure what to call whoever he spoke of. I was sure my father was one of the *them*, but I didn't know who else the man meant.

"I am told you are ill," he said. "Can you tell me what ails you?"

He looked at me, waiting for a response. I suddenly remembered I had a small notepad in my pocket. I reached for it, maneuvering in the car to grab it from my back pocket. Soon, I found that while I still had the notepad, I no longer had a pen. My kidnapper studied me from the corner of his eye. *Maybe I would still have something to write with if I hadn't been thrown over his shoulder and jostled around like a rag doll.*

"Listen, I understand with what just happened how you wouldn't want to speak to me. It appears as though I am a dangerous man, and perhaps that is true, but I swear to you I mean you no harm. I would like to help you if you can tell me what's wrong."

I couldn't explain why, but my anger lessened whenever he spoke. He had a strange effect on me. I felt my glare melt away, and I pointed toward the notepad making a writing motion. Then I grabbed at my throat to convey I couldn't talk.

His brow furrowed. "You cannot speak?" He asked.

I shook my head no.

"Have you ever been able to speak?" He asked.

I rolled my eyes and nodded yes. Then I made a writing motion again. I could explain better if I could write—or if he would stop driving, I thought. Clearly, though, he wasn't going to pull off the road.

"This isn't my car, so I don't know if there's a pen somewhere, but maybe check the glove box," he suggested.

I opened the glove box and dug around. Nothing. I closed it, then looked to the man's large arm resting. His eyes were on the road, so I softly tapped his arm. I needed him to move his arm so I could search further. When I touched him, however, he reacted as though he'd been struck by lightning. The man pulled his arm back, and his eyes grew wide. It took a moment for him to realize what I wanted.

Once he moved his arm, I rifled through the console and triumphantly found a pen with no cap. *I hope it works.* I lifted the pen up to him, displaying the treasure, before closing the arm rest. For some reason, I found myself nearly smiling at the man again.

His expression suddenly grew somber, and he broke eye contact. I turned my attention back to the task at hand.

I had to scribble the pen tip on some paper several times, but eventually, the ink started to flow. I wrote the first thing on my mind: "Brain tumor." It was the answer to his question and the reason for the strange and terrible things that happened the past few weeks. As

I stared down at my words on the paper, tears welled in my eyes. I couldn't muster the strength to show the words to this stranger. It was too much; I was overwhelmed. I was in so much pain, and not only afraid of my current situation, but also of what was to come. With all that transpired recently, I lost everything.

I heard a gasp escape me as I struggled to hold back tears. If I started to cry now, I might never stop. I had to calm myself. I took a deep breath and batted my eyes, refusing to let the tears fall. As I did, the man reached for my hand. He hadn't seen what I had written yet; his empathy stemmed from how emotional I became. I nearly jumped from my seat as it felt like electricity ran through me at his touch. He squeezed my hand slightly before letting go. This simple, kind gesture nearly made me burst into tears.

I gathered myself before writing the next word—"dying."

I showed my captor. He was able to take his eyes off the road long enough to glance at what I wrote. I watched the color drain from his face. *Why would he care whether I live or die?*

I sensed my kidnapper struggled with what to say next. He also seemed very affected by my news. *Do I know this man?* Had I completely forgotten an encounter I had with him in the past? He felt so familiar to me—so safe. *But he is not familiar or safe,* I reminded myself. My mind could not be trusted any longer, so I flipped the page on the small notepad and wrote, "Have we met before?"

He laughed a brief, but somehow sad laugh when he read my question. "You could say that," the man answered.

This is frustrating. I didn't like communicating only through written word. It had been a chore with my father, and it was laborious now too. Then, I thought of my father with a bit of despair. *What happened to him?*

I wrote my next word—"EXPLAIN!" I showed it to the stranger now, just as I had showed it to my father several times at the hidden library. The man next to me took a deep breath in, then sighed.

"This may not make much sense to you now," he said, "but yes, we have met many times before."

I pointed to the word on my page again; this time, underlining it for emphasis. I needed this man to further explain, well—everything. Before he could answer, I flipped the page and wrote "My father?" Then I stared at the man.

"Do you mean the man back at the hotel?" the man asked. "Tahrell? Is Tahrell your father?"

I nodded yes. My captor's eyes darted back toward me wide with panic as he nearly swerved off of the road at my response. *Why did he look at me like that?* I didn't remember much from the past few days, but I did remember that my father told me his real name was Tahrell.

The man with me gathered himself and apologized.

"I'm sure what happened back at the hotel didn't look good, and it's difficult to explain," he said. "I think *your father* should be alright, and if he is, I am certain we will see him again very soon."

Why did he say "your father" with an added emphasis? I flipped back to the previous page, prompting him to explain—again. To my surprise, my kidnapper pulled the car over to the side of the road. Without explanation, he got out of the car and walked toward the rolling fields surrounding us.

Hop in the driver's seat and leave him. The thought was tempting, but with my current condition, I didn't know what would happen. I no longer trusted that my mind wouldn't fail me.

I watched the man's large frame pace back and forth—a solitary being in a canvas of lush green fields. He looked so out of place, and not just because it was so desolate here. Tension built within him. He looked back at me, then tore his gaze away, exasperated. I got out of the vehicle, feeling drawn to him for some absurd reason. As I got closer, he looked at me. His eyes had shifted to hues of blues and greens, and he appeared grief-stricken. He studied my face for a moment, then sighed and closed his eyes.

"I'm sorry. I ... I'm not quite sure how to begin," the man said.

His head hung a bit as if in despair. A small tendril of his long hair fell, but he made no move to brush it out of his face. My fingers twitched as if I wanted to be the one to tuck his hair behind his ear. My hand moved toward his face before I could stop myself.

"When time passes as it does for me, it is difficult to remember the beginning, but I will try. For your sake, I will try. After all of the pain I'm sure I have caused you, I owe you that much. Perhaps it will give you comfort to hear the pain it will cause *me* to retell it now."

Why should it give me comfort for him to be in pain? I didn't understand. I didn't think he was referring to when he took me from my father. *Is there a deeper meaning to what he's saying?* I could sense this was difficult for him. For the first time since this whirlwind of events started, my gut told me I was about to get some *real* answers— answers that weren't loaded with riddles. I nodded, trying to prompt him to continue.

"I believe there is a way for you to view my memor—" he stopped. "What I mean to say is ... there may be a way for me to let your mind see what I have seen—just as I have seen it—or experienced it rather. But you must allow yourself to relax, if you are able. I need to form somewhat of a link between us in order for this to work."

Fear oozed within me. *What is he planning to do?* I knew once I decided to give him my trust, I could not go back.

"I know you have to no reason to trust me, but if I can make you understand, then everything that has been happening to you will make sense. You see, I need your help."

He reached for my hand, and I felt that jolt of energy run through me again. I pulled my hand from his. This man had taken me from my father. He kidnapped me and I didn't know what else he could be capable of. I wanted answers, but I didn't know the cost of that information.

"It won't hurt," he said.

It wasn't the pain I was afraid of. It was the thought, buried deep down, that once I knew the truth, my world would change. *I have been fighting this. I wasn't ready before, but now my time is nearly up and this may be the only chance left for me to get some answers. Now or never, Senia.* No matter how frightened I was, I had to try. I stepped back toward the man. When we were face to face, I reluctantly set my hand in his. A strange sensation ran up my spine. When we touched, it was as if we formed a connection—some kind of link—between us.

"I will not start from the beginning," he said. "That would be too difficult to grasp just now. Instead, I will start by explaining my penance, and then maybe after learning what I have been through, you can learn to forgive me for what I did to earn it."

At those last words, pain erupted in my head, then was gone in an instant. "Remember," said a woman's voice in my head.

CHAPTER 29

SENIA

I watched the visions Carrick, which I now knew his name to be, shared through our strange link. I somehow saw it all directly through his eyes, but also reliving it myself. *How can this all be possible?* It wasn't. *I have a brain tumor. I am dying.* I knew that was the logical explanation for this experience, but Carrick's story was so enthralling, and I was fully immersed in it. I knew I must have lost my mind, but I was too weak to do anything about it.

What was once a sharp pain in my head became so constant that it was a mere distraction to my concentration. I became enveloped in the kidnapper's memory until I felt like I was part of it. It was a form of medication that allowed my mind to escape the pain. Still, I grew weaker. Carrick's voice lulled me into a trance, and I became one with the story as though it was all that mattered. Deep down inside me, I knew that his story was *all* that mattered.

My emotions took over. I felt a sadness for Carrick and the hopeless story he shared. I had grown familiar with sadness and hopelessness. I felt hopeless myself, so it was easy to empathize with Carrick.

When I saw the vision of Carrick arriving in Lacuna, it appeared that he tried to retrace my steps. I remembered the café, a hospital, and the hotel. All these people and places were a blur, but I also knew I had been there. *Why was he searching for me?*

211

I heard the chime of the elevator and felt as though it vibrated through my body. I saw through Carrick's eyes and I thought about the wrongness of it. *This is not what I look like. I know I was the one to get off that elevator. I remember smiling at him, but I don't look like that girl. Do I?*

The memory ended, and I felt groggy like I had been in a deep sleep. I was aware of my own body again, and noticed I was standing in a field in the middle of nowhere. Carrick was still grasping my hands.

Was this supposed make sense to me now? He thinks I am this woman, but clearly, I'm not the woman—Eirene—he's been searching for. I felt myself getting ready to fall, but Carrick held me up. True concern was etched on his face, and his eyes were a deep indigo swirled with gold.

I'm confused. Where am I, and who is this man? I felt a sickening panic build as I struggled to recall what just happened. I pushed myself out of the man's grip and took a step back. I tried to speak, but nothing came out. *Calm down. Breathe. Try to find a solution.* I noticed I have a pen and small notebook in my back pocket. *I have been using this to communicate.*

"What is your name?" I wrote and then turned it to the man in front of me. Even though I couldn't speak it, I felt as though I should at least know his name and try to piece together what happened. I showed him the notepad. He looked into my eyes with a strange expression. What was it? Pity? Remorse?

He still did not answer my question, so I thought maybe there was some confusion. Had I written it down wrong? He seemed unsure about the question, so I flipped the pad back toward me to make sure I wrote my question down right. Weak as my mind felt, it was difficult to be sure. My writing had changed to faint scribbles, but it still seemed legible. I flipped it back toward him. *Does he not want me to know his name, or is he concerned because he already told me and I forgot?*

Something changed in the man's expression as he studied me. It barely registered to me, lightheaded as I felt, but it was there—worry. His face was etched with worry. Worry for me, I thought. I didn't know why it made me so happy that this man was worried about me, but it did. For a moment, I could pretend that someone cared for me. I felt content, and my mind began to fade. My world went dark, but I remained conscious.

"Carrick! My name is Carrick!" I heard the man say.

At the sound of his name, my vision went from black to bright. I saw with unseeing eyes as if in a dream, a multitude of vibrant lights and colors I had never known. I saw foreign lands and faces racing through my mind all at once—and him. I saw Carrick, colorful eyes lovingly-looking at me, and I felt content. *This is what I always wanted.*

In an instant, Carrick's eyes changed. They turned dark, and he began to loom over me as a shadow blocking out the light—blocking out *my* light. My heart raced as the terror and panic ran through me. My ears rang until they hurt; his scream overwhelmed me. I covered my ears as the sound pierced through. I heard another voice. "Not yet," it whispered. "Not yet. Remember."

I jolted back to my reality. I thought Carrick had been shaking me, possibly screaming at me. I was alert now, heart thumping in my chest, reassuring me that I was still alive. That was it, though, I thought to myself. I alternated between feelings of relief and panic.

That had been the end for me, but something brought me back. That voice, I thought. I had heard that woman's voice before.

Unsure at first, Carrick hesitantly reached for my shoulder and rested his hand there as if to reassure me. I felt an electric pull at the light touch. I caught a vibrant flash of light out of the corner of my eye.

Thunder and lightning crashed around us as heavy rain pelted us. Carrick's colorful eyes left mine; his panic was visible in his posture. *I've seen Carrick move in this panicked fashion before. Wait, when did I see that?* For a moment, I ignored the situation around me and allowed myself to celebrate the small triumph of realizing I remembered his name. Not only that, but he seemed familiar to me. I was interrupted by another jolt of fear as a large figure landed—as if from the sky—in front of us.

Carrick turned toward me. "Run! Now!" he shouted.

I staggered, trying to make it to my feet. The rain felt as though it would crush me. I could hear Carrick shouting as if from a great distance. The storm raged around me and muffled whatever he tried to tell me. I crawled on my hands and knees, fighting to create distance between myself and the assailant. My vision blurred both from within and from the rain.

The ground shook beneath me, then I watched as the lightning unnaturally spiraled like a barbed wire.

This isn't real. None of this can be real. Fight. Fight against it.

The winds threatened to make me lose my footing again, but I strained against it and rather than fleeing as I had been, I made the decision to turn back toward Carrick. I could see he was screaming at me. He had the assailant by the throat; in turn, the assailant had a grasp on Carrick as well. The attacker turned toward me then, and I found myself looking at another familiar face. I pushed my soaking hair away from my eyes and blinked again. *Paige?* It was Paige; I was sure of it.

Two sets of colorful eyes met my own and watched as I slowly made my way toward them rather than fleeing the threat. Carrick screamed in earnest now. Just as suddenly as it had started, the storm stopped. I marched toward the two of them.

Carrick removed his grip from Paige's throat, and in a sudden jerk, freed himself from her grasp. He rushed toward me. I wanted to run to him as well, but as I began to stride toward Carrick, someone grabbed my arm from behind, stopping me in my tracks.

Carrick skidded to a halt as I felt hands gently wrap around the back of my neck. I felt the strange sensation of both the familiarity of those hands and the terror they now invoked. I turned my head to get a look at the person who stopped me.

Father. Even as relief flooded in, I felt a terrible sense of dread and unease. The energy between my father and I changed. He made no move to comfort me, and as I tried to move, he only tightened his grip. I was forced to remain looking forward at Carrick, who now cautiously had his hands raised as if in surrender. More than ever, I wish I had my voice so I could ask what the hell was going on. ⸲

The exertion of fighting against the storm began to hit me, and I swayed in my father's grasp. His hold was like a vice around the back of my neck. Paige joined Carrick. It appeared they were in a standoff for some reason I couldn't piece together, but I was clearly at the center of it.

"Be easy, Carrick. We want the same thing," my father said.

Carrick's eyes flared at that and he shouted back, "We do *not* want the same thing, Tahrell! Let her go!" He advanced toward me again.

In response to Carrick's threatening stance, Tahrell tightened his grip on me. His other hand shot up, prompting Carrick to stop.

"As ever, you forget yourself, Watcher," Tahrell said. "Remain where you are, and for once in your life, listen before you act."

Carrick stopped, but his nostrils and eyes flared in anger.

Paige took a step toward Carrick. "Listen to him, Brother. As far as Eirene is concerned, we *do* want the same thing. There is much you do not know."

Eirene. That name echoed in my mind. *Eirene, remember.* I tried to clear my mind. I tried to think of anything else. *What did Paige say? Brother? Carrick is Paige's brother?* My mind searched for any sort of memory I could muster about the two of them. What did these two siblings have to do with me and my father? Whoever Eirene was— that was the key.

I could hear my heart pounding in my head now. This was new. This wasn't the faint and weak feeling from my illness. This was a thrumming of new energy, like strength building inside me. The searing pain returned to my head and my body convulsed, but Tahrell's grip on me remained. I stayed on my feet, the pain blending into the thrumming. I fought the pain, silently pleading for it to stop.

I convulsed again as the world began to fade around me. I saw Carrick's eyes change; the colors fluctuated in worry. *Worry for me,* I thought. My father loosened his grip on me and quickly whispered in my ear. I didn't hear what he said.

My father cradled my head and gently laid my body on the ground before moving his hands to my temples. He closed his eyes in concentration. I watched his mouth move, but could not make out the words. *I can't hear*, I thought. *Hysteria took over. I can't speak or hear anything, and my vision is gone too.* I had to make the searing pain in my head stop.

I made myself go somewhere else. I made myself disappear in my mind, for it was the only way to stop that pain.

CHAPTER 30

CARRICK

I rushed toward Eirene as I saw her go limp in Tahrell's arms. Tahrell now had both hands on her head, eyes closed in concentration. Tahrell yelled at me to stop.

"Wait! Please, wait! She lives." Tahrell's tone changed from someone who had the upper hand to someone in a full panic.

He is afraid—afraid of what I might do.

Tahrell blocked my path to Eirene. Arden joined him.

"Brother, please listen to him," she said.

"Get out of my way, Arden," I demanded.

Anger and fear coursed through me like the Khassos power itself. I knew not what I could do; my only thought was about Eirene helplessly laying by the monster who destroyed us. I shoved past Arden.

"Brother! Listen!" She pleaded. "Carrick, please!"

"Do not call me that, Arden! You are no sister of mine!" I screamed at her in a fit of rage. "You knew! You knew his plans this entire time and lied to my face. How could you side with Tahrell after all he's done? I am no longer your brother, so remove that endearment from your lips, traitor."

Tahrell made himself a shield in front of Eirene.

"Move out of my way, Tahrell," I instructed.

"I will not." He straightened his posture in defiance.

217

This demon ruined our lives and now has the gall to stand between me and Eirene after all of this time? The ground rumbled beneath us, quaking in rhythm with my own pounding heartbeat—thrumming with my very pulse. Tahrell remained in place, staring me down in challenge for her.

"You know what I am, Tahrell," I said. "My very name is death and destruction. Move out of my way, or this breath will be your last."

"Easy. I have no wish to harm her, Carrick, but time is of the essence. You must listen to me. We need her alive. If she should die here," Tahrell hesitated. "Well, if she should die here, then I believe it will be too late for us both. Eirene will not be born again. There will be no world for her to come back to unless we find a way to bring her back to ours."

This was my greatest fear. *Eirene wouldn't return in a new form? Is he telling the truth?* I no longer trusted what Arden told me, and I never could trust Tahrell, so what *should* I believe?

"If Eirene is able to sever her link with Erreta, then she can return as a Sator once more?" I asked.

"It is difficult to say, Watcher. Only Eirene truly understands the powers of the Sators. As you know, her memories of her true self are gone. Well, they were gone until recently." Tahrell took a breath. "Eirene began to leave a trail, not in this life, but in previous lifespans. We believe she left them for you. Arden, however, was the one who began to piece it together. We believe Eirene knew her memories would be lost, but she left small creations—as if in a trail—leading us to her. Who knows? Maybe leading her to her next self. Either way, Eirene has the power of the Sator in her still, and as you know, that is invaluable."

I looked to Arden.

"What did they promise you in return, Arden?" I asked. "What price did you put on Eirene and I?"

"The Council of Five made an agreement with me in which I will be allowed to return home and my penance completed," Arden replied.

There it was—the explanation I'd dreaded. Deep down, however, I knew it to be true. The Council promised her a way out. Why should she not take it after all this time? I had promised her as much when I thought we were working together.

"I suppose you do deserve that much, Arden," I said. "But I speak from experience when I tell you that you will never be able to live with yourself after such a betrayal. How could you work with him?"

"Do not speak to me of betrayal, Carrick!" Arden shouted. "You speak of love and loss as if you and Eirene are the only ones who suffered because of your actions. Yet your one true love is alive. Where is mine, Carrick? And now, we offer you a way for her to *continue* living. That is far more than she deserves!"

"It will all be over soon," Tahrell interrupted. He set his hand on Arden's shoulder as if to console her.

The mere sight of Tahrell's hand resting on my sister's shoulder revolted me, but I allowed myself to hope that what she said was true—that there would be a way for Eirene to live on as her true self once more. *Is bargaining with this monster the only way?*

"What do you ask of me?" I asked. "How can we save Eirene?"

Tahrell exhaled a deep breath. "Your part in this is two-fold, Watcher. This form that Eirene has taken is dying. She is in a sleep state now, but we will lose her soon. Eirene must remember herself before Senia's life ends. This world is ending—as it must. But if this world goes, Eirene goes with it—unless she can unbind herself."

"Wait, unbind herself?" I asked. "What do you mean? You sent her here to serve her penance."

"I fear you never fully understood your punishments, Carrick. We didn't take Eirene's memories from her. She did that to herself."

"I'm done with your lies, Tahrell," I said. "Eirene wouldn't intentionally erase me from her memory, no matter how painful. She wouldn't."

Would she though? Arden had suggested the same thing.

Tahrell laughed. "You really don't know, do you? Eirene struck a deal with the Council, one that saved your life."

I blanched at that, unable to hide my shock. "No. That is not what happened," I said. "I was there, Tahrell. I was there, and so was Arden."

"Do you think Eirene was not given more credence than you two?" Tahrell asked. "She was the only remaining Sator, after all. Thanks to you," Tahrell smirked.

It took all my control not to smash his face in. I had to listen to him now; I had no choice. If he could return Eirene—if he could save her—then I had to control myself.

"Though you all were to be punished somehow, we needed Eirene. Yes, you were punished for what you did, but truly you were studying the Erretas—as was Eirene. You served a new purpose for us this way. We did not know how Eirene would be able to create without Kallan, or another Sator. We just knew if Eirene lived, then her half of the Sator power remained. This was not just a punishment, but a means of keeping you all contained. That way, if the opportunity ever arose, we would have the possibility of returning Eirene to the power she once held. More importantly, we could return our people to what we once were."

"Eirene agreed to become a Watcher herself. The Council thought she posed little threat as a Watcher without Kallan, and it was a way to keep track of her, so we agreed. She bargained for your life and Arden's as well by convincing us that she would quietly go to her penance and study the Erretas until she found a way to replicate what they made—a sustainable planet for us to inhabit. We did not think she could ever regain the power she had as a Sator without Kallan, but we had to try. You all had to serve a penance for what you had done. We know now that she never intended on staying a Watcher," Tahrell stopped a moment.

"Eirene attempted an escape, and to save you, during her first cycle as a Watcher. She tried to create, and create she did, I suppose. Something went awry though, and she burned herself out as a Watcher because she attempted to use her full power in Erreta. This event is what we believe caused her memory loss and her permanent link to Erreta. She became unable to travel back and forth as you and the other Watchers do. She was reborn on Erreta lifetime after lifetime, never returning to us, but a Sator is more than just a being as you and I are. A Sator is an energy itself, unique in its power and survival. Time passed, and we thought the power was lost to her forever.

"I believe, had Eirene been in her true form, that she would've succeeded. Unfortunately, she was in the delicate form a Watcher takes, so she was unsuccessful." Tahrell looked me in the eye. "So, you see, Watcher, this was of her own doing. She broke the bargain with the Council and remained locked in this world, paying her penance as she well deserved. We thought her powers were lost to us. We held onto hope that somehow the power of the Sator could be returned to Anatan again. Eirene should *not* have been able to create at all without Kallan. She eventually found a way—as you now know—and is still very much capable. Thanks to Arden, we have figured out why."

I glared at Arden.

"That is why you two stand here in your true forms. I attempted to make Eirene regain her memories by using the Panoptis to try and return our Sator to her true self. At that point, though, she was bound to Erreta and no longer bound to the Panoptis in the same way you and the others are. I eventually altered and used the Panoptis myself, thinking I could guide Eirene back to remembering herself, but I was obviously unsuccessful. So, here she lies, a broken, dying Erretas. And here we stand, returned to ourselves. If anyone has the power to return Eirene to us, it is you, Carrick. What better way for us to achieve our goal than for you to be your true self?

"So you see, we do want the same thing. The power is there within her, but she must remember it to be able to use it. And you are the only one who has ever helped her remember," Tahrell said. "We have tried and failed. I have divulged information and led her to her own memories. I have told her of our true origins, but nothing has returned her to us. We need you to make her remember, Carrick. Then she can go on as she always should have—creating and building new worlds. If you can make her remember, you can save her and make her whole again."

This is too much. Can this be true? How can I trust anything Tahrell says, or Arden, for that matter? For all I knew, this was yet another trap. Was I willing to risk Eirene and the lives of the Erretas on the word of these two? I glanced down at Eirene, lying there, looking lifeless. She was trapped within a broken Erretas body and looked much the same as her brother had so long ago. How different everything would be if we still had Kallan, and it was my fault he was gone. It was all my fault.

"We cannot be what we once were without Kallan. You cannot replace him, Tahrell," I said.

Arden and Tahrell exchanged glances.

"There is more," Arden said. "We have learned much in our studies. The power of the Sators has always been a living energy. It is life itself, and a power of that magnitude does not die out. It is how the power of the Khassos works as well—a transfer of energy from one force to another. Only certain beings can hold such a power. It was the only reason I could agree to this plan, Carrick. It was the only way I could live with myself, knowing Eirene would be allowed to return."

"Arden, what are you saying?" I asked.

"Kallan lives on through Eirene. That is how she could create here. When you killed Kallan, we now believe his Sator energy transferred to the only other living Sator. So, Eirene no longer needs a partner. We believe both of their powers reside within her, and they have all along. She just didn't know who she was, let alone what she was capable of."

I stared at the woman who was once my sister. *Both powers lie within this small Erretas girl?* The power of one Sator alone was enough, but the power of two? No wonder this girl was dying. How could an Erretas body contain such power?

"We have also learned why the Erretas are so different from the others who failed. We know why they are unique. We have discovered that we—well, we discovered that our people came from them. We are descendants of the Erretas."

How could this be? I came to Erreta with Eirene; we discovered this place together. It is what changed everything.

"I have lived among them for generations. If this were true, how would I not know?" I asked.

"They do not know themselves," Tahrell answered. "Well, very few of them know. They do not want it known that they failed before—that they caused their own destruction and barely survived it to rebuild again. They want to live as they do now. They cannot sustain themselves as they were. The Erretas advanced too much. They made life on their own, and it ruined them. If they knew we existed, the results would be catastrophic. We cannot let that information be known to our own kind either. If our people were to learn that we were made by beings as simple as the Erretas—that there was something before the Sators—it would change everything. It would change our very way of living."

"It would change your position of power, you mean," I stated.

"It would change all of our positions of power, Watcher," Tahrell said. "I propose that we become the *only* power."

A feeling of dread ran through me. I knew now what Tahrell required of me.

"You said my part was two-fold. You require much more of me."

"Yes. The Council of Five will pardon your sister for the part she played here and Eirene because they must. But your crimes cannot be forgiven," Tahrell said. "You must remain here. The origin of our kind must remain here as well. Our people can never know where we came from. That knowledge must stay between us. Erreta will fail of its own volition, regardless, but we mustn't leave any trace of our origins. The Erretas and all of their history must be destroyed for us to go on, and you will be the one to destroy it. You must do what you were created to do, Carrick. You must become a Khassos once more and end the Erretas."

CHAPTER 31

CARRICK

What can I do? If Tahrell found a way for Eirene to live the life I had taken from her, then I have to give her that chance. No matter what Tahrell did to us, and no matter what would happen to me now, I could not be selfish a second time. Arden, too, deserved a better fate. My anger changed to thoughts of hope. If my enemy was the one to deliver my redemption, after all of this time, then I couldn't dismiss him because of our past. Why then did it cut like a knife to think of them going on without me? Could I sacrifice myself—as Kallan had—after all this time?

Was it right to allow Eirene and Arden a chance at the expense of an entire people, or was my resolve as a Khassos returning to me? Could I witness the destruction of another world, one I had become so attached to?

As it has always been for me, I found none of my decisions had been my own. I lived lifetime after lifetime because of decisions made by someone else. Even before my penance, my life had never truly belonged to me. I was created for the sole purpose of serving my people. It was only fitting that it should be my end.

What would Eirene want? What would she do if we succeeded and returned her only for her to watch the destruction of the very people she fought to save? If the decision was hers, would Eirene sacrifice herself to let this world go on? I had to decide now, and the only thing I knew for certain was that I needed Eirene—the true Eirene—to go forward. If anyone could solve this, it was her. She would find a way, so I would do what I must, but how could I make her remember?

"I have tried to no avail to make Eirene remember. I have even gone so far as to share my memories with her directly, but she still recalls nothing. What more can I do, Tahrell?"

The realization hit me like a ton of bricks. There was another way, but it—oh it would be dangerous.

"I have an idea," I proposed. I think your two-fold plan should become one."

Tahrell cocked his head in question.

"She is bound to this world. We need to break that connection," I said. "I think the way to bring her back is to start the destruction of Erreta."

Tahrell's eyes shone in triumph. "Perhaps you are right, Khassos."

It was not lost on me that he called me Khassos or that I made another irreparable decision, but time was running out.

"I will need assurances."

"Go on," Tahrell prompted.

"Once Arden and I begin, how will you make it out in time with Eirene? How will you be able to return to our realm? Last I checked, the Great Corridor was demolished."

"I designed the system myself," Tahrell responded. There is another way."

"Not good enough, Tahrell. What is this other way? What is your means of transport home? Tell me, or I don't cooperate."

He glared at me. "I carry a key of sorts."

"Show me."

Tahrell hardened his expression further, but then pulled out a small object from within his coat. It was a small flat-shaped disc made of some sort of metal. It was no bigger than the palm of his hand. He revealed it to me as if in surrender.

"Show me how it works," I pushed.

Tahrell sneered then; he could barely contain his impatience.

"Show me how it works, Tahrell."

Tahrell pressed the disc to his palm facing toward me. He held it in place with his thumb before pressing down on it. As he did, the object illuminated to a blue glow. It was as if a screen was present in the very air before us, displaying images similar to the orbs I broke in the Great Corridor not so long ago. I saw each orb represented another realm, and there in the center, glowing brightest of all, was ours.

"To show you further would send us back without her," Tahrell said. "She is still bound." He pressed down on the key again and the images disappeared. "It only opens at my touch."

I looked to the ground below them; the small Erretas body remained unmoving. My heart ached at the sight of her so helpless and frail. Home was within reach for her. I had to succeed. I had to make Eirene remember so she could make things right.

"And if she does not remember? If I should fail?" I asked.

"Then she will remain bound to Erreta. I cannot take her back. I have tried; believe me, I have tried."

"Well, then, let's make sure that she does. Let us begin."

CHAPTER 32

SENIA

Pain. It was within me and outside of me. It was everywhere. The pain tried to force its way out of me, and I thought I would surely split in two with the effort of it. I reached outside of myself for anything that wasn't searing pain. I tried first to feel around outside of the pain. I reached out, but all I felt was the tremble beneath me. It was another pain, the pain of my world crying out as power writhed through it. Even the pain outside of my own body felt as though it was part of me, like I was linked to everything surrounding me, and it was crying out for me to save it.

I tried, instead, to hear again, but there was only silence. I could only hear the pain; whether it was my own or not, I could no longer tell. That all-consuming pain screamed within me and outside of me. Still, I struggled for something more than pain.

I tried next to see, but my pain was blinding. Still, I fought against it, though I knew not what I was fighting.

Where had this pain come from? Why should I be in such agony? I felt as though I were tethered by some invisible force, contained by something I should be able to overcome. *Am I not powerful? Am I not the maker of all things? Who then can make something more powerful than me? There was once another, but he is gone now. Who can overcome a Sator? No one. No one holds such a power as I do.*

The pain changed then; it grew stronger, though I thought such a thing could not be possible. It grew around me first, outside of my own body. I felt the very existence around me crying out, ready to break open. *I have felt this feeling before.* I watched as parts of my creation, parts of me, were destroyed in front of my very eyes over and over again until I could no longer bear it. I knew it was happening again, and I would not allow it. I embraced the agony then and let it do as it would within me. I let it surge through me like it was my own power rather than pain. I stopped fighting it and, instead, let it build to an even stronger level. It built within me until it threatened to split my mind in two.

Pain seared in my head until I found myself reaching out to it and grasping my own head to contain it. As soon as I did, the realization hit me that I felt my own head. *I can feel! I can feel again!* Once I knew that, I knew more. I could smell the smoke and death around me. I then heard the disturbance around me, the quaking of the ground beneath me, the noise of the storm raging, and the ground breaking.

I opened my eyes and saw. I starred up at a blackened sky that lit up with a crack of lightning. I saw it with my own eyes and nearly wept at the agony and ecstasy of it. The sky was divided into sections, displayed like a grid in great detail. I saw what was there to the naked eye, but I also saw what was beyond that. I saw an array of color and life that made up that blackness. I saw within it, and I saw through it. It cried out to me. Erreta cried out in pain—the very pain I felt. *I can no longer lay here weak. I have to stop it. I have to stop the pain.*

I lifted my head and saw his dark eyes looking down at me with concern. Then I felt more than pain. I felt hatred that had been hidden within me for so long. I felt hatred for the suffering he'd caused and the countless lifetimes lost to me and worlds of others because of him. I saw him, and I hated him. Then I loved him for helping me feel anything other than pain. I broke through it then. I thought surely my head split open, so I lifted my hand to it to reassure myself.

I made myself stand, meeting him face to face. I glared at him, but he responded with a grin. It was strange to see him smile; it looked wrong on him. *How dare he grin at me?* A chill ran through me. *What can possibly make someone like him grin with such delight?* I looked down at myself, but what I saw was wrong.

"What have you done, Tahrell?" I asked.

I spoke with my own voice, and it shocked me to hear it. *I regained my own voice, but this is not my body.*

Tahrell grinned even wider, and my stomach dropped at the sight.

"It would seem, I have accomplished the impossible," he replied. "I have yet again outdone myself. It is good to see you, Sator." He bowed his head in reverence to me.

"Do not mock me. What is going on?" I asked. "Why are you here? *How* are you here?"

"Where do I begin, Sator?" Tahrell's eyes bounced around, searching. He opened his mouth to speak again, but was interrupted by the crack of thunder and lightning.

I looked beyond him to the demolition happening around us; my heart began to race. *This is the work of the Khassos.* My head throbbed. I let my head hang, clutching it as I stood. *How do I know that word?* Khassos and Sator. The words came into my mind, and I knew them. I took a step, then staggered. The ground shook beneath me. *This is familiar. This is me. This is the real me, and yet I still felt distant. Something is missing.*

I felt another presence before I saw it. I lifted my head from my hand. When I looked, he was there. We locked eyes. This man ... this man kidnapped me. This man told me of his life. He told me everything, and I remember. I couldn't make myself look away from him. I wanted to be near him with every fiber of my being. He starred at me unmoving, waiting. Waiting for what?

"Sator," Tahrell said. When I did not respond, he called out, "Senia?"

The wind howled around us, and yet I felt frozen, unable to make myself move. I waited for what would come next, knowing it would change everything. The voice behind me called out again, but I barely heard. Instead, I saw the man in front of me.

"Eirene," he mouthed.

That is me. That is my name. I felt my name, and I fell to my knees.

In an instant, I knew him. I knew everything we went through. I didn't see it flash through me in a series of memories flooding back in. All the memories were already there and had always been. I knew lifetimes. I knew myself. I knew how much Carrick loved me and how much he sacrificed for me. I knew it all, and the weight of it crushed me.

Raw emotion poured out of me like the bursting of a dam. Before I could stop it, I sobbed. Carrick kept his distance, allowing me the space he kept during our entire last encounter together. He could not hold me when I didn't know who he was. He had to bear the nearness of me this entire time, trying to make me remember. My chest ached with the thought of the pain it must have caused him to do that alone. The sobs racked my body with the release of it all. I shook, head in my hands, until I couldn't stand not to touch him for another second.

I rushed toward him. Carrick barely had time to open his arms for me before I slammed myself into his embrace, burying my head in his chest and gasping for breaths between sobs.

I lifted my eyes to meet his and saw that his were also filled with tears. I brushed a lock of hair from his brow as I had when we were ourselves, showing him with this simple gesture that I was myself again and that I knew him. I let my hand rest on his cheek, holding his face. My love allowed his head to drop and rest on mine so that our foreheads touched. It was as if the very weight of holding his head was too much for him now.

The world around us faded away. Carrick held my face in his hands, looking at me as though nothing else mattered. Nothing did matter just then. He looked into my eyes, both of us drinking in the wonderful nearness of each other. He kissed me then with all his might until I couldn't tell which tears were his and which were mine.

He stopped, tearing himself away from me as though it pained him to do so. I clung to him, not wanting to let go.

"Don't let go of me," I pleaded. "Don't ever leave me again!"

Carrick embraced me, clutching me to his chest and stroking my hair.

"It will be alright," he said. "I will never leave you again, Eirene. Never again."

He held my head to his chest. "I would spend eternity like this with you," he whispered. "Just you and me, and I'm sorry, but Eirene, we need to act fast. This world is ending faster than it should have, and it's my fault."

My heart pounded in earnest again.

"Arden and I have started the destruction of Erreta. Arden found evidence in her time as a Watcher that Erreta would not go on, but there is another world—one I am told the Erretas will not get to, but our people will inhabit it in their stead. This world is ending now, and you must unbind yourself from it to survive. You can leave now. You can finally return to our people. You can finally go home."

I separated myself from him just enough to look up at him. "You and I both know that is not our home," I said. "How can I stop this, Carrick?"

"It is already done, my love. They would perish no matter what we did here, but you have the chance now to live on as you did before, with the power of the Sator returned to you. Eirene, you are no longer just a Sator, you are *the Sator*. You possess Kallan's power as well now. It runs through you."

Kallan's power? How can that be? Before I had time to respond, we were interrupted.

Tahrell cleared his throat behind me. "I am sorry to interrupt, Sator, but time is pressing. You see, we have struck a bargain, these Khassos and I; one they have begun to fulfill but need you to finish."

I searched Carrick's face for reassurance, but it was not there.

"You must go with him, Eirene. He is the only way to return," Carrick said. "He is your only hope of living."

"No," I said for all parties to hear.

"This is what we must do, Eirene. This is the only way," Carrick said. "I will uphold my end of the bargain, and you will return as a Sator. Only you can fix this, Eirene. Only you can save them. I have faith in you."

My heart grew heavy all over again for I knew what Tahrell meant to do. He meant for Carrick to stay here. He meant to take him away from me again, and I would not allow it.

"No," I said again.

"Eirene, it is the only way. If you stay here, you die. He must bring you back, or we lose you forever."

"No!" I shouted right into Carrick's face. "I will not leave you! We will not be parted again."

"Think beyond us, my love. You are needed by many," Carrick said. "You *must* go on. No. You *will* go on because they cannot do it without you. It is the only way you live, and I know you will find a way to go on without me."

I pulled Carrick's head down toward me, his colorful eyes shining.

"Think beyond us? All that I have done has been to protect them! Whatever he's told you, Carrick, it isn't true. Erreta was not ending. Tahrell wants them gone and needs a new home for the Anatani. I have never been bound to this world. My mere presence here has been what has been saving the Erretas from destruction all this time. Tahrell used you and Arden, and now he wants to use me as well. Do you not see that it has all been a lie since the beginning? *We* will find another way. I will not be without you any longer. Don't do as he says. We are greater than him. We don't need him for anything."

Carrick's colorful eyes widened with realization. He kissed my forehead. "You're right," he whispered. "We don't need him for anything."

Carrick walked past me, striding with purpose toward Tahrell. Without hesitation, Carrick grabbed Tahrell's coat and removed what looked like a Corridor key. Tahrell looked terrified.

"Get your hands off of me," Tahrell shouted. "I have told you, Watcher. The key is useless without me. It only opens at my touch."

Carrick held the key up with one hand, studying it closer. With the other hand, Carrick snapped Tahrell's neck with a flick of his wrist. Tahrell's body convulsed before collapsing to the ground. Carrick spit on the ground where Tahrell's body laid.

"I need your touch, not you," Carrick said. He walked back toward me, key in hand.

I watched Carrick's expression change from happiness to sheer horror; I felt the force of her hand rip through me. I endured death many times before, and you know when it happens. You don't feel the pain at first, only the shock. I didn't feel the pain yet, just the shock as I collapsed. In my true form, she could not have hurt me, but this body—with so little strength left— it could not take the strain.

I knew it was over; I knew before my body hit the ground. Had Carrick not been there with me, the pain so visible in his colorful, beautiful eyes, I might have almost welcomed an end to it all, but that was not the fate I was offered. The world turned sideways around me as I fell. My eyes never left his.

My poor Carrick, who was fated to watch me die over and over again. This would be the last time; at least there was a comfort in that. Carrick cried out a guttural noise from another time, a time long lost to us as he ran toward me. I heard him scream at Arden.

CHAPTER 33

CARRICK

"Arden, no! No! No! No!" This wasn't happening. I couldn't think. I couldn't breathe. I ran to Eirene and fell to the ground, holding her body to my chest before I knew what I was doing. The light was already gone from Eirene's eyes. It was too late. Her body lay limp in my arms.

My mind wouldn't let me see it at first. I didn't fully grasp what happened. *I will not let this be true.* I rocked back and forth with Eirene in my arms. Tears came so fast I could barely see her. I kept wiping my eyes because I would not allow myself to stop looking at her.

"Shhh, hush now," I said as I rocked Eirene back and forth, but she could not hear me. "I will never leave you again. I told you I wouldn't, and I meant it. I will never leave you again."

Eirene didn't respond. She didn't move. She didn't open her beautiful eyes. She didn't breathe.

She was dead. Eirene was dead, and when I let my mind realize it, the numbness went away. Pain I had never known consumed me. My body shook with grief. I lost all of my senses for a time, then I heard myself make a noise I didn't recognize as my own. I howled like an animal. I gripped Eirene tighter and tighter. I held her like I could somehow meld her into me and give her life once again. I wanted to join her. I wanted her to be one with me, but there was nothing I could do. In that moment, I felt myself break.

I crushed people and worlds alike, felt them split and break apart beneath my touch. That's what it was to be a Khassos—to destroy and destroy until there was nothing left. So that's what I did. I let myself be destroyed.

The power of the Khassos roared within and around me. I felt it flow through the very veins of Erreta. I was part of this world and now it would become part of me. I never let her go. I held Eirene tighter, drawing my power through the ground we lay on. I drew on more power than I ever held, not knowing or caring where it came from. My surroundings warped around me. I would destroy it all. Existence itself could burn for all I cared. I was going to take them all with me.

I had to say goodbye to Eirene one last time. *No, she is going with me.*

"It is how it has always been for the two of us, my love. Khassos and Sator," I said. "So now you must create something in me once more, and I must destroy."

I saw Arden a short distance away from me. She reached toward Tahrell's body, struggling to move as I melted the earth around us away. *Too late, Arden. You are too late.*

I would not allow Arden to be the last sight I saw, so I loosened my hold just enough to look once more at Eirene. I brushed a strand of hair from her face, letting my thumb run over her cheek as my last tear fell. I let go and let the Khassos consume me. The world detonated around me, and still, I held her to me as the power broke through, exploding my very being until I was no more.

Epilogue

Lyris

I bolted upright, gasping for breath. I wheezed, trying to suck in air over and over. I looked to my surroundings and vaguely registered the blurry image of someone looking down at me. I had to tell them ... someone ... before it was too late.

"I was Her!" I croaked out. "I was Eirene! You have to tell someone." I gasped for air. "It's important! Anatan depends on it!" I said the last words barely audible to my own ears before collapsing and losing consciousness.

Acknowledgments

I debated for years if I should pursue writing this story. I was so nervous to let anyone read what I had come up with, but finally took a chance and let someone read my very poorly written rough draft. That person was my friend and editor, Erika.

I would not have had the courage or confidence to complete this book without you walking me through every step of the process and giving me the encouragement I needed. I truly could not have done any of this without you. I'm so grateful not only for your patience, but your talent as well. You helped me make something I could be proud of.

To my poor beta reader and husband, I apologize for how much I have agonized over what to do with this book. I have gone back and forth between excitement and self-doubt ad nauseam and you have been there with me every step of the way.

You are the best partner in life I could ask for and I don't know what I would do without you. You make me laugh or smile every single day, and you always have since we were 11 years old. Thanks for making my life so much better and for the endless love and support you've given me.

Thank you Peter, Karla, and the team at Publify Consulting for your guidance and answering my endless questions. You have been such a reassuring presence for me to lean on during this process.

9 781736 951347